PRAISE FOR *THERE'S ONLY O[NE]*

'Few do raw, authentic, almost pa[...]
than David F. Ross, and this is grassroots football laid bare
(literally, in one of Ross's many hilarious vignettes). It's a novel that
deals with more profound themes. But this author makes fitba'
seem the perfect setting' Patrick Barclay, *The Times*

'David Ross has carved out an enduring place for himself among
contemporary Scottish novelists' Alastair Mabbott,
Herald Scotland

'It's a brave writer who tackles despair and disappointment in this
era of blind and aimless positivity ... I can't stand football, but I
found this a deeply compelling story about ambition, failure and
interpersonal history' Ewan Morrison, author of *Nina X*

'A brilliant, bittersweet story that captures the rawness of strained
relationships, set against the struggles of a failing lower-league
football team. Ross's best novel yet' Stuart Cosgrove

'Triumph and tragedy are inexorably woven together, with the
former only offering brief respite before reality returns. In life, as in
sport, it's the hope that kills you ... In case you were in any doubt,
There's Only One Danny Garvey proves David F. Ross is in the
Premier League of writers' Alistair Braidwood, *Scots Whay Hae*

'It's an amazing book, brilliantly interwoven, giving me the same
feeling I had reading James Kelman when I was younger' Douglas
MacIntyre, *Creeping Bent*

'Ross tends to eschew purple prose in favour of the black-and-blue
kind, and here, it's as raw as a raked stud on a shin'
George Paterson

'Ross brilliantly captures the hopes, dreams and some of the
nightmares that are part of people's everyday lives, and the unique
power tha[...]
Kevin Ton[...]

'Ross's fifth novel is his most mature and his most accomplished to date. Maybe he hasn't realised it yet but he's now given himself an even bigger problem – how exactly does he follow *There's Only One Danny Garvey*?' Sergio Burns, *Ayrshire Magazine*

'It's great when a book surprises you. This is a story with a punch, clouded by memory and regret. For all its gut-punching sharpness, it ends up being a pretty beautiful story' The Bookbag

'If you enjoyed *Shuggie Bain*, you will adore this ... filled with honesty and written with a tenderness that is faultless, *There's Only One Danny Garvey* is one of the best books I've read in years' Random Things through My Letterbox

'No words will EVER be good enough for this incredible book. Intense. Heartbreaking. Passionate' Swirl & Thread

'Has all of the author's beautifully formed tapestry of human existence ... but it tips the balance between comedy and tragedy in a truly devastating way. I closed the cover rooted to the spot, stunned into immobility by the desperate, heart-rending power of the ending' Live Many Lives

'A story of loyalty, family, of past transgressions and of atonement. It explores the fragility of both mind and body; a story of hope but also of ultimate sadness ... had me absolutely enthralled from the off ... a beautiful narrative in which even the more difficult elements are handled with care and understanding, and that has a real capacity to surprise' Jen Med's Book Reviews

'Took me back to an almost forgotten time when vengeance was still in vogue and young DJs remained wilfully "uncool". Just brilliant' Bobby Bluebell

'Ross has a brave and distinctive voice that is sure to appeal to men and women across the country' Culture for Kicks

'Ross has written a great coming-of-age novel that is full of wonderful prose and characters who are instantly likeable' Literature for Lads

'Ross is a genius with these comic moments and creating the perfect nostalgic read' Northern Crime

'It is funny, fresh and damned entertaining' Grab This Book

'This book evoked such intense emotions – I had a lump in my throat, tears in my eyes and a giggle in my belly' Chapter in My Life

'Highly engaging and both a fun and moving read' Book Drunk

'A book I'd strongly recommend, great summer reading or just great reading, if you don't want to wait' Blue Book Balloon

'Heartbreaking, poignant, and ferociously funny' Espresso Coco

'I love a book that can make me laugh out loud in one chapter and make me an emotional wreck in the next ... this has had this effect on me' Segnalibro

'If you like Irvine Welsh you need to read David F. Ross, not as much grit but certainly of the same calibre ... absolutely I will be reading this author again' Always Reading

'It's a cracking tale and I've thoroughly enjoyed being along for the ride' The Book Trail

'The dark humour in these books paints a truthful and perceptive portrait of Scottish men of a certain age, and the blend of humour and poignancy hits just the right balance' On the Shelf Books

'Ultimately an uplifting story of hope. And a bloody funny one at that' Mumbling About

'I cannot wait for what David Ross decides to do next. I'm sure I'm not the only one thinking that' Christopher Clark Sports

'The writing in this book excels because it takes what would ordinarily be page upon page of humour and one-liners, keeps them, embraces them and yet at the same time the story is poignantly crafted, the wit balanced out with pure, genuine emotion' Reviewed the Book

'This novel was a revelation for me, a breath of fresh air and I can honestly say I have never read anything like it' My Chestnut Reading Tree

'David F. Ross has a talent for social angst, and it's this I'd love to see more of in the future' A Novel Book

'A tragic comedy of deep family difficulties and comedic coping mechanisms, it makes for a strikingly authentic and enjoyable read' Publish Things

'A ride down memory lane ... funny, witty, and extremely well written' Trip Fiction

'An absolute must-read' By the Letter Book Reviews

'Emotionally resonant and absolutely unforgettable. Highly recommended!' Liz Loves Books

'David Ross definitely has a way of putting the human into his characters, they live and breathe, and you feel every emotion with them' Reading Writes

'It's gritty, poignant and darkly funny' Misti Moo Book Reviews

'Full of energy and humour and races forward with a punchy rhythm ... It balances humour with heart to perfection to create a compulsive read' Stacy Is Reading

'An evocative, insightful must-read and I cannot recommend it highly enough' Hair Past a Freckle

'An enjoyable helter-skelter ride of multiple perspectives with an exceptionally strong sense of place' Claire Thinking

'A thoroughly gritty, uncompromising and entertaining throwback' Raven Crime Reads

'This is a great book, a poignant and funny blast, and I can highly recommend it' The Crime Novel Reader

'Alongside the humour there is also sadness ... It is a long time since I've read anything like it' Steph's Book Blog

'This novel would be perfect for adapting for the TV ... Enjoy the grit, the rudeness and the fabulous seventies setting' Tales before Bedtime

ABOUT THE AUTHOR

David F. Ross was born in Glasgow in 1964. His debut novel, *The Last Days of Disco*, was shortlisted for the Authors' Club Best First Novel Award, and received exceptional critical acclaim, as did the other two books in the Disco Days Trilogy – *The Rise & Fall of the Miraculous Vespas* and *The Man Who Loved Islands* – and his most recent book, *Welcome to the Heady Heights*. He is a regular contributor to *Nutmeg* magazine, and in 2020 he wrote the screenplay for the film *Miraculous*, based on his own novel. Follow David on Twitter @dfr10 and his website: davidfross.co.uk.

There's Only One Danny Garvey

DAVID F. ROSS

**ORENDA
BOOKS**

Orenda Books
16 Carson Road
West Dulwich
London SE21 8HU
www.orendabooks.co.uk

First published in the United Kingdom by Orenda Books, 2021
Copyright © David F. Ross, 2021

A catalogue record for this book is available from the British Library.

ISBN 978-1-913193-50-8
eISBN 978-1-913193-51-5

Typeset in Garamond by typesetter.org.uk

Printed and bound by CPI Group (UK) Ltd, Croydon CR0 4YY

*For sal*e and distribution, please contact info@orendabooks.co.uk or visit
www.orendabooks.co.uk

For Nathan Ross,
and everyone who cares about the grass roots.

'Mother I tried please believe me, I'm doing the best that I can. I'm ashamed of the things I've been put through, I'm ashamed of the person I am.'
  —Joy Division, 'Isolation'

'A man who gives a good account of himself is probably lying, since any life when viewed from the inside is simply a series of defeats.'
  —George Orwell

There's Only One Danny Garvey

'Aul' Jock Reid ... he's no' right in the heid. His wife's a hoor, an' his daughter's deid.'

Groups of youngsters and seagulls are rummaging around on the site of the old Barshaw tip. Piles of discarded rubbish are spread into every corner, only prevented from spilling outside the perimeter of the tip by a chain-link fence, which is straining with the effort. The tip is on the edge of the village and has long been abandoned by the local council, but its unlocked gates allow random dumping to continue unchecked.

An elderly man, familiar to the small humans, wanders in. He is barefoot and wearing pyjamas, although it's midday. That cruel and senseless refrain sings out. Chanted to get a rise out of a troubled old man prone to unpredictable outbursts that make the Barshaw youngsters laugh, that briefly relieve them of the interminable boredom of summer holidays.

The chant follows him around. But the old man takes no notice of it, or of us; the tuneless, baiting choir. He is – as always in recent months – miles away. Most likely, I can now appreciate, in a private, painless world where he doesn't have to deal with his granddaughter's abduction; or the terrible torment of knowing the entire community is convinced he was responsible for it.

Presumed dead. Unsolved child murder.

Or his daughter's subsequent suicide.

He is smiling, I notice. Something else has caught his attention. He ambles towards a partially hidden, upright wooden box. He clears it of the debris and black bin bags that conceal it. His feet submerged in a brown puddle of sludge, he gently lifts a hinged panel. He starts massaging the black and white keys. The most majestic, mournful, colourful sound drifts across this swampy wasteland. It has me transfixed. Even the squawking birds fall silent. It is the first music to make me cry without my understanding why.

The others jeer. Make fun of me. Call me a *daft wee fucken lassie*. We get a chasing from clumsy policemen. They have arrived with the old man's concerned wife and a blanket to wrap him in. They drive him away. Through the rear passenger window, he is still smiling.

It's a recurring memory that has stayed with me, haunting me since I left this place thirteen years ago. And yet, something about that illusion is more real, more tangible and more pivotal to me than every moment since.

I was eight when he played the piano for me. I'm twenty-nine now.

One
Higgy

May 1996

—Christ almighty, this ground's a dump. For the semi-pros, I mean ... obviously not in comparison to ours back in Barshaw. Compared to The Barn, it's like fucking Wembley or something. Haven't been here for, what, five years? Since the last time they got in touch. It seems like less. He knows I'm coming, but he'll act like he didn't. Part of the game, me begging. Begging for him to come back. To come home.

I see it immediately for what it is; my complicated past and my short-term future, amalgamating in human form and sweating profusely in a garish green shell-suit. Stumbling down the old, empty ash-and-gravel terracing. Unsure of itself. Hesitant and anxious. A nylon-clad fire hazard. If only I'd been quicker to realise. If only I'd sparked a careless match. Might've saved a lot of trouble.

But, unavoidably, Higgy's here. Here to reclaim me. To drag me backwards. Backwards in time. Back to the bridge.

'Hullo son. How've ye been this last ... what'll it be? Five year?'

—I came because his bosses asked me to. Danny didn't want me here. He never does. It was a dark time for him back then, five years ago. One of many.

He was here three seasons ago. Trying, then as now, to persuade me to return. Time passes more rapidly at his stage of life, so I don't correct him. He shows up when he's hiding from something or running from it. It's a pattern. 'About that, aye,' I say.

'Ye've no' changed.' He's talking about appearances.

'Bollocks. We've aw changed. Some just fucken hide it better, that's aw.'

That's undeniably true. After twenty-five, the mould's set for everybody. For all he has aged, it's still obviously, outwardly him. The same man I've known my whole life. Inside? Well, that remains to be seen.

'Ye headin' up north? Plannin' on doin' a bit ae hikin' around the Cairngorms?' I see him puzzled. Then it dawns on him that I've clocked his rucksack. He sighs, then attempts a smile.

—I've brought a bag. Figured it might take a few days to get him to trust me. Trust was always something hard-earned with Danny.

'They treatin' ye awright?' he asks, as if I was in my brother Raymond's shoes.

'Nae complaints.'

'What's gonnae happen next season? There'll need tae be cuts tae the budget, club goin' down, an' that.'

'Probably. Cross that bridge when ah come tae it.' *Another* bridge. The direction of my life's been influenced by bridges. Particularly the one in Barshaw, the tiny Ayrshire village where I was born. Where I'm now urged to return, tail somewhat between my legs.

'Look son, can we go somewhere? Get a wee chat goin'?'

'Here's fine. Ah've got the nets tae bring in anyways.'

'Can ye no' make the team dae that for ye?'

'It's part ae ma job. Ah dinnae mind it.'

He laughs. Nervously. He's reaching. Looking up. Searching for a foothold. He thinks he's found one.

'The young boys played well. Good movement off the baw, an' that.'

'Aye.'

'Last game ae the season, tae. Minds usually on bloody Benidorm, eh?'

—He's always been a difficult person to reach. He was always a quiet kid. You never knew what he was thinking. Always somebody you had to drag the words out of, even in the good times. The silent insolence, his ma used to say. Keeping all that in ... it can't do him any good. When things get difficult, he hides ... withdraws into himself like a wee bear going into hibernation. When the wee girl in his primary-school class disappeared – must've been around 1972 – it was a major thing around here. She was never found. Danny went missing the same day. Somebody in the crowd out looking for both of them found him down under the Barshaw Bridge. He'd been out all night. Libby was absolutely frantic. The police were furious at us for wasting their time.

Raymond rattled Danny's jaw when he got hold of him, and Danny didn't speak to anybody for months and months after that. About a year, in fact. They had these social workers coming around constantly, right at a time when Libby was struggling badly, too.

We had teachers, doctors, therapists, even a child psychologist all look at him. Some nights, you'd listen at the door and you'd hear him, in his room, talking away to himself. Talking to her: to wee Louise-Anne, the missing girl. But he'd say nothing to anybody else. Not a word. Then, just when I thought he'd be taken off Libby, he suddenly opened up as if nothing had happened. It was strange. Things were fine then. Until the next time.

I look at him. He's wondering what to say next. Stumbling over the words like a drunk with amnesia trying to recite a poorly rehearsed soliloquy.

—I should've tried to get him more help back then. But I was too wrapped up in looking after his ma. Trying to keep the worst of it

from the social workers, to keep them together, him and his brother. To not have them split up and put into care. I often wonder if we did the right thing by him.

'Ye must be right chuffed wi' aw the attention, despite everythin' else.'

'It's no' about me.' I say this and mean it. Football is about the players; that's until their manager fails them. Until he loses the dressing room. But this unexpected cup run has brought uncomfortable exposure. Scouts from the big clubs are following our progress. Looking to swoop in and land the young talent we've groomed.

—It still staggers me that he's doing this; developing youngsters. Imparting knowledge. Showing leadership. And doing it well, too. He's a good coach, there's no doubt of that.

The football was always his coping mechanism. Regardless of the domestic carnage that was going on around him, Danny always focused on the pitch. Watching him play, you'd never have known about the problems he had; about the overdoses he witnessed, or those endless bouts of screaming at his brother.

'But ye'll be lookin' forward tae takin' them at Hampden, eh?'

I nod at this. Pointless denying that it's satisfying to have navigated ten emotional, sometimes tortuous, rounds to reach the national youth-team final.

I'd always been told I was special. Not by my closest family, obviously. But by Higgy, and others who watched me play. Never questioned it. Not when barrelling around the muddy pitches of Scotland as a lauded and sought-after youth player. Not when the big clubs turned up on the doorstep with S-forms and a pen, and bouquets for my mam. Not even when Deek Henderson asked me to touch his cock the week before my debut for the Bridge. And certainly not when scoring in the cup against Auchinleck

Talbot when I was sixteen. Whenever I pulled on the number-ten shirt, I was special. They all said it.

I look across the rutted turf. Sigh deeply. I turn to look down at the stooping, stunted shell I spent my teenage years calling uncle.

'Look, Higgy, nae offence but ye could've phoned tae bum me for tickets tae the final. Why the fuck are ye *really* here?' I say it with more anger than I intended. He's just Raymond's fucking messenger after all.

—Fuck me, it's freezing up here. He can't be wedded to this, surely? I want him to come back. Back to the Bridge. It'll do him good, ultimately. People here are worried about him just like they were before. Five years ago, during the summer break following his first season as Arbroath's youth team coach, Danny was found to be defacing books at the local library. He was finding it hard to get over the injury that ended his professional chances. He needed real help back then, but we weren't close enough to him to see it. He'd been ripping pages out of novels and sellotaping them into medical textbooks. Scoring out names in books and writing 'Louise-Anne Macdonald was here' all over them. He got caught and charged. He told the club's directors that he was just bored; it was something that had passed the time. The club paid the fine. Made it go away. His young team was very successful, but few considered or cared about the mental toll the job was taking on him. They didn't want their wee boat rocked. The club doctor thinks he's overworking himself again, that he needs a clean break. I think he just needs to see his ma, his brother. Focus on helping our village club. I suspect he knows this, but he's making me work for it.

He doesn't answer. A floodlight bursts into life. It isn't dark but the sudden dull sound of it kicking in takes us both by surprise. A weekend test of the electrical circuits following the embarrassment of last week's cup-tie cancellation. He takes off his bunnet. The wind lifts the wispy strands from one side of his head and wafts them straight up like a flip-top bin lid. He quickly scratches the scalp. Skin flakes. He pulls the hat back on, maybe hoping that I haven't noticed.

'Ah've mind ae a match here ... must've been sixty-seven or that.' He's reaching for another ledge, another branch that he must hope won't come away by the roots. 'You'd just been born. Me an' Deek brought Raymond.' My face offers no clues about either man's name being raised. 'It was his first-ever game. Away tae fucken Arbroath. In torrential rain. Jesus! If that's no' enough tae put ye off fitba for life, ah dunno what is.'

I look at my boots. I conceal a smile as I remember Raymond telling me years later how much he hated that game. The cold. A thunderstorm. Daft auld Higgy telling him that was just God rearranging his furniture. Then him gagging from the sickening, stale smell of the smokies that polluted the car on the long journey back home.

'It was bloody Baltic back then anaw. We were leavin' the ground in the rain an' walkin' back tae the motor. Despite his fingers bein' blue wi' the cold, wee Raymond asked for a pokey hat. The smile on his face when the boy handed it down tae him. He was that excited; like Santa Claus himself had gie'd him it. Then he turns an' trips ower a kerb. It was aw ower his jacket. Ah don't think he'd even licked the bloody thing. Poor wee bastard. He's lyin' there, in the mud, covered in ice cream. Greetin'. He just wouldnae get up. Stubborn as fuck, even then. Aw these strangers watchin'. Ah was affronted.'

Jesus Christ. Fighting every impulse not to, I reach out an arm. I put it around my uncle's shoulder. I resign myself to this; knowing what's coming. His voice is breaking.

'That fucken ice-cream cone ... why did ah no' just go back an' get him another one?'

At regular intervals – typically following another of Raymond's lapses in judgement – Higgy would drag out the ice-cream cone

defence; the pivotal point at which he believed Raymond's destructive life course was set. It conveniently shifted responsibility
for his actions from my brother and placed them at the feet of the
principal martyr to the cause: Saint Higgy of the Blessed Bridge.
My brother disappeared the night they got back from the match
in Arbroath. Squeezed himself out of the bedroom window at
Higgy's place. He was missing for twenty-four hours. A policeman
found him asleep under the Barshaw Bridge. He was suffering
from mild hypothermia.

—*Raymond doesn't even know I'm here. I didn't even discuss my
suggestion of the Barshaw Bridge manager's position with him. But
it might pay to let Danny think I did. There's a lot of unfinished business between the three of them, Danny, Raymond and their ma. I
just wanted to bring Danny home.*

'Why could ah no' take better care ae the two ae ye'se?' he wails.
   'Cos it wisnae your fucken responsibility!' I yell in response.
   'The poor wee fella. His da'd just beat it ... an' Libby wis done.
Ah shouldae stepped in, like ah did wi' you.'
   He has a skewed view of the history. Libby is our mother;
Raymond and me. She's the love of Higgy's life, God fucking help
him. He's not our *real* uncle; it's just easier for us to call him that
– it avoids more painful truths. We are four points of a compass
determinedly pointing away from the centre. Trying to escape that
centrifugal force that periodically drags us back to confrontation.
Only Higgy seems unable to resist it.
   'Fuck off, Higgy. Libby's always been her ain worst enemy,' I
say. 'Olympic-level selfishness, hers is.' Sackcloth and ashes. Both
of us. What a fucking pair. I pity him his cloistered existence in a
tiny working-class village where fuck all happens and the only
thing you have is time; to regret, to relive, to put the few 'what-
ifs' on a pedestal. But am I any better? The environment is
different, that's all. Isolation takes hold of me now in colder air.

Words ricochet around my head, flipped incessantly like a steelie in a pinball machine. *Ashamed of the things I've been put through. Ashamed of the person I am.*

A headache is forming. Starts at the base of the skull and quickly works its way towards the temples, like an amphibious army invading a pristine beach. I haven't had one of them in a while and I silently curse this old bastard for bringing it on.

'We've missed ye, Danny. We need ... we *want* ye tae come back, son. Back tae the Bridge.' It's a rehearsed statement. Planted there by a Janus-faced cunt with a PhD in advanced manipulation. I withdraw the arm. Raymond's behind this. I know it.

'That's no' gonnae happen,' I tell him. He knows why. Same reasons as the last time he tried.

'Jesus, Danny, it was donkey's years ago, son. Water under...'

I rummage around in the pocket of my tracksuit. I retrieve a pack of cigarettes and my tiny lighter. I'm trying to give up but failing heroically. It takes a few sparks, but I light the small, white nicotine stick. I fleetingly visualise a smoking pile of green nylon ashes, but I dispose of the lighter, fulfilling its destiny. His tone changes.

'Danny, the Bridge needs a new manager. It's gonnae be a tough season ahead, nae doubt, but it's a good opportunity for somebody.'

'Good. *Somebody*'ll be fucken happy then.'

'We want ye to come home, boy. Yer mam...'

I turn sharply at this; a line crossed. Raise a finger. Challenging him to say another word. None comes. Higgy pulls up his collar and shoves his hands into his pockets. A stiff North Sea breeze billows in suddenly, like a shoulder charge from a fifteen-stone centre half. It catches us off-guard.

'How can ye even stand it up here?' he says. 'It's fucken freezin'. Just as well my baws are past their sell-by date. They've just dropped at my feet.' The guns of the invading army in my head fall silent. He grimaces, then smiles. It takes time, but eventually I do too. He isn't wrong about the weather. Even at milder times, the cold seems to wire straight through the ribcage, its sharp, bony fingers compressing the lungs. He'll know I'm not happy here. Futile trying to deny it. Would it really be any worse back in Barshaw?

'Christ's sake, you live in Barshaw, no' fucken Barbados,' I say to him.

'Come back tae the Bridge, son. The club needs ye.' Higgy sits on the rough timber slats of the dug-out bench. He looks exhausted. 'Fuck it, ah *need* ye! Imagine it ... you an' me, back at the Bridge. Turnin' it aw around. It's a big chance for ye, son. An opportunity tae—'

'Tae whit? Apologise? Atone? Fix things wi' folk that ah let down. That's whit ye mean, int'it?'

He slumps, head in hands. He looks like he might cry.

'Ah'm desperate, Danny.' The daft auld cunt.

—I knew he'd come home.

He knew I'd comply. A subtle twisting of the grapple hold Raymond has on me via this weak, pitiful man ... the closest thing I have to a father. It may be that Raymond has grown a conscience over Libby. The vacancy at the Bridge a chance to absolve himself of his guilt, but through me, since he's behind bars? But this also seems unlikely. Prison may have changed him, but he can't rid himself of his self-centred streak.

Higgy stays with me for the week. My mother's medication is being changed so she has daily carers coming in, therefore Higgy doesn't need to be around. He tells me he's allowed himself a wee break. A week's holiday in Arbroath. Sleeping on the worn sofa of my tiny rented flat. With its broken front window frame and the wind that whistles relentlessly through it like a drunken, tuneless lounge crooner forgetting the words of his own songs.

—Jesus, he lives like a monk, this boy. The room is meticulously laid out. He could evacuate this place in ten minutes and not leave a trace. Maybe that's the point. No television, only a few books, his records and a radio. He always lost himself in his music. When he was upset or hiding ... or even when his team won and he'd played well, the radio was his thing. Hidden away in a room, on his own. His brother was the opposite. Raymond craved attention; needed to be the centre of everything, regardless of the personal cost.

'Long ye been in this place?' He means the flat, not the town.

'Couple ae seasons, mibbe,' I reply, having to think about it, and still not sure I'm right.

'It's aw'right though, eh?'

'It's fine.'

'Close enough tae walk tae work though. Ah used tae love that.' In all the time I've known Higgy, he's never worked a regular job. Window cleaning and odd-jobbing funded the years following my youth teams' games in the far-flung outposts of Scotland. Libby won't have paid him to run after her these last few years, that's for sure. And with the Bridge's current predicament – which he has started to educate me on – it's certain that he wouldn't be on the meagre payroll there. A beneficiary of the state, God fucking help him.

'Yeah. Ah enjoy takin' the bike,' I say.

He looks at me strangely, as if I've just cracked a joke that isn't particularly funny. 'Ye gie up the wee motor, then?' he asks. It jolts me. I don't answer. 'Probably wise.'

Over the course of the two days since I made the decision to return to Barshaw, Higgy has investigated this living space like Columbo building a murder-case theory. There is nothing to reveal though. I live, by choice, in a very spartan way. There are no indications of my past life. Apart from the vinyl – my one indulgence – it's as if I only exist in the present tense. He acknowledged this when he first walked in.

'Nae telly?'

'No time for it,' I told him.

'What about the fitba,' he asked. 'Ye no' thought ae gettin' a dish?'

'Can see any games ah want at the club. An' ah don't have tae pay for it there.'

Forty-eight hours later and he's exhausting my patience. And wearing out the stylus of my record player. With little else to do, Higgy has unsuccessfully attempted to understand how anyone could content themselves with friends like Morrissey and Marr, Ian Curtis and Nick Cave without reaching for a cut-throat razor. We choose our friends, not our relatives.

—This town, my God ... I thought Barshaw was bad, but Arbroath? It feels like weeks since I got here. Danny coaches his young team and I stay here, listening to his favourite music; songs that make me want to slit my wrists.

He's lonely here. His attitude's a dead giveaway. No wonder he's under a cloud. But he's promised to return. To attend the interview with the Barshaw committee. After his youth team's cup final, of course. He was forced to run out on one before, thirteen years ago. I can't expect him to do the same thing again.

Higgy's staying for his own reasons. But also to ensure that I give Arbroath's director my notice. I'll stay for the youth cup final. But that's to be my last game. Unless Arbroath cancel my contract early. They won't do that because the youth cup final is a glimmer of light in an otherwise dismal season for the seniors. Those on the board couldn't give a fuck as long as the youngsters are still winning. Changing the coaching team now, ahead of a major final, would just be unsettling for young players becoming used to routine. Older players manipulate the position of managers and coaches to suit their own individual or collective agendas. It's a skill that the youth players haven't yet mastered, and why I prefer working with them.

The first team has been relegated. The players gave up months ago. The manager took the rap and the early pay-off, as they always do. But the damage was done. A hefty fine is sure to descend following the floodlighting failure that resulted in the postponement of the cup tie. And a lifelong fan is suing the club for emotional distress; a broken nose resulting from a stray shot hit during a warm-up ... as opposed to the more general distress of following the first team. It's a good time for me to be getting out. I just wish there was somewhere more worthwhile to go.

We sit and eat. A pie and chips from the seafront. *Louder Than Bombs* sets the tone: *'If you have five seconds to spare, then I'll tell you the story of my life.'*

'What's the script, then?' I ask.

'What d'ye mean? Wi' me?'

'Naw. Wi' the Bridge,' I say.

He *ahs,* as if I'd just translated from a foreign language. 'Bad biscuits,' he says, conspiratorially. 'Been on the slide for about six year. Slow, like ... but every season, slippin' further.'

I knew nothing of the club these last two seasons. The black dog is myopic. It only looks inwards.

—We're a fucking laughingstock, and that's the truth. Tiny wee village, always punching above its weight. Had some great teams, great players ... young Danny being one of them. But last year? Fuck sake...

'Ah knew right fae the kick-off that he was a rank bad yin,' he says, referring to the previous Barshaw Bridge FC manager.

'That right?'

'Aye.' His brows furrow like wartime trenches. 'He swans in eighteen months ago, aw Fancy Dan ... a suit an' a cigar. Like he wis the Junior league Malcolm Allison.' Higgy's blood pressure is up now, no question. His disgust at such middle-class appropriation can't be hidden. His words curl and corrode. They need to be spat out. But once done, he composes himself.

'First few games were total bloody chaos. Whole team clueless, an' him effin' an' blindin' at everybody fae the dugout. Somethin' just wisnae right. It wis embarrassin'. He's got the wee Irish lad O'Halloran at right back!' He pauses here, holding out his palms. 'Ah mean, for fuck's sake, Danny.'

I have no knowledge of Sean O'Halloran, or for that matter, Adie McGinty, the outgoing team manager. But I nod along anyway.

'Fucken McGinty ... man. Close tae ruinin' the Bridge.' Not for the first time since he's been here, it feels like Higgy might cry. I'm intrigued by this; the heightened anguish over something so superficial. I've often witnessed it at the fag-end of the game in Scotland. Maybe there's more to it this time.

—There are few things I love more than life itself: his ma ... and God help me, this daft wee inconsequential local team. Soon, Libby will be gone. Her boys, an' my team are it for me. There's nothing else. Nothing.

I never quite felt the way Higgy does about football. Certainly not after the injury. Before that, I loved playing. I loved the feeling of superiority it offered for ninety-plus minutes. I loved being in total control with the ball at my feet. It was an escape from all the other tortures. But I was never obsessed with it, like Higgy is. I suspected there were other things in life that were more important. I just didn't have the access to them.

But for Higgy, the club is his reason for existing. Without it, he simply fades away. Sometimes I envy him his life spent on an island with like-minded people, where rational thinking is displaced by passion and loyalty.

'Weren't gettin' any decisions. Players were leavin', naebody'd go an' watch the team...' He gulps. Lowers his voice. 'An' then, the fucken scandal. It's just about sunk us.'

I understood little of why Barshaw Bridge were even contemplating me as their new manager. Until this next revelation, that is.

—I had to tell him.

'Knows fuck all about fitba, does McGinty. Stupid bastard kept forgettin' it's three points for a win now. Second half ae the season, he's playin' for a draw every bloody game. We're in the bottom three. Four games tae go. Eck Dunbar, the striker, punches the Hurlford Juniors goalie square in the face, then boots him in the baws, and spits on him for good measure. Sent off. Banned for three games. We've got two or three other yins out injured. A draw an' a four nil humpin' away at the Glens leave us needin' tae win the last game ae the season tae avoid gettin' relegated.' He draws air in deeply, as if reliving this might be the end of him.

'Dunbar's a big hairy bastard. Long ginger hair, an' wi' a beard like the Big Yin. Palest skin ye've ever seen tae, like he's been coated in white emulsion.' He sees my confusion. 'McGinty per-suades him tae shave the beard off, get a number one buzzcut, an' spend the whole week oan a sunbed. Slathers aw this dark-brown fake tan stuff ower him tae. The boy looks like a bloody Brazilian. Christ, when he turned up that last Saturday, ah didnae recognise him either. McGinty lists him as a trialist.'

Higgy pauses. Sips the beer from his can.

'Tight match, nothin' in it for the first three quarters. A goal's aw we need, ah'm thinkin'. One bloody goal, an' we're stayin' up. The baw bursts through an' our new trialist's after it. He's past their centre half. The big bastard reaches out an' grabs at Dunbar's shorts. Well ... that wis it!'

'*What* wis it?'

'They'd sprayed the tan everywhere except his arse an' his bol-locks!' Higgy's enraged still, but I can't not laugh at this. 'The shorts are aw ripped tae bits an' the bloody clown's chasin' their defender wi' his big white knob hingin' out, an' a big massive white arse ... swingin' punches, an' bawlin' the odds at the ref for haudin' up a red.'

Fielding ineligible or unregistered players happens a lot in the lower leagues of grass-roots football, but Higgy reinforces the severity of this one.

'Dunbar's aw'ready oan a polis charge ae common assault for the nuttin' the goalie yin. For Christ's sake, Duncan Ferguson's no' long out the jail for less. On the way off, somebody shouts "Yer da sells Avon" at him. Big bloody eejit launches himself intae the crowd, feet first. Very near kills this guy.'

Eck Dunbar won't be coming back. He had vanished – taking several wallets with him – long before the final whistle. 'Good riddance,' mutters Higgy. The club will start the new season down a division and with a points deduction as a further penalty. This wipes the smile from my face. But Higgy isn't finished.

—Don't judge me just because you think I should've told him all of this before he handed his notice in at Arbroath. Don't kid yourself on you'd have acted differently.

'After the game, the ref finds a brown envelope wi' a stiff roll ae twenties in it. There's a note wi' it, signed fae our chairman, pleadin' for him no' tae report us. How fucken stupid did they think we were, eh?'

'What d'ye mean,' I ask. This last bit has me baffled. Higgy's desperation to get it off his chest means his account has more holes in it than one of the nets. However, what's crystal clear is that the blame for this botched attempt to bribe the officials falls squarely at one man's feet.

'It wis bloody McGinty. Ah'm tellin' ye, he wis absolutely off his head at the end. A complete mental case.' Higgy is laying it on thick. Hard to separate the fact from the exaggerated fiction.

'Never told me aw this before,' I say.

'Tellin' ye now!' he comes back, defences up.

I'm piecing it together: The Bridge need someone cheap, (relatively) young and part of a time in the club's history when it overachieved. A prodigal.

Higgy pipes up with my name – prompted from afar by Raymond – and Barshaw Bridge FC can make a grovelling appeal for leniency to the SFA. Which brings us to…

'So, what's the damage?'

'Dunbar *sine died*,' says Higgy. He sighs. 'But he went oan the run fae the polis anyway. Naebody knows where the daft bastard is now. McGinty banned fae fitba for five year.' He takes a deep breath. 'An' the Bridge docked nine points fae the start ae next season.'

It's my turn for anger. 'What, an' ye couldnae've fucken mentioned that right off the bat?'

'Ah thought ye'd turn it down,' he says.

'An' ye'd have fucken thought right then, ya sneaky wee bastard.' I get up. The chair tips over behind me.

Higgy looks crestfallen. He'd know I'd have found out sooner or later. Having reluctantly said yes to returning, he'll assume I won't go back on that. Even if I wanted to, the option to stay has been removed. My contract was up in the summer and there has been no rush by my employers to renew it. Higgy doesn't know this, but it's the reason for my aggravation. After a prolonged silence, Higgy apologises. Then his tears *do* flow. My anger eventually subsides. It's only a game, after all. Nine points is an Everest ascent in bare feet and without crampons for the current Barshaw Bridge FC. It's three straight wins. Although I'm not returning for the glory, it forces me to reassess what even modest success with the team might look like.

There's little else to say. The decision has already been made. In truth, I'm fucking miserable here in the cold north-east. And where else would I go? My choice of downbeat soundtrack merely reflects it. Brief moments of fulfilment, swamped by the more insistent guilt, regret and loneliness. I'd already reckoned it was time for a change, but lacked any form of impetus.

Although it kills me to admit it, I owe Higgy a lot. He told me stories of the great Barshaw teams of the past; of wonder goals

and wonder player
young enough to
it was not just po
the local team. I'
the game. It was
the Barshaw pit
up my power an

But I'm not
longing nowhe
that I ran fron
But if providir
live for beyon
purpose, may

street, one-dimensional place an
ferent normality. Not a h
emotionally safer.
The place is exactly
wards rural commun
been ten years, I r
I imagine i
eighty years
their cou
rustin
my

The car slows.

'Left here, is it?' He's still going too fast.

'Aye. But ye need tae watch. It's a sharp turn just beyond the hump.'

'Fuck sake,' says the taxi driver. He breaks sharply. I knew he would and I've braced myself for it.

Barshaw Bridge. The awkward, twisting, dangerous access the village football club is named after. A hump-backed death trap, as I can personally attest. A narrow approach shaped exactly like the metal catch on that wee elasticated snake belt I wore as a child. Too fast and you're right into the low, dark stone wall. Too slow, and you risk oncoming vehicles not seeing you in time. Catch-22.

'Ah see what ye mean. That's an accident waitin' tae happen, eh?' He laughs. Not coming close to the truth of his observation.

'Aye.' I look out the window. We drive up the gradual incline. The density of the trees that line the road, until it widens enough to permit two vehicles to pass each other. Even now, at this late stage, I contemplate the car taking me straight through this one-

d out the other side. Back to a dif-
ppy one, admittedly; just a bit

s I recall it. The pace of change in back-
ties like Barshaw is barely detectable. It's only
mind myself.

looking exactly like this on the day, more than
ago, when five young recruits left the village to serve
try; the only addition being the stained stone pillar and
plaque to their memory in the centre of Main Street. I hear
older brother: *Lucky bastards*, he'd say, as he sat on the plinth
rinking pale ale. *At least they didnae have tae fucken come back
tae this shitehole.*

We drive past Ollie's, the butcher's, where Raymond nicked a
whole haunch of beef while a pal distracted the owner. Next door,
Bogart's Hypermarket is closed. A queue has formed outside its
door. The biggest shop – although that isn't saying much – re-
opening after lunch, like it's still processing ration books. The
baker's was run by a jovial man called Ernie. Looking through the
window, I can see that it still is.

Past a tiny vennel and there's Dave Bamford's newsagent, where
I had a paper round. When my bike got stolen from the yard
behind it, Libby had to drive me about, and took my wages.
There's the brick wall with white goalposts painted on it. The
word 'End' is painted where you might expect a goalie to stand
when facing a penalty kick. I'd always be down here battering a
Mitre 5 at the middle letter. Bending the ball around carefully
placed dustbins until daylight faded and I couldn't see the posts
anymore, or when someone came out and complained at the
racket I was making so late in the day.

I'd fingered Alison Currie in that same dimly lit waste ground.
There isn't a commemorative blue plaque on the wall there. Just a
newly installed security camera. I contemplate running into her
after all these years. Would I recognise her? What would I say?

Would she remember me the way I do her? That the smell of her on my fingers had repulsed me and made me gag. But not enough to stop me losing my virginity to her a week later.

The built structures of Barshaw developed around its church. Its identity spilled from the other place of worship: The King's Arms. Hard, blackened, pitted mining men falling into personal decline as the coal industry collapsed and in the daylight above ground, where they forged a different type of covenant with God. Trouble prospers when uneducated men have too much time on their hands.

And at the far end of Main Street, just beyond the soon-to-be-redundant school gates, over on the elevated left plateau, is the football ground; the emotional (broken) heart of the village. It seems smaller than I remember. Down to Arbroath's pitch at Gayfield being bigger, no doubt, rather than me being smaller when I last played on it.

I was eleven the first time. A schools' cup final. Barshaw Primary's first – and to date, only. It was a wonder there were enough boys from the village school to make up the numbers, never mind have us all co-ordinated enough to win the four games needed to lift the cup. But we did. The coaching extended to an excitable male teacher yelling 'pass it to Garvey' or 'shoot, Danny!' every five minutes. He'd argue it worked. I scored four.

Prophetic classroom banners proclaimed *Garvey Will Burst Your Net*. I took one home to pin to the ceiling above my bed. I felt special. Libby threw it out. Raymond retrieved it the next day before the lorry took it. He took money off me for it. I kept it hidden under my bed until I left Libby's place.

Ours wasn't a happy home filled with laughter. Kids should laugh a lot. I didn't. Not inside it, anyway.

I get out of the car. A man watches me. He leans on the corner wall of the pub, as if preventing its imminent collapse, rather than the other way around. Maybe each needs the support of the other. He stares. He seems concerned. He shouts: am I alright? which seems strange in the context of me just arriving. Something vaguely memorable about him, but that will happen a lot. Hard to determine whether *I've* been recognised. Maybe the uniqueness of a taxi dropping someone off here is the remarkable thing.

I wait; staring for what seems like hours. Imagining myself occupying these narrow streets, brushing up against that monotonous grey roughcast.

There's been a load of compromisin', on the road to this fucking horizon.

'Bud? Mate?' The driver; out the car and nudging me out of the daydream. 'Ah need tae shoot, pal.'

'Aye. Sorry.'

I pay the driver and advise him to return to the seventy-six, taking the northern route that skirts the long north bank of the river. It'll add about twenty minutes but it's far safer than the Russian Roulette of the bridge, I advise him. I watch the car become a tiny purple dot before it disappears into the haze.

I walk towards the pitch, drawn there magnetically. The propped-up man still stares. When I reach the perimeter fence, I look back. He seems to be following.

'Danny, son. Ye made it.' The shout comes from the back of the huts. It's Higgy; my sponsor and landlord for the next two weeks.

I still have no idea why I agreed to this. It won't end well. It can't. When I left, I never expected to return. But Deek Henderson dying changed all that. Ten years ago, I came back for his funeral. Raymond didn't want me to. He said it would open a whole series of buried emotions, that it wouldn't benefit anyone, least of all me. I told him I didn't know what he was talking about, and he said that that was the way it should stay. Despite everything else he did, Deek Henderson had given me my chance. When others were saying I was far too young, far too weak for the rigors of the junior game, he said he trusted me. And he'd stuck by the promise he made me. I felt I owed him. But even so, I didn't stay long at the funeral. In and out. Alone. Didn't go to the graveside.

Didn't catch up with old school friends or team-mates. Didn't spend any time reminiscing. Didn't go and see my mother.

Now she is dying. She knows the cause of it and the likely time-scale. A season at best.

Being involved in football makes you think differently about the passing of time. You think in seasons, not years. Starting in August and finishing in May. Fuck all in between. The boredom and depression of the summer shutdown. Alone and with nothing to do. And, paradoxically, the time when the darkness sets in. Christmas, another unwelcome intrusion. Especially a white one with games being called off. The real time; the *remaining* time, as-sessed in quarters. A mathematical strategy for plotting progress in incremental stages.

At best, Libby, my mam, might make it to the quarter-final stages of the various cups. Anything else would be injury time and up to the discretion of the ref. It's out of her hands.

～

And now I'm back here with him. Higgy's house; as chaotic and uncoordinated as the man himself. As cluttered and shambolic as I remember it. Being in the midst of it makes me feel ill and dis-located.

'Ye got a suit?' he asks.

'No.'

'Want a loan ae yin?'

I look at him; a fat, dumpy silhouette against the low, late light from his front window. My physical opposite. 'Ye fucken serious?'

'No' mine. Christ, ah dinnae have a suit. The one Raymond used—'

I interrupt him. 'For court appearances?'

'Well ... aye. Ah suppose.' He sighs. 'Nae point in it goin' tae waste though.'

In typical fashion, I am now turning up to be interviewed for

a job I don't want, wearing a stolen suit my imprisoned brother
has no further use for.

◠

Higgy has a TV set the size of a small car. A 'gift' from Raymond,
he says. It is perched on a low table, looking like a world-record
'clean-and-jerk' lift by a tiny weightlifter. He has the contrast
dialled up. The exaggerated colours prompt a sharp headache and
remind me how little I've missed television.

We watch a buoyant England team destroy a lacklustre
Holland, and then debate the merits of New Order's 'World in
Motion' song from Italia 90. Higgy thinks a football song should
be like 'Ally's Tartan Army'; a knees-up novelty sing-along that's
a bit of a laugh. Not something that takes itself too seriously.

The likelihood that the hosts will win these European Cham-
pionships aggravates Higgy.

'Bloody hypocrites. Aw these right-wing politicians and chin-
less royals desperate tae be seen at the matches cos the country
looks like it might lift a trophy. They've spent the last ten years
victimisin' their own fans. Fucken stigmatisin' the entire game.'

And he's right. These glory-hunting cunts wrapping themselves
in the flag as they watch from secure goldfish bowls full of free
hospitality; the same ones that condemn the fans for Hillsbor-
ough, that send truncheon-wielding police on horses to batter and
corral. That send in the Alsatians, straining at the leash. Hooligans
on the terraces, but the vandals are in the plush seats. I thought I
couldn't care less, but the partisan coverage is getting to me too.

'An' they bloody commentators ... bangin' on about 1966 every
five minutes. Does ma nut in, so it does.' Football irritates him so
much, yet he can't turn it off.

'That'll aw stop if they win,' I offer.

'Ach, Christ sake! They'd be unbearable. Un-*bloody*-bearable,'
he emphasises. 'Really thought *we* had a wee chance tae.'

—Didn't realise how much I missed him. Missed just sitting here, watching the football and talking about the game. Used to be Match of the Day. *Danny loved it. With Raymond, it was always the boxing. Ali, Frazier, 'Hitman' Hearns. Never had much time for the football. But a fight ... he'd always sit in for that. Danny wasn't one for kicking every kind of ball around the house, but Raymond ... he was forever punching things. Walls, doors. His brother. Me. Danny used other, more subtle ways to hurt people.*

I didn't see the match he's referring to. The Paul Gascoigne goal that sunk Scotland has been shown six times already in the pre-match build-up. The hysteria is escalating. The English-based newspapers are full of jingoistic language. Photos of Saint George flags drape terraced houses up and down their country. The government might be fucked but don't worry, lads ... *it's coming home!* It feels like the Falklands all over again. We turn it off and discuss options for the Bridge.

'So,' I say. 'Who's left in the squad?'

—He was ten years old, and the first of the pro clubs came calling. The granda of a boy in his primary-school class was a Celtic scout. He knew Danny was a potential contender. While others scraped off layers of skin on the unforgiving full-size blaes pitch, Danny glided over it. Through school teams and S-forms, Scottish Boys caps and then the start with the Bridge when he was only sixteen. But that put some of the bigger clubs off. Raymond decided for Danny, masking his determination to maintain control over his younger brother by insisting that our local village team needed him. Can't deny Raymond was probably motivated by more selfish ambitions. 'There'll be plenty ae time an' money later,' he'd regularly say. Danny was an elegant young midfielder in his short time at the Bridge. Slaloming past the hardened, stocky, thick-veined legs of those twice his age. He scored eleven goals in eight games. He stood out. He had panache. He was tall and strong for his age, and despite the junior levels, plenty were taking notice.

He has a renewed purpose. Like he's recaptured something vital from his youth. Higgy brings a pristine pad of lined paper from his kitchen. It hasn't been used. He'll have bought it weeks ago, anticipating this moment.

'Here ye go, boss.' He earnestly hands me a wee blue Labrokes pen. Like we're Clough and Taylor planning a new campaign.

Using one of his own, he marks out a rectangle. He draws a line across the middle. Then he adds a perfect circle and the two penalty boxes. He's taking his time over the proportions to make it accurate. He turns it and slides it over to me, like a pupil submitting maths homework. I almost expect him to put an 'x' and 'y' along the edges before using an equation to work out their equivalents.

'Did ye know only psychopaths can draw perfect circles?'

He makes a weird, nervous laughing noise at this. 'That right?' he says.

'Naw. They're just convinced they can.' I stare him out. 'Jesus. Ah'm just kiddin'.' He waits, as if my permission is needed for him to continue. I nod, and he does.

'McIntosh – the goalie – he's a good shot stopper, but see crosses? As much use as bloody Dracula.' Higgy folds his arms as if to reinforce this.

'Right,' I say. 'Worth keepin' though?'

'Ah'd say so, aye. He still struggles wi' the pass-back rule. Four times last year, the daft bastard picks it up. An' he's a lazy fucker tae ... an' a bit too fond ae the drink, but we can work on the attitude.'

If they are all this flawed, it's going to be a very long season.

Higgy has the fire in his eyes. That expectant glow before a new season starts. The period in which unconstrained dreams thrive before reality kills them. It's endearing.

'Back line's a real problem. Nae connection between any ae them. We need tae fix that first,' he says, before mindfully adding, '...in my opinion, that is.'

We discuss the current middle-to-front resources before Higgy lays it on the line for me. The scale of the task ahead.

—We had some good players at the start of last year. Young players, fast ones; those that thought on their feet. We had the makings of something exciting. By the end though, many had left, broken by the chaos of McGinty's tactics. The last time I felt this was back in early eighty-three. The year Danny broke into the team. That's what makes the disaster of last season's end so fucking utterly painful.

'There's eighteen signed. Twelve'll come back … thirteen maybe. Four ae them just aren't good enough, Danny.' He is putting lines through wee circles on the paper. Indications from this are that I'd need a striker, an attacking midfielder and a centre half. The very spine of a starting eleven.

None of this will be simple. Barshaw Bridge is tainted. Believed to be on an antiquated life-support system or on death row, depending whether you believe the committee were complicit in the recent scandal. Logic suggests they couldn't have been, and this has probably saved the club.

—The four guys on the board knew nothing about McGinty's palm-greasing antics with match officials. God, most of the team were unaware of it. I'm certain of this. I've been involved with this club for nearly thirty years. Since my granda looked after the ground. You learn about people; learn their motivations and their weaknesses. The chairman's only error was trusting what Adie McGinty told him.

Despite some questionable decision-making, Higgy tells me, the committee – and the unpaid sub-committee, which includes him – have put in endless hours, come rain or shine, purely for the benefit of the club. They got something back, no doubt. It offered them purpose and self-validation. A reason to believe for men still holding on to the fading glories of their youth. Men in the depths of mid-life, with nothing to do but watch *The Bill* while waiting for the grave. The club is an escape for those too intimidated by the golf club, and too poor for it.

How to attract players that are exciting enough to bring the meagre core support back to watch? Stretched finances find new priorities when the local team has been relegated. It will be challenging to regain the spirit of the early eighties, when the club was part of the village identity struggling but unbowed; an outlet for a prescient socialist community aware what Thatcher had planned for the mines, the only mass employer in the area.

The club was the community's passion back then. Upwards of three hundred people – male *and* female – supported the home games I played in during that memorable season.

A few weeks back inside Higgy's narrow perspective and I understand what it means to him, and what it could mean to others here with little else to hope for. They yearn for something that they can belong to. A cause. Survival; a mid-table finish; a big home draw in a national or regional cup – I sense that the fucking bunting would be out if even one of those could be delivered. Challenging indeed, but what have I got left to lose?

It's this, and Higgy's incessant pleading, that has convinced me to return. I must still address the issues of the past; *my* past. If I don't – irrespective of results on the pitch – there's no future for me.

⌒

—*There hasn't been a word out of him since he got up. Every question or remark I've made gets ignored. He's always had these periods where he just retreats into himself. It's like he's in a trance; impossible to reach. I hope today isn't another one of those times.*

Thirteen seasons have passed, but I walk into this dilapidated place known to everyone as The Barn like I was returning to it after a disappointing two-week summer break. I'm anxious. Sweating. Not about the job – about the interview; the kind of social situation I dread. I wander down the narrow corridor. It hasn't seen fresh paint since Higgy volunteered to decorate three months before I left. The carpets are new, strangely enough. Loud and headache-inducing, admittedly, but new.

I pass the office, a large cupboard rammed with everything from cleaners' mops, detergent supplies and cans of petrol, to last season's team strips, balls and training equipment. It smells like something has crawled in there and died. Months ago.

The changing rooms are exactly as I remember them. Cold, dark, windowless and stinking of a mix of stale body odour and Ralgex spray. The showers drip. The urinal trough is dented in the middle, leaving a puddle at the opposite end from the drain. And the light switch has gone on strike. I make a mental note to swap the home and away dressing rooms for next season. There's not much to choose between them but I'd rather we benefitted from a working radiator when winter hits.

The season we got to the league cup final, a small army of volunteers materialised. The facilities were transformed. *Amazing what a wee bit of spit, polish and elbow grease can achieve,* they'd say proudly. A selfless backroom team, galvanised by the unfettered joy of an unexpected cup run.

Failure, on the other hand, is like a rot that sets into everything and everyone. A blanket of gloom descending on a whole community of desperate men. For this is a corner of community life that is almost exclusively male. A pervading depression descends. There's too much invested. Too little self-control on the sidelines when that investment bears nothing. Fans arguing and fighting amongst themselves. As if the village didn't have enough to contend with.

—I came in three hours ago. I hoovered the committee-room carpet, after spreading this powdery freshener stuff that I'd seen advertised. It smells like a bloody perfume counter. I dusted. I scrubbed. I laid

out clean glasses and placed the chairs for the committee tight to-
gether, like a defensive wall facing a Beckham free kick. I put the
heater on, to shift the chill that makes your fingers go blue. It's a new
season. New hope. I hope the interviewing panel notice.

The committee room is the biggest space in the small, rectangular
complex. As soon as the door opens, fresh Shake n' Vac wafts up
my nostrils, as powerful as smelling salts. An electric heater makes
the room feel like the Amazon. The panel of four face me. None
were here when I played for the club. To their right is the window
onto the pitch. It is cracked. Brown tape runs along the fissure
on the inside. To their left are the wooden wall panels decorated
with the names of captains and players-of-the-year going back to
the dawn of the twentieth century. Two young Barshaw sons who
didn't return from a war are also commemorated. Alongside
them is Bill Shankly, who briefly played here. Further along is
mine. The club's last great young hope, who abandoned it on the
eve of their only cup-final appearance of recent times. I'm surprised it hasn't been chiselled out, like one from an earlier era
seems to have been.

They know me but I only know one of them. A ball not yet
kicked in anger and I see the defeat in their faces. Sense the heavy
gloom that is polluting the air. They are going through the
motions. No-one will touch this job. They know I know this. But
still, there's a formality to undergo. Rules are rules.

William Kidd is the chairman. He took over early last season.
He's new to the area. He doesn't have the deep roots of the others.
But he has money. And that's more important. He runs a small
carpet-fitting business called Kidd's Carpets. They run regular
adverts on the local radio station with the ridiculous tagline 'Piles
better'. Their logo is everywhere around the ground and on the
club's red strips. I asked Higgy how much money Kidd has put in.
He didn't know the sum but he feels the need to reaffirm just how
hard Kidd's small team have worked to raise money for the club

over the last year. Higgy vouches for the chairman like he was a Mob boss's consigliere. But it's the depth of Billy the Kidd's pockets that I'm primarily interested in, not the benevolence of his character.

Other second-division clubs like Ardeer, Muirkirk, Troon or Craigmark can muster finances to change the squad. Barshaw has a tiny fraction of that to work with. We'll be relying on gate money – if we can attract a crowd – and intermittent sponsorship from The King's Arms. And the tireless fundraising of its committee members, main and sub. The only other route is favours, but reciprocity is in short supply here, like everything else.

—I gaze out the window, and suddenly, there I see him. Number ten. Running rings around fat midfielders. He was in total control on this pitch. No hiding here. No anxious looks over the shoulder. Senses attuned to everything. He didn't shout or cajole back then. He was quiet. Calm. Composed. An old head on young shoulders, it was regularly said. Danny could see not only three or four passes ahead, but three or four minutes. That's a long time in a passage of play. Especially in Scotland where genetics hinder. Fitter, stronger, harder, taller. *The only attributes that matter.*

The committee file in. I can't sit in while Danny talks to them, but I'm convinced he'll be fine. The job's his unless he decides he doesn't want it. He's interested, I can tell from all the questions he's been asking. He hasn't mentioned Raymond. Plenty of time for that later.

The door closes. I go out for a walk around the pitch to pass some time.

'Mr Garvey. Hullo. Alright if we call ye Daniel?' Billy the Kidd is a bald ball of meat and whisky, as wide as he is tall.

'Danny,' I reply.

'Ah, yes … Danny,' says the chairman. He probably thinks I should've grown out of Danny. Become something more adult. Daniel, en route to the middle-aged era of Dan.

'We'll take some notes, if that's okay.' Mr Kidd jerks his head sharply to one side and I follow its direction towards the corner. One of the seated men opens a notepad.

Behind him, a young woman stands so close to a curtain that at first, I think it's what she's wearing. She has long dark hair; it almost reaches the clipboard she is holding. The committee introduced themselves as I came in, but no-one refers to her.

'Ah hear ye were quite the prospect when ye last pulled on the shirt, eh?' It's a stupid icebreaker on anybody's terms. He sounds like a disappointed headmaster about to admonish a former star pupil. It draws my gaze back from the corner of the room.

I don't answer. *The past is a foreign country*, and all that bollocks.

'So … Danny, why do you want this job?'

I resist the urge to tell him that I don't. That my reasons for being back here are nothing to do with the club. That it's simply a convenient staging post in the journey out of the dark place that I'm stuck in.

'I think ah know how tae win,' I say, generalising.

The committee react like it was the Gettysburg Address. Nods and smiles. The woman writes. Job done for them. Billy the Kidd gets up and goes to the cabinet. He opens a door and brings out a decanter. He pours a whisky for each of his colleagues. They are celebrating. After one answered question.

'Well, that's our number-one priority, son,' says Phil Dick, the only one here that I remember. Phil's wife Senga was my primary-seven teacher. She was – as you might expect – known as 'Suckma'. Scrubbing this off the red-brick toilet walls became a full-time job for the janitors. A letter was once given to every child outlining that Mrs Dick was reverting to her maiden name of Brown. It didn't help her. Suckma Brown was arguably funnier.

I briefly consider asking if she's still teaching. But I don't.

'4-4-2 … or 4-3-3?' poses Bert Thompson, club secretary, as if we're holed up in a bank vault and he's whispering combination alternatives. I see the numbers written on his notepad. His pen is now poised, ready to record my reponse.

'Dunno. Ah'd need tae assess the players. See how adaptable they are.'

'Good man,' he says, winking at the chairman; his one rehearsed question has been addressed. The chairman offers me a plastic cup. I decline.

'Higgy's been keepin' an eye on yer progress wi' the Arbroath kids.' I glance over at the corner. The woman is staring out of the window. Probably watching Higgy pacing the touchline. 'You're his recommendation, ah'm sure ye'll gather.'

'Aye,' I say, to fill the gap he leaves.

'We had a couple ae options,' says the chairman. I don't believe him. Higgy would've told me. Gilhooly, last season's captain, was sounded out, but he told Phil Dick that he'd rather 'get a short back an' sides off a combine harvester'.

'Ye've made a few waves up there. The *Press & Journal* feature. We thought we'd best get in quick afore Man United come callin'.' They laugh; not at me, and not in the condescending way this sounds.

'Ah think Fergie's probably pretty safe,' I say, smiling.

They are delighted at this because it opens the door to the real reason why I'm being interviewed for a single candidate post.

'Whit's he like then, big Alex?' asks Treasurer Des Bryson, on behalf of the males present. Beaming, expectant faces.

Best not to let them down. I conceal the truth and appropriate an apocryphal story that they'll recount at dinner parties for years. 'He came to the house. Back in eighty-three. Right after the Talbot semi-final,' I tell them. 'They're preparin' for the Cup Winners' Cup final an' he still finds time tae drive aw the way tae Barshaw tae persuade a sixteen-year-old tae sign for his club.'

This staggers them, and it would have staggered me too, had it been the truth.

'He told me I'd be nurtured at the Dons. Looked after an''

developed properly. He said I'd be a future Scotland captain under his direction,' I tell them. 'When he said that, I knew it was the club for me.'

Aberdeen was the option available to me that put the most distance between me and the consequences of what happened on the night of the Talbot game. Alex Ferguson didn't come personally to pluck me from teenage obscurity. That's the truth. But that's not the tale I'm telling.

'What a fella,' says the chairman.

Their faces ooze admiration at the class of the man whose picture I'm painting. The cut of him. The exquisite taste of him. I'm certain Billy the Kidd will be contemplating the possibility of me persuading my old boss to revisit Barshaw. Hand out a commemorative medal or two. Record a line praising the luxurious comfort of a Kidd carpet. Uttering the words 'Piles better'.

'Aw, Christ, son ... that's brilliant!' Phil Dick slaps his thighs when I lie about Alex Ferguson driving me personally to Arbroath ten years ago; one of his last acts before taking over at Old Trafford.

I'm not the man they think I am.

⌒

They ask me to step out for half an hour or so to allow them to consult their notes. Less than five minutes later, I'm back in the room. The woman has gone, her purpose there seemingly at an end. I'm shaking hands with my new employers. They talk mobile phones. I've never had or used one. A modest clothing allowance to buy a suit I'll never wear from Bert Thompson's brother's shop in Ayr. They probably think I need one. I decided against wearing Raymond's. Death is the only justifiable reason for dressing up. They offer the use of a pool car with a designated parking space that I'll never use, and a hundred a month. It's a third of what I was on at Arbroath but I'm not paying rent at Higgy's. And there's a free carpet for Libby's place in return for some regular Kidd's Carpets promotion duties. It's more than I thought they'd have to offer.

I'll be able to access payments for players of five to twenty pounds a week paid as travelling expenses to avoid the tax. Signing-on fees, at a modest level, if I can use my contacts and lure anyone decent from the bigger leagues – even if they're just on loan.

They show me the office. My new office. I remember Deek Henderson sitting in there, in tears. Pleading with me not to go to Aberdeen before the final. Apologising. Talking about the stress he had been under. Begging me not to tell anyone about him and what he had asked me to do.

I'd already told Raymond, of course. He cooked up a plan. I'd get my shot in the first team, and he'd get a few quid out of Deek to pay for our silence. I already knew I was good enough to play but my brother didn't see it that way.

I lift a rotting plant from the desk and throw it in the bin. Through the small window, I watch Higgy continue to circum-navigate the pitch. I leave him to it.

It's just us. Me and the awkward, uncertain playing squad I've just inherited. Minus a couple of young midfielders who are in Spain on holiday. A kid wearing what looks like a space helmet plays on his bike on the other side of the pitch. Higgy is off somewhere. Checking on Libby. Meeting an old acquaintance. Who knows?

I look at them. Say nothing. The younger ones fidget, snigger. The older ones remain cynically remote. They've seen it all before; a new broom. Different ideas, same outcomes. Some of them joined in the last months of the crisis season just past; a campaign in which Barshaw FC barely won a game, and the team's manager resorted to bribery and cheating to avoid relegation. It's surprising any of them returned. They're here because, despite everything, they love playing. Crave the draw of being part of a gang, regardless of how dysfunctional it is.

I'm looking intently at the words on a piece of paper. They were written days ago by Higgy. As I read, I imagine him laughing out loud at his own descriptions.

> *Keepers: we've only got the one right now.*
> **Tony McIntosh** *– Like Goram. Great shit-stopper. Don't leave any pies lying around tho.*

Higgy's handwriting makes it hard to know if he meant to write *shot-stopper* or not.

> *Defenders:*
> **Davie Russell** *– This yin's a good yin. When he can get here.*
> **Mark Buchan** *– a cripple with legs dipped in tar, wearing ice. skates with the laces tied th'gither's got more grace and speed.*
> **Paddy Gilhooly** *– aircraft carriers turn quicker.*
> **'Dib' Ramage** *– New Youngster. Worth a chance.*
> **Stevie Smith** *– The better of two evils.*
>
> *Mids:*
> **Sean O'Halloran** *– McGinty had him as a defender???? But he's the best natural ba' player in the club. Build the team round him.*
> **Luke Lorimer** *– Shy kid. Needs more self confidence. He fits carpets with Kidds.*
> **Micky Minns** *– Thinks he's Michael Laudrup. More like yon Michael O'Fattly ... That Lord of the Dance cunt.*
> **Fraser Boland** *– Promising. Came along with Lorimer.*

Higgy searching out a highlighter pen to draw further attention to Sean O'Halloran tells me that he regularly put forward his theory last year to widespread ignorance.

Strikers:
'Flute' Strawhorn – *A total cunt. A rabid Orange yin into the bargain.*
Jaz Sinclair – *This yin played with Ayr United. He's a good plasterer, I'll give him that. But a bloody disaster as a fitba player.*
'Huck' Finnegan – *A decent shot. He's got that in his locker. (Along wi' 50 Embassy Regal, 1000s ae bettin' slips and photos ae his teammates wives in the scud.)*

The remainder are categorised with reference to the wooden slats he figures they'll spend most of the season warming.

Planks:
Cyril Smith – *I know! About as much fucken use too. Him and Stevie are twins. He's got a motor.*
Andy Meikle – *Fucken hopeless. But his auntie runs the laundry and we get the strips washed for cheap.*
Dougie Wilson – *Jury's out. Came from the Glens. Meant to be good. Fits carpets.*

They all live locally; they won't have any excuses for not being able to get to training when unpredictable weather hits. I've gathered them together early. Season doesn't start for five weeks. They seem surprised. Like they expected the club to fold. Curiosity and fuck all else to do on this mid-summer Sunday morning has made them turn up.

They aren't in differentiating kit, but I immediately know McIntosh before I ask them to introduce themselves. *A bit fond ae the drink*, Higgy has warned. He's the one three from left with long, curly hair. He smells like a brewery and looks like the Pillsbury Dough Boy's fat sister. No wonder he's hopeless at cross balls, having to hoist that belly off the ground to reach for them.

They stand in a line, not in a group. Mouthy ones in the middle. Shy ones at the edges. It reminds me of the primary school teams

I played in. Twelve selected as a minimum, because, despite the absence of talent, you still needed a sub ... just in case. The 'in case' scenarios rarely came though.

I ask them to introduce themselves. Mainly to determine if the 'Meikle' is the one I think it is. It is. That'll have to be dealt with carefully. The two missing are Lorimer and Boland. In Magaluf. Together. I look at them more intently, *my* squad. Apart from two, I'd guessed them correctly from Higgy's pinpoint descriptions.

'Gaffer?' That still sounds bizarre. It's a term I associate with the hierarchy of the unions, not football. At Arbroath, I was 'Mr Garvey' to the players, like I was one of their school P.E. teachers.

'When wis you here, again?' The lower-league equivalent of 'show us yer medals'. It's Gilhooly asking. The current captain. The questioning will be a way of delaying the training, rather than any real interest in my playing history. However, I indulge it.

'Ah was in the team that beat Talbot tae get to the league cup final. 1983.' I suspect he already knows this. But we're feeling each other out. It's about what they'll get away with, how strict the new man will be. Will he be worse than the last? Will he make us run further?

'Left before the final, though, eh?' A challenge from my over-weight goalkeeper, or an acknowledgement?

'Aye,' I reply. 'Ah did.'

'Must've been a tough yin, that,' says Micky Minns.

'How?' asks Gilhooly of his team-mate. 'A chance tae get out ae this fucken dump an' make some solid dough playin' fitba for a pro team? Ye widnae ae seen me for fucken dust, pal.' Maybe the captain will be an ally. Every manager needs one on the pitch.

'Played for Scotland, din't ye?' says Gilhooly. He sounds impressed. He's a veteran of this team. He's been here since 1985; a traumatic year for Barshaw Bridge FC. And for me. The year of the injury. Inevitably, I'm asked about it. I rarely think about it now, but since I have their attention. And yours...

The day after the semi-final against the Talbot, Raymond

phoned a scout at Aberdeen whose number he'd kept. A meeting was hastily arranged. Raymond travelled across the country with me and Higgy. Three buses. The two of them studied my first formal contract like they were Harvard lawyers, protecting their own interests. I signed it because they hadn't a fucking clue whether it was good or bad. They only saw the money; minuscule in comparison to what the other boys said Miller or McLeish were on. But it was like a pools coupon win for a couple of opportunistic Ayrshire chancers.

The Aberdeen youth coaches turned me into a right fullback – the white Viv Anderson, they called me. A year and seven months after I left the village, I was playing for the Dons youth team and up in Banff. A friendly against Deveronvale.

A freezing cold February morning. A dismally poor first half. We were a goal down. It should've been more. I was up against a great wee player; a lightning-fast *jinky* winger. He was running me ragged. The conduit for all their chances. Our manager told me to let him know I was there in the second half; to *do him*. He was bombing towards me, making a move to go outside. I saw a big lunging slide tackle. I launched into it. A terrible crunching and twisting, and astonishing pain surged immediately from my hip, groin and stomach. My right leg was diagonally behind my back and my right boot was behind my left ear. Like an Action Man bent shapeless by a destructive child.

The referee stopped the game. None of that kicking it out from sporting opponents in those days. *Play to the whistle, no matter fucking what.*

Nothing changed for my beneficiaries back home. No-one came to see me during my isolated recovery. I didn't want them to anyway. My money was still being transferred so they were alright.

Rehabilitation was slow, but I made it back; as far as Aberdeen's reserves. A substitute performance lasting twenty minutes in a nothing, end-of-season game against a poor Rangers second team in an empty Ibrox. But I had long lost the early swaggering self-confidence. The elegance. The balance. The interest. All supplanted by the crippling fear of it happening again. Gone was the focused determination necessary for progress. It was simply a series of defeats. I was just another one of thousands of young contenders desperate to be a footballer, getting barracked from the terracing, week after week, by twenty-stone beer-bellied balloons, convinced they could do better. I wasn't special anymore.

I didn't fit in either. Couldn't contribute to the speed and brutality of the changing-room banter. I withdrew from my teammates. When the darkness descended, I listened to the records that had become my only companions. I read more. Educated myself beyond my English and P.E. 'O' levels. When the cast was removed, I spent more time in the local library than I did in the gym. Just turned eighteen and searching for renewed purpose. Trying to work out what I was for.

Aberdeen let me go. Arbroath picked up the pieces. I played only sporadically for the first team. I was encouraged to do the coaching badges and then took over the youth-team responsibilities when I was just twenty-three. Since the injury, life has passed by in a monotonous blur, although I omit that revelation from my testimony.

Minns seems unconvinced.

'Why'd you really leave, eh?' As if none of the foregoing had made a dent.

The truth is, I had changed completely and catastrophically before leaving Barshaw. I went north to escape. To try to be a better version of myself.

My team have lost interest in this cross-examination. They don't give a fuck. They're footballers. Shorter attention spans than toddlers. Their only interest is themselves. As it should be.

'Right,' I shout. 'Up the fucken hill an' back. Sprints. Go!'

Orders. It's what they understand.

The kid in the helmet hasn't moved in over an hour.

Meikle is the last to leave. He's a quiet one. Just like me. He has said nothing to me, nor anyone else that I'm aware of. But he knows me. He knows my family name.

'You aw'right there?' I ask him as he struggles through the door with the laundry kit bag.

'Eh ... aye. Ah am ... em, Mister Garvey.'

'How's yer brother?'

'Which yin?'

'Scud ... *Scott*.' He must've known I would inquire.

'Ach. No' great. See him about, an' that, but he keeps well away, like.'

'Ah'm sorry about that,' I say. I hope he knows I mean it, but it doesn't register much.

'Cheers,' he says, then leaves, pulling the door closed behind him.

Scott Meikle and I were friends, briefly. Until my brother Raymond put him in intensive care.

There will be a lot more apologising and appeasing to be done over this coming season.

I could've avoided her. I could've been here for the whole season; the last few months of her life, and not encountered her. No hiding under the Barshaw Bridge necessary now. Libby, you see, can't leave the house. If many in Barshaw are prisoners of economic circumstance, she's in permanent solitary confinement.

But I do the right thing. I visit. Reluctantly. Had to get my bearings first; realign my memorial compass.

—Danny walks beside me silently, his head down. I can't read him. He's still the same inscrutable kid. I'm sure Libby was more protective

of Raymond because he seemed to need it more, not because she loved Danny less. Despite being much younger, Danny always seemed the more stable, the more emotionally independent. Raymond's brash outward charm was just a front for his lack of confidence. How wrong I was about them. Still, I'm pleased he's here, even if I do have to put up with his hurtful jibes. I'm happy for Libby. She deserves a bit of temporary happiness. We all do.

Three months it's taken. That's how long I've been back here. So three months, plus thirteen years, give or take, of Higgy's exhortations. Peter Higgins, the faithful manservant; the carrier of the torch. What a fucking dunce. I tell him he's wasted his life waiting on her hand and foot like a courtier. A brief shard of anger like he's stood on a tiny glass fragment, and then it quickly dissipates. You can toy with him. It's all too easy though, to be honest. He keeps it all in. Anger isn't his thing. Never has been. He can't sustain it against anyone, more's the pity. And it's mainly pity I feel for him now. Maybe he's the reason I came back. Despite everything, this club is all that has ever offered him joy. He deserves a result. I suppose I owe him one.

'Dinnae keep her waitin', son,' he says to me.

'Why, she got somewhere else tae be?' I reply.

'Christ sake, Danny, ye know what ah mean. Stop bein' so...' He tails off. He can't say it. He wants to tell me to stop being so much of a cunt.

I sigh, take the petrol-station flowers he bought earlier and head up the hill towards the small terraced house I was born in. The one the two of us have been staring at for over fifteen minutes.

The net curtain twitches as I approach the door with its flaking green paint. There are still remnants of the blue I'd started to cover it with twenty years ago, before she caught me and clipped my ear for it. I push back the stiff, metal letterbox cover. It stays open, silent. Not returning to its original position. It needs oiling. It must never get used.

Even though she watched me approach and she knew I was coming Libby still edges the door open little more than an inch. She's checking it's me. And this is after several noisy bolts and locks are released. This is Raymond's legacy.

—I wave to her but she doesn't see me. I'm used to that now. She doesn't have long left. I know she just wants to know Danny will be fine. That both of them will be okay. Plenty of times, I urged her to tell Danny about his father, but she always said she couldn't. She's too ashamed, even after all this time. It would explain a lot for him, I told her. He wouldn't blame her. It might help him come to terms with her passing. Help him release some of that pent-up emotion; something he definitely needs to do. But she disagrees. Too much water under the bridge, she says. Better to just keep the past where it is. That's her decision and while I can't completely agree with it, I have to respect her wishes. I leave them to it. I'll come back later. Make sure she's okay.

Four years ago, two men from Galston broke into Libby's house in the middle of the night. They were looking for my brother. He owed them money. Fed up waiting for it, they'd come to collect. Raymond didn't show, but one of the two remained in the house for hours. He terrorised Libby in ways that Higgy finds impossible to describe. The mind being perhaps the most brutal prison of all, she now can't leave the very place where that assault took place.

'Yer tall, son,' she says, looking up at me. A voice with the texture of cement being mixed. The first words spoken in this, the new normal. It's a strange opening; as far back as I can remember, I've been tall. She seems to have shrunk. Maybe this is a way of her acknowledging that before I do.

'Aye. Eatin' well an' that,' I tell her.

'What's he been feedin' ye then?'

'Naw, no' at Higgy's, back in Arbroath. Christ, his cooking skill extends tae the Findus Crispy Pancake range an' nae further.'

Her eyes widen. Nostrils flare slightly. It's as if a noxious gas was suddenly forced down the wee clear tubes that are feeding oxygen to her. She steps back and light from the front window catches her, holding her in its spotlight.

She sees me looking at her forearms, at the still-visible welts from years of stubbed-out cigarettes. Those indications of just how much she must've detested herself. There are tiny holes in the midst of yellowing bruises where needles have searched for veins. They remind me of the ones years ago where all her money used to go.

Yer mammy's just a wee bit upset the now, boys. Grab yer stuff an' ye'se can come an' stay wi' me until she's a bit better. And off we'd go to Higgy's holiday home down the road for anything up to a fortnight at a time. And I wouldn't see her. Raymond would go back to deliver messages. He always cared more. There's no point in denying it.

Seeing her now only prompts memories of the countless times she disappointed me. It should've been the other way around.

I remember Libby turning up late and drunk at a school parents' evening. Higgy, who was acting dad, dragged her away and left me to suffer the looks of pity and scorn.

I remember coming home from school on numerous occasions to find her unconscious in the midst of her own vomit. The rehearsed three-point plan being put into action: phone an ambulance, call Higgy, hunt for Raymond.

And I remember her out in the street in her nightie, fighting with a neighbour, pulling hair and yelling obscenities for everyone around to witness.

The spectre of the woman she was back then can be seen in the angular bones of her face. They're like tent poles fighting a wind, holding up the sagging tarpaulin of her skin. I look again at those wiry arms that once seemed so defiant. She pulls her loose sleeves down. She returns to the subject of food, as if it's all we ever had in common.

'Ah've mind ae ye refusin' tae eat nothin' other than mince out ae a can.' She smiles ruefully at this. Her recollections are different from mine. Suffice to say, I barely remember that.

'My horizons have broadened a wee bit since then,' I say.

'But yer back now,' she says sharply. A rebuke? A regret? A smug *telt ye ye'd never amount tae anythin'*? It's hard to tell. Her delivery has a resigned weariness.

'Aye.'

'Ye applying for a place?' she asks.

'No,' I reply, laughing at the thought. 'Ah'm only on a season's deal. Higgy's place is aw'right. He insisted anyway.'

She clocks me looking round, imagining the room without the medical paraphernalia that sustains her life. Trying to remember, or to see what's changed. Pictures of Raymond. It's not a shrine but the absence of any of me makes it feel like I'm visiting one. I'm not bitter about this. Raymond was her first child; the pinnacle of her achievement. I was just an inconvenient mistake that coincided with her downward domestic slide.

There's a more recent photograph of Raymond. He's holding a child. They are both laughing. Happy. I'm certain it's Damian but I'm not asking. It must've been taken a short time before he went away. There are none featuring the boy's mother. I pick it up.

'He's a good boy. Dinnae see much ae him now though.' She could be talking about either of the people in the picture. 'Quiet, y'know. A bit like you were. Nancy'll no' bring him anymore.'

'Why's that?' I ask.

'Cos she's a spiteful bitch,' Libby says. It's a calm response. No anger, just matter-of-fact commentary. 'The boy's no' right. Sure she blames us for that.' The 'us' in this statement is curious. It can't possibly include me since I haven't met Nancy or Damian, but Libby is circling the wagons. Implying that it's our whole family name that's being traduced.

Libby and Raymond have this in common. They are both masters of manipulation. A personal response to their unreasonable behaviour is transformed into an all-out attack on all of us. Libby can't blame Raymond for anything. She convinces herself that there's a good reason for his actions: he's looking out for her. Or me.

Always the victim, never his fault.

I finally sit on the torn, faded sofa that I was once warned not to touch, like it was on temporary loan from the Louvre. It was bought with Kensitas tokens, a result of a determined habit that will soon kill her.

Libby coughs. It sounds guttural and painful.

'How are ye, anyway?' The ultimate in pass-the-time clichés, but fifteen minutes in and I'm running out of things to say. There's a big fucking elephant in the room. We avoid directly engaging with it for fear it'll crush us.

'Much better,' she replies, clearing an airway and drawing on her second B&H in ten minutes. She looks dreadful. Skeletal and translucent. The sunlight from the front window is behind her, and her blackened organs are almost visible. 'They'd gie'd me pills ... for the weather. Vitamin D,' she says. 'Tae make it sunny.'

'Aye?' I say, unable to mask the surprise; unable to see that she's trying to be funny.

'Oh aye. Been leafing through the brochures,' she says. 'Planning a cruise. They Scandinavian Fjords look nice.' For once, there's no meanness, no self-pity and I laugh at the absurdity. She does too. I feel immediately sad for her. I can't help it. Trapped amongst the bitter memories and the framed reminders of Raymond and of what might've been.

'Ye been behavin' yerself up there?' And there it is; that accusatory stance. Stooped maybe, but still defiant and up for a fight.

'What d'ye mean?' I ask, surprised. I can't imagine she cares all that much. I wouldn't, if I was her, approaching the end of the road.

'The books an' that,' she says. 'That aw in the past now, ah hope.'

I'm suddenly on the defensive. Her tone – frail though she is – takes me back to days when I was being accused of something I hadn't done. Taunting old Jock Reid over his granddaughter, or goading Raymond into stabbing Scud Meikle. I briefly consider asking her about my father; about why she'd never talk about him. But I hold it back. I'd just be resorting to her level, and I'm above all that now. I'm a grown-up.

'Aye,' I say. 'Ah'm done wi' all that nonsense.'

I should offer you some familial context here. My understanding of it comes soley from Raymond, but it's all I have. Any attempts to dig deeper were always shut down. The three of them have always harboured some great secret they refuse to share with me. Libby is my mother. And Raymond's. But we have different fathers. Eddie MacAvoy – *his* dad – was the love of Libby's life. He was a man unable to reciprocate. His love for himself was far too great for any altruism. He drifted from one place to another. From one woman to the next; something that can't be hidden for long in a small village.

Raymond hated his dad. Libby excused her man's every failing, but the one that did the damage was Eddie's disdain for his son. During an extended separation, Libby fell pregnant with me. The circus was in town. My father? A waltzer operator from somewhere near Swindon. Was I the result of a pity fuck? A desperate attempt to draw the jealous Eddie back in. Any time I enquired further, Higgy jumped in and diverted me. I never knew what fucking business it was of his, but whenever I raised questions about my father he acted like an aggressive linebacker protecting Quarterback Libby. Even Raymond clammed up around them. In the end, I asked simply because I enjoyed watching the adults squirm. As if my father was some serial murderer like Bible John. Eventually, though, tormenting them got boring. I just gave up asking. Raymond would join the dots for me. He was probably lying, but I was past caring.

According to Raymond my existence drove Eddie MacAvoy

away for good. Eddie moved to Glasgow two months after I was born. I suspect Libby has never really forgiven me; for this and for the 'sins' that drove Raymond – the one last connection with Eddie, and therefore the only slim hope of his return – away. But we'll get to those later.

Higgy and Libby went to school together. Like many villagers born within a short distance of each other neither seem able to escape the curious hold Barshaw has over them. Both suffered the early death of a parent; Libby's mum was run over and killed by a drunk driver when Libby was fifteen. Higgy's dad suffered a heart attack and died down the pits when Higgy was only four. Along with the rest of his family, he watched the men bring his dad to the surface. Libby's dad descended into alcoholism and was sectioned for his own protection. She was eighteen. Higgy was essentially an only child, born to elderly parents. His mum was forty-eight when she had him. His two brothers made a better life for themselves in Australia. Higgy stayed, he once told me, not to look after his mum, but to look after Libby, who needed him more.

Libby was a good-looking young woman. Wild and hard to handle, and consequently never short of male company. But age withers and the good times became desperate times. I don't remember any of the good times. They predate me. Drugs and alcohol were her constant companions during my preteen years. Higgy had picked up the broken fragments and glued them back together when Eddie departed. But the pieces didn't fit the same. The cracks were too evident. If Higgy had fallen for someone less outwardly attractive, he'd be in a different place. Despite everything, he still loves her. I can't be sure if he's ever told her. Her self-absorption would have destroyed anyone else, but not Higgy. As faithful and loyal as a guide dog for the blind.

There is simultaneously nothing I want to ask her, and lots that I want to say. But when the words start to form in my head, I can't speak them. After all these years. I'm not looking for apologies, or even understanding. Just acceptance that I exist and that at some point in the dim and distant past, I meant something to her.

We sit and eat. Or at least I eat. Libby merely moves the tiny morsels of steak pie to different locations on the plate. There's no sound other than that coming from the TV set in the corner. We watch the opening ceremony of the Olympic Games. It's a garish American spectacle that moves at a slower pace than my newly in-herited goalkeeper running up a steep incline. But it passes the time.

Libby gives up after an hour. She goes to her bed at the rear of the room. Asks me to stay until morning and then let myself out, and that she'll maybe *see me later*.

I stay and watch until a shuffling, shambling, shaking Muhammad Ali lights the flame inside a cauldron that looks like a giant McDonald's French fries' carton. It's emotional and pitiful and gaudy and tasteless. I switch it off, and lay down on her sofa, listening to her shallow breathing with unexpected tears in my eyes.

I can't maintain stubborn resentment. Not towards Libby, Higgy. Not even toward Raymond. It's too exhausting. Even when things were at their worst with my brother, I remained intent on pleasing him. He has a hypnotic effect on people. Like an Ayrshire Rasputin weaving a charismatic spell on those he comes into contact with.

⌂

—He wasn't in a good place after visiting his mam. I think the shock of seeing her so dependent on others has affected him more than he thought it would. My house must be suffocating him. I've got to get him out of here. Need to fill the spaces between training and games with something that occupies his mind, or he'll sink back into the depths. He must be

fearing what people think of him now. That they'll remember the highs of that cup semi-final, and then the crushing defeat in the final after he'd left. Back then there were some who blamed him. It was a long time ago, but he'll have to face them sooner rather than later.

'Fancy a pint, son? C'mon ... it'll do ye good.'

Higgy knows I don't drink. Not with the pills. But I fetch a jacket. He's probably right. I can't get Libby out of my head, so I need a distraction, and there's also the expectation that I make myself visible. The football club revolves around The King's Arms, its unofficial sponsor. It's a fortnight since I officially became the team's manager, and Higgy claims the regulars are interested in hearing my plans for the season. Or at least the first quarter of it. He suspects that's when the interest level will drop off.

The ten-minute walk features a few respectful nods and one 'aw'right Danny?' from a lad I'm sure I was in the Boys Brigade with but whose name I can't recall.

Higgy is swelled. Chest out with pride. As if he's the little Dutch boy who saved Haarlem by putting his finger in the dyke. He walks purposefully, striding into the pub first. He holds the door open for me. I half expect a showbiz announcement from him: *An' now, ladies an' ennulmen, boys an' girls, all the way from Arbroath ... it's the one, the only ... DANNY GARVEY!*

There are five people inside the pub. Including us. And a heavily moustachioed barman who resembles Live Aid-era Freddie Mercury. No-one looks up. No-one cares.

'Still early,' says Higgy. He must feel the need to temper my disappointment. I'm not disappointed. I'm fucking relieved.

'A pint ae lager, Alf,' he orders. He looks at me.

'A Coke please, mate,' I say, and then: 'Draught's fine,' when asked to pick between that or a bottle.

'This is Danny. Danny Garvey,' says Higgy to Alf, but loudly enough for the others to hear. I imagine it's how Higgy would introduce a mail-order bride he'd recently purchased.

'That right?' Alf observes. It impresses me that he couldn't give a fuck. I think he and I will get on fine.

We sit in a corner, under a television. Another couple of Higgy's fictional acquaintances, Kevin and Sally Webster, are having a heated argument that goes over our heads.

Half an hour passes; half an hour where Higgy does little other than scribble tactical ideas on Post-it Notes while nursing his pint. I visit the wall-mounted jukebox three times. Predictably, it's a bland, chart-based collection dominated by Celine Dion, Mariah Carey and George Michael. I spot 'Wonderwall' and punch the code, but I'm too late to notice it's the lounge-lizard version by The Mike Flowers Pops. I hope the two barflys and Alf won't associate me with it.

'Live Forever' restores some credibility. In my head at least, since no-one else is even listening. Ironically, 'It's a Shame about Ray' by The Lemonheads is the best of the rest.

'Got a couple ae boys interested,' says Higgy. 'Heard it fae an auld contact.'

'Aye?' I reply. My voice makes me sound more interested than I am.

'Suggested they come down on Thursday. That aw'right, son?'

'Why no'?' I say to him.

Higgy smiles contentedly. The deal struck with the club has Higgy as my unofficial assistant. He doesn't have a desk or an official title, and he's not getting a new carpet, but he's been smiling contentedly ever since. His position validated and any expenditure that I approve will get remunerated.

He's the soul of this club. He's been on the sub-committee since the early seventies. If you asked him to paint the walls of every fucking surface around the pitch with a toothbrush, he'd do it without hesitation. He deserves this boost. It will almost certainly be the last season he'll get something in return for his unflinching commitment.

'How's it goin', Higster?' says a young man, holding the door open for five others of varying ages as they enter. I look at all of them and they stare at me. There's no mutual recognition until the last man glances over.

'Fuck me!' he says. 'Danny fucken Garvey. That really you?' The voice hasn't changed much. A wee bit deeper. A bit more of a gravelly edge to it.

'How ye, Dennis?' I ask. We sat together in third-year English.

'Better for seein' you, ya cunt!' he says. 'Boys ... this is the legendary Danny Garvey. Whit a fucken prospect he wis, man,' he proclaims, as if I wasn't there. 'Greatest goal ah've ever seen at the Bridge. Against the Talbot. Ayrshire Cup semi-final. This yin beats three ... like the cunts had their feet cased in concrete ... easy as that.' Dennis swivels his hips. The boys nod approvingly. 'Runs in on the keeper,' he says, his voice quieter now. 'Then does he no' just fucken dink it ower him?'

'That right, son,' says the oldest. 'Ma brother wis at that game. Talked about that goal for weeks after. Wis that you, right enough?'

'Aye,' I say.

'Back tae see yer ma?' Dennis asks.

'Naw,' says Higgy, on my behalf. 'Well, aye ... but Danny here's the new gaffer at the Bridge. Ah'm his number two.'

'Fuck sake! Gen?'

'Aye,' I say, beginning to feel that I could make it through the rest of the evening with this one word.

'Jesus,' says a second man. 'Talk about a dead end, son,' he sniggers. He is crag-faced and has curly, knotted shoulder-length hair that looks like the shredded tape from an unwound C90.

'Aye,' I repeat, warming to the challenge. I'm varying the tone at least.

—*These men. I know them all. Knew their dads and their uncles. I also know Rocco Quinn, the big, dark-haired one at the back. I wish I didn't.*

They pull their seats closer and sit around our tiny table like it was an impromptu press conference. One refuses the seat brought over for him.

'Ye'se aw comin' a week on Saturday?' Higgy asks them. 'First game ae the season.'

They look relieved. As if he'd been talking about a party invite and they'd had to think fast.

'Doubt it,' says the one who looks like Plug from *The Bash Street Kids*. 'Ah've got the bairns on a Saturday. Lets Effie go tae the bingo, an' that.' He speaks with a right-sided drawl that indicates a mild stroke is still having an effect.

'Bring them,' says Higgy, hopefully. 'In for nothin'.'

'Should fucken hope so, after that bloody disgrace ae last year,' says C90-head.

'You Ray Garvey's brother?' I was wondering how long it would be before this would be asked. It comes from the only man who was yet to speak. The one who has been staring at me since my name was uttered. The one man still standing. The one with heavily tattooed sallow skin. Hair dripping wet, although it hasn't rained for days. A chin that has almost certainly taken a fair few bare-knuckled jabs in its time.

'Aye,' I say. Brevity still seems appropriate given the edge behind the query.

'Cunt owes me,' he says.

A silence follows, and seems to take root and immediately grow out of control.

—*Rocco Quinn is one to be avoided. Maybe if Raymond had avoided him, he'd be here. Drinking with us.*

Eventually ... 'So, where ye been hidin' out, Dan?' asks Dennis.

'He wis up in Arbroath,' says Higgy.

'You his fucken translator then?' says my brother's creditor. 'Cunt no' speak for hi'self?'

The game ends. Four–nil to me. 'Coachin' the youth team up there,' I say. Straight to Dennis, no-one else.

'Aye?' he says. Four–one. A late away goal against the run of play. Final whistle.

'After the Dons finished, ah went tae Arbroath. Played on for a wee bit, but the injury wis too bad. Did the badges at Largs wi' Roxburgh's class. Started coachin' the youths...' I look down, uncomfortable at my own candour.

'...an' took them tae the final ae the Scottish.' By the looks on their faces, they regard Higgy's interruptions with the same contempt as an early ringing of the last-orders bell.

'An' now ah'm here,' I say. I curse myself for not lacing the words with more dripping irony.

Dennis's comrades get up. They head to the pool table. The lingering stares gradually diminish. Higgy goes for a piss.

'Ne'er mind Rocco,' Dennis leans in to whisper. 'He's like that wi' everybody. A good cunt though.'

I've forgotten how every male in Ayrshire is a cunt. It's the delivered grade of good or badness that defines your relationship with other male cunts.

'Ye'll need tae come round tae the house for one ae our parties,' says Dennis. 'Catch up proper an' that.'

'Okay,' I say, hoping it's an offer he'll forget.

'Meet the wife, like,' he adds. 'She'll have mind ae ye tae, sure.' I know before he utters it.

'Alison. Alison *Currie*, she was then,' he says. 'Remember her?'

⌂

Warm sunlight flits across my face and wakes me. The broken slats in Higgy's dusty blinds grant it entry. I look at the clock. 5.15 am. At least I've slept a bit. At the worst of the bad times, I'd have had four hours of watching the clock lumber towards this point in the day. I get up, get dressed and head out for a run. As part of the negotiating stance, I have acceded to the committee and registered myself with the SFA as a player. I have no intention of ever pulling on the strip, however much they want me to. But if I expect the team to work harder over a season, I should lead by example.

A milk float drifts slowly through the low-lying mist that covers much of the village. It is awkwardly pulling a barrow with newspapers in it, and has a small ginger cat for a passenger. Other than one dog enthusiastically shagging another, it's the only sign of activity I witness. With Sparklehorse in my ears, it's like the unsettling opening scene of a David Lynch movie. I imagine the boring surface normality concealing a dark, frightening underbelly.

I always enjoyed early-morning training. Especially when doing it alone to build up stamina after the injury. The privacy of the music. The clarity of thought that the early-morning air seems to bring. Before the rest of humanity rise and pollute it.

I run for an hour. I surprise myself at how easy it feels, although I haven't really pushed it. The peripheral routes around this place are predominantly flat. Despite Libby's ghostly presence regularly invading my thoughts, I'm starting to warm to this peculiar position I've found myself in. This may change after I've been to see Raymond for the first time in over ten years. This is his third spell inside, but Raymond will agree with Libby's implication that we're all to blame for his current stint in Barlinnie.

Higgy is up when I get back. Just. His yawning, crumpled face resembles a grey sock puppet on the arm of someone suffering a seizure.

'Ye been out?' he asks.

'Ye just watched me come in,' I reply.

'Ach. Aye,' he says, wiping the sleep from his eyes.

'Just get yer tea an' then we're goin' up tae The Barn.'

'Aye, aw'right.' He yawns again. 'Ah'll see ye there, son. Ah've got somethin' tae dae first.'

It's the first proper day of full training. A Sunday, normally the loneliest day of the week in football, although the satellite telly companies are doing their level best to fix that. I've made it a Sunday to ensure as many as possible are available. We have a squad of sixteen at present. Only Davie Russell – a fireman – is unavailable today due to his shift patterns. This will be a problem throughout the season. Auchinleck Talbot or Glenafton may be able to exert greater influence over players' employers, but Barshaw Bridge are now only one rung above amateur-league status.

I have the clubhouse keys. No-one else is due at the ground for another hour. The church bell rings in the distance. Insistent and annoying. I'm in the office. I close the window and put a cassette in the tape recorder I've brought with me from Arbroath. It was a gift from the youth team at the end of last season, after the cup final win at Hampden.

I press 'play'. Sonic Youth's 'Teenage Riot' comes on, and I make a note on the pad about using it to test the PA system, if we still have one.

The list of tasks is growing:

- Fix the leaks in the flat roof above the Committee Room
- Get the changing-room toilet drains unblocked
- Buy a typewriter
- Speak to a printer about the programmes
- Get around local businesses looking for additional sponsorship or donations
- Contact Kilmarnock FC or Ayr United. Ask if they have any second-hand training kits. Or young professional players to loan out for the experience
- Get boards up around the perimeter fencing to stop people watching without paying
- Get the fucking grass cut to a length where it might be possible to play proper football on it
- Talk to whoever does the food and hot drinks on a match day
- Get some coverage in the local media

There are numerous others circulating in my brain. I'm taking it seriously. I'm not sure I know why. But it is occupying me. It'll pass the season, and then I can take it from there.

Higgy appears. Someone is with him. Higgy has been out and about, scouting. Job Centres. The sports centres. Waste ground where bored teenagers are kicking a ball around for something to do.

—Danny's a good coach, with good ideas about how the game should be played. Easy to impose that on youngsters; the ones still desperate to impress, and with a wee bit of the fear in them. But he'll struggle to discipline the older ones; the veterans that know it all and couldn't change their ways even if they believed the new man was right. Some square pegs need to fit into round holes. We don't have the time to reshape them. They'll need to be battered in with a big fucking mallet.

'Danny, this is Harry Doyle. Thought he could mibbe help us.' Harry's a stout fella. Far too old, even for this level, although advancing age didn't hold Stanley Matthews back.

Higgy has an eye for a player, I'll give him that. And I need to hope he can still see. But on this evidence his judgement may be in question.

'Harry's ex-army. Played in goal for Whitburn before signing up.' The penny drops. I get the inference immediately: I'm likely to be too soft. Especially on the older players. Higgy has obviously given this a lot of thought. I've underestimated him.

'Hullo Harry.'

'Mr Garvey,' says Harry, with a nod that's just a few degrees short of a royal bow.

'Danny, mate. Just call me Danny.'

'Right ... boss,' he replies. Harry's demeanour implies a lifetime of following orders. No questions asked. Just point him in the direction of the man you want killed. Maybe he could really help me.

I hear the players start to drift in to the far changing room. It's just after 11.00 am. Several will be late. The new Barshaw Bridge FC management team wanders through. Most don't even notice us coming in. I listen to various conversations happening simultaneously. Almost all are about football. One, developing quietly in the corner, isn't. It concludes in a punch-line involving the Pope.

The speed of the turn from light, topical observation to sharp sectarian aggression isn't totally surprising. I recall it from my own time here. A dressing room is *Lord of the Flies* with bigger lads. The tension. The pressure to integrate. The low-grade bullying of those who don't. It is always there, mostly under the surface, but it doesn't take much for the volcano to erupt. Gilhooly pushes Buchan. He stumbles backwards and turns an ankle on a stray boot that's been concealed under the training tops. My two centre backs – Buchan and Gilhooly – at each other's throats, needing to be pulled apart by younger teammates. It doesn't bode well. All eventually return to their seats. Tensions simmer. Buchan groans and flexes his foot.

'Mornin', I say, quietly. As if the fracas hadn't been witnessed.

No-one answers. A door opens behind me. Finnegan squeezes past us. He's more than half an hour late. The squad snigger as he sits down an' whispers, 'What've ah missed?' to Jaz Sinclair seated to his left.

Before I can speak again, Harry Doyle strolls slowly into the middle of the small room. He stands on the bibs. I look down, noticing shiny steel-toe-capped boots under his joggy bottoms. He edges closer to Finnegan.

'Hey, you ... is it still March?' he asks innocently.

Finnegan looks around; a child being singled out for an inevitable belting by an assistant head teacher. 'Eh?' He laughs, hoping not to lose face.

'Did the clocks go forward last night, an' we aw just missed it?'

It dawns on Finnegan. 'Who are you, mister?' he inquires.

'Ah'm Doyle,' he says calmly, holding out a hand.

Finnegan laughs again. Looks around for a reaction before he takes it. I watch Harry's forearm expand. The tattoos on it appear to come to life. Rather than an introductory handshake, his goal-keeping shovel tightens and the grip crushes. The ink darkens. The lion roars. Higgy whispers to me that he met Harry at the nursing home their mothers reside in. He was tearing strips off an orderly.

'Ah'm yer new trainer, son.'

Finnegan's expression drops. No nervous childish laughter this time. Harry applies the pressure. The moisture in Finnegan's body is being squeezed upwards, released from his reddening eyes.

'Mist ... hey, yer fucken hurtin' me, ya cunt!'

'An' if you show up late for anythin' tae dae wi' this team again, then ah'll rip yer fucken head off an' shite down yer neck!' Harry Doyle bawls this message right into the younger man's face. It's a statement of intent to all of them.

Higgy glances up at me. This isn't my way of doing things, but I'm used to dealing with young players on the rise. This bunch of gamblers, chancers, has-beens and drunks are used to simply going through the motions. It makes me wonder why they've been showing up every week, to be harangued by a handful of old men who see coaching as little more than a hobby. To be embarrassed by the skill and pace of younger, better, hungrier opponents. And to be verbally abused by the likes of Sergeant Major Harry Doyle.

Their answer would surely be the same as mine: because they know nothing else. They *have* nothing else to do.

They file out silently. I'm certain some won't return after today, preferring to look for another club. I can only hope it's the older ones. The first match of the season is less than two weeks away. There's not much time to act. Or react.

My list of tasks is growing longer. It's pinned to the white board in my new office, covering the faint, long, blue diagonal arrows that betray the poverty of football ideologies from seasons past. There's so much to do if this isn't going to be a disaster.

Before training starts, I formally appoint Harry Doyle as my assistant coach. I tell him there's little money available. He tells me he doesn't want any, and I'm relieved. Harry's a recovering alcoholic. He needs this for the discipline it requires. His life went off the rails without the rigours of army life. He's played football. Knows the basic drills. He'll work them hard. Prepare them for the season ahead.

The two young players Higgy mentioned – Harry's nephew and his neighbour's boy – are keen to play. Harry has other useful connections. He'll see to half of the items on my list. He doesn't tell me how, and I don't enquire further. My first free transfer into the club may well turn out to be my best.

Two

Damo.

Wednesday night. An evening training session. Our first since I took over; the previous ones all held in the unforgiving glare of weekend daylight. The full squad – bar the injured Buchan – is on time and out on the pitch ten minutes before 7.00 pm. I hide my surprise as I greet the team. Harry Doyle has already roped in conscripts from Alcoholics Anonymous meetings and the grass is looking greener than it has since I returned to the village. 'There are loads of folk looking for a focus,' he's told me. Desperate hours to be filled. And it's not just the handymen. Two youngsters have come with him tonight as trialists. 'Sons of addicts,' he admits. Harry Doyle desperately wants to save people. He's just a different type of keeper from the one he was before.

'Right, gather in,' I shout.

The squad come to heel after Harry's ear-piercing whistle. Only three days and it's already becoming like a satisfying episode of *One Man and His Dog*.

'Attack against defence,' I instruct, and they groan. 'But wi' a difference.'

I drag out some long ropes sourced from army surplus.

'Ramage, Russell, Gilhooly, Smith ... step up.'

They edge forward. Cautiously.

'Tie the ropes round yer waist,' I instruct.

'Well, fucken move it,' yells Harry. 'We've no' got aw night!'

They comply. Once they're in their positions along the edge of the eighteen-yard box, I tighten the ropes a bit. Several in the squad snigger.

'Strikers win matches, but defences win ye trophies. If we're gonnae be harder tae beat, it needs tae start wi' some better organisation at the back. See the table fitba at The King's Arms? The players are organised.'

Gilhooly laughs. He must think I'm taking the piss.

'Big gaps in the back four are where ye lost so many goals last season. Ah've seen the tapes. Lose an' early goal an' the discipline goes aw tae fuck.'

Higgy nods, his video-recording of the matches finally justified, and not – as some have alleged – for his own personal private pleasure.

The first fifteen minutes is unsurprisingly chaotic. The midfielders and strikers move the balls around the pitch in a horseshoe formation, finding easy gaps. The heavier Gilhooly grips the ropes and topples his slender central partner; Smith and Ramage get yanked inwards unexpectedly. Gradually, they begin to anticipate. They take their lead from the captain. They begin to understand. They move like a co-ordinated team of four. Soon, they'll do this instinctively. They won't need ropes.

I leave them to Harry Doyle's corner drills, aimed at protecting McIntosh, the keeper. Harry commands Gilhooly and Davie Russell to attack the ball in the air so that he doesn't need to come for it. Higgy and I head to the other half of the park. Short passing between the cones. Sean O'Halloran is a stand-out. He says little and reminds me of how I addressed a pass. How I anticipated the irregularities of the surface. His touch – the instinctive way he caresses the ball – is excellent.

The two new lads – Gilmour and Peters – are midfielders. Harry informed me they didn't know each other prior to his intervention, but they play with a telepathy that's intriguing. I watch the smaller, slighter Gilmour hit short, angular passes to Peters without lifting his head. Peters takes them on the half-turn and moves away from his opponent with ease. It's early days, and the capability to turn training-ground skills into match-winning abilities has defeated many a young player. But for the level we'll be playing at, there's some real hope here.

We finish with shooting practice. Hugh Finnegan is blasting balls like a cannon sheared off its moorings. High, wide and reckless. No control or composure. We've boarded up the centre part of the space between the posts. This is about improving the accuracy. I watch him closely and see that at the point of connection he closes his eyes.

'Haw, wee man. Kick us the baws back down, eh?' Finnegan shouts towards a kid on the top of the hill behind the goals. The kid ignores him.

—*Laudrup, Ravanelli, Shearer, Juninho, McManaman, Redknapp, Schmeichel, Beckham, Gullit, Zola, Vialli. Ravanelli's got a fat belly. Ravanelli's got a fat belly.*

Sinclair and Strawhorn fare better, until we move the boards and they appear unable to adjust to it.

—*Strawhorn has never scored a free kick. Strawhorn has never scored a free kick.*

'For fuck's sake!' Higgy laments the lack of goals that has infected the forwards like a virus.

—*For fuck's sake! Strawhorn has never scored a free-kick.*

'Practice is the only way,' I say.

'What if that's aw they've got though. What if they cannae improve?' ponders Higgy.

For twenty minutes, we stand silently, and watch balls disappear into the descending gloom behind the goal.

'Right … that'll dae for the night,' I shout as the light fades. The three forwards head back to join their colleagues. They all sit in the centre circle. Waiting for me. Waiting for the instruction to leave.

I've wandered behind the goal to retrieve the balls that my strikers have squandered. The little kid is still there. He's the one I saw before – the kid who wears some kind of space helmet. He's about ten and on his own. I look at my watch.

'Ye aw'right there, wee man?' I ask. He doesn't answer. 'What's yer name, son?'

It occurs to me that it might not be a boy. The visor is down, preventing a proper look at the face behind it.

'What's that ye've got?' I ask.

The kid has something gripped tightly. The fingers unfurl to show a tiny football figure on a green circular base. He has a painted red top with white shorts, just like the Barshaw Bridge strip. The figure has a large caricature of a head, but it's identifiable as Fabrizio Ravanelli, the Italian striker who plays in the English league, for Middlesbrough.

The visor opens.

'Ravanelli ... got a fat belly,' says the kid. I'm sure it's a boy.

I laugh. And he says it again, several times. It isn't a song, but he repeats it with rhythm as if it was a chorus. Or a football chant.

—I don't know the man. I don't like men I don't know. He doesn't have a beard.

'He's Ravanelli ... an' he's got a fat belly!' I sing.

The kid stops abruptly. He gets up and runs.

'Hey pal, your bike!' I shout into the trees.

'Danny'.

I turn. It's Higgy from the edge of the pitch.

'Everybody's waitin',' he shouts.

I look again for the little spaceman but there's no-one there. I'm left with the balls and a kid's bicycle.

The doorbell rings. A few short bursts at first … and then re-peatedly. The person ringing it is angry or aggrieved. If Higgy was here, I'd leave it to him. But he's not. He's at the prison, visiting Raymond.

I approach Higgy's front door with caution. The brief en-counter with Rocco Quinn has unnerved me. I headed home from The King's on edge the night I met him. I had anticipated some local anger at my return. I left the club in the lurch in 1983, like a reluctant groom running out on a pregnant bride as she waits at the altar. Barshaw was beaten 6-1 in the final. Perhaps unlikely that I'd have made any difference on the day. Those bad memories have apparently faded, though. No-one seems to care. But there's something else going on with Rocco. Something I fear my brother's involvement could yet drag me into.

I nervously shout 'Yes?' from behind the door. A glimpse into Libby's world.

'Hey, Garvey! You got my boy's bike?' A female voice. Still angry and aggrieved, but for reasons that I can deal with. I open the door.

'Where the fuck is it?' The young woman is small, pretty and not what I was expecting. There's no rolling pin. No thick cotton socks rolled down corned-beef legs overlapping dog-chewed slippers. She looks like she should be on *TFI Friday* fronting an indie band, being fawned over by Chris Evans.

'It's up at the club. Just let me get m—'

'You're the brother, then,' she says. The season ahead is likely to be defined by the agendas lying behind this statement of fact.

'I'm Danny.' I hold out an open hand. Hers remain closed; par-tially concealed by folded arms.

'Ah know who ye are.'

'Look, the boy just up an' left his bike at the side ae the pitch last night. Ah didnae take it off him.'

'He said somebody shouted at him. Wis that you?'

'Naw. Jesus … ah wis talkin' tae him! He wis singin' this wee song. Just seemed a bit late for him to be out there on his own.'

'Whit's that supposed tae mean?'

'Nothin'. Jesus Christ, hen, it's just that weans can go missin'.' The words seem to chill my tongue as they come out.

At this, she steps closer. Right onto the front step. Her arms fall to her side. Fists clenched. Maximum rage level reached.

'No' as regularly as their fathers though … an' don't dare bloody *hen,* me!' she yells. 'You bloody Garveys…' The conclusion to this remains unsaid.

'Nancy?' I ask. The mention of her name seems to draw some of the ire. 'Look, why don't ye come in a minute, eh? Let me get the keys an' my shoes an' that?'

She won't sit. Or accept the offer of a tea. Fair enough.

'Where's the boy just now?' I ask. There's a *what's it tae you* look that I'd anticipated. 'I got him this,' I say as a means of explanation. I hold out a small football figure I bought at Bamford's earlier when I was out for the rolls. 'He was showin' me the one he had last night.'

Nancy looks at the caricatured figure of Paul Gascoigne as if she was Eve being handed the apple.

'Thanks, but ah cannae take it.' She's still trying to be angry but struggling to maintain it.

'Why not?'

'The last thing he needs is another one ae you lot lettin' him down,' she says. She's calmer now. And has taken a seat of sorts; on the arm of Higgy's chair.

'Nancy, until about ten minutes ago, ah didnae even know it was *him* the other night.' She seems to accept this. 'He had a helmet on, for God's sake. The visor wis down for most ae it. He was just a kid hangin' about behind the goals, y'know?'

She slides off the arm and into the seat proper. There's a deep, exhausted sigh. The sound of the anger leaving her body.

'He loves the fitba. Higgy used tae let him intae the ground. Then that stopped. Ray's doin' probably, like every other bloody thing he tries tae control.'

I almost say *ye dinnae know that half ae it, hen*. But stop myself, since I suspect she does.

'An' now somebody's boarded up the fence. He's no' gonna be able to watch it at all.'

Better not to confess to that right now.

I get my trainers. Pick up the keys, and we head up to the club. She's not what I would've pictured. No make-up on a face that doesn't need it. Sparkling brown eyes. Warm, tanned skin that would be more at home in Naples or Rome than the Ayrshire valley. The same black hair as her son had in the picture in Libby's living room.

We walk past Nancy's house; the one she shares with her mum, who is watching Damian. He sees her from the window and waves.

'Hang on a minute.' Nancy goes up the path, opens the door and the boy in the space helmet comes out.

He holds on to the belt around her jeans, not her hand.

'Damo, this is Danny,' she says. 'Yer *uncle* Danny.'

—*He's big and tall. I don't like tall men. I don't like men with beards. This one doesn't have a beard. I won't have a beard.*

⌒

We watch him ride his bike at speed down the steep, grassy slope at the edge of the pitch.

'Jesus … he's no' feart, is he?'

'No, he's not. A bit too gallus at times,' she says. I look to see if she's smiling. She isn't.

'How d'ye mean?' I ask, mainly to keep the conversation in motion.

'He has no sense ae danger.' She pauses, like she's desperate to capture it properly but struggling. 'Most weans his age don't stick their fingers in plug sockets. They've grown out ae that. They know it'll hurt them. Damo would still do that kinda shit if we weren't watchin' him constantly.' She looks worn. Still pretty, but like an oil painting found buried under rubble.

'You take him out there?' I ask. 'Tae the prison?'

She shakes her head. 'Took him once. It's too far.' Her head bows.

There's an awkward silence. Neither of us seem to have the social skills to navigate these black holes. It sucks us in, and we say nothing as we watch the boy perform the same manoeuvre repeatedly. Like it's a video tape of him that we keep rewinding. He must've completed that circuit well over a hundred times before Nancy says:

'He struggles at the school.'

That isn't a surprise.

'What, wi' the lessons ye mean?'

'Some ae them,' she says. 'It's more ... the general gettin' on wi' the other kids. Teachers don't know what tae dae wi' him.'

'Ach, ah wis a bit like that,' I say. She rounds on me before I can add: *He'll probably grow out ae it.* 'Kids aw develop at different rates, don't they?' I observe instead.

'Is that right, Danny? she says, loudly enough for me to look around to see if anyone is close enough to hear. 'Popular kid, were ye? The best fitba player in every year ye were in ... plus a big brother that'd batter anybody that looked at ye the wrong way. He's got none ae that, so don't bloody tell me you an' him are the same.'

I expect her to get up and leave. To have had enough of this ad hoc social-work consultation. But she doesn't.

'Raymond ... your brother, he idolises you!' she says. 'You, up there on yer pedestal. The great Danny Garvey. Nothin' tae touch ye. If only there wis a wee bit ae space up there for his son.'

I want to tell her she's wrong. I want her to know my version of the truth about Raymond. About all the things he did to me; to keep control of me. But this isn't the time.

—*My mum's over there. With that man. The one that doesn't have a beard. She's been talking to him for a long time. She doesn't notice me. I like going up and down the hill on my bike. I'm bored now.*

Damo comes off the bike. I make a sudden move, but Nancy holds my forearm. It's either a reminder that he isn't my concern, or an indication that he must learn to be more independent. We wait. After a few moments he gets up. The helmet turns and the visor looks over at us. And then he starts on the hill again.

—*He's my daddy's brother, Mum said. I can't remember what my daddy was like. Except that he had a beard. And dirty fingernails. And he smelled of the toilet. And once he came to the house and blood was running down from his head. And Mum shouted at him. And then she shouted at me. He left and I was crying.*

'Look, ah'm sorry,' she says eventually. 'It's been a stressful few months. Ah took him out ae school, last time there was an incident wi' the other kids. Six months ago. An' now they want him tae go tae a special school, after the summer.' There it is ... that fucking word again: 'special'. Being used to cover the multitude of our sins, Damian and me.

'Ye sure that's the right thing?' I ask. The words are out before the brain catches up. And like a critical, over-familiar judgement, not in the politely inquisitive manner of someone she's just met.

'What did you say?' She's angry. Rightly. A stupid question. 'You're here five fucken minutes an' you're an expert on my kid. That it, Uncle Bulgaria?' she challenges. Her eyes widen.

'No ... naw, ah ... em,' I stammer. Up against the ropes.

'*Naw ... ah, hmm, ah ...* fuck off!' She is slight but like Harry

Doyle's inked lions, she seems to expand when angry. I spend the next few minutes clumsily apologising for the missteps, until she reduces in size.

'Was Raymond livin' at yours, before?' I ask. Asking almost any other question feels like navigating undiscovered landmines, so I proceed cautiously. Surprisingly, I make it through intact.

'He was around, here an' there,' she says. 'It got tae be too unsettlin' for Damo.'

'Can imagine.'

Even when he was younger, Raymond flitted from house to house. For the last two years I was living here, there wasn't a week when my brother spent all seven nights under the same roof. He was always on the move. *Duckin' an' divin'*. Of course, months of his youth were spent in a detention centre. I often wondered if his desire not to be pinned down is a reaction to all the time he was incarcerated.

'So how is it wi' you an' him now, then?' I'm still in danger of stepping too far.

'Well, we get peace, y'know?' Then she turns the questioning around. 'Ye seen him yet?'

'Naw,' I reply.

'Ye've been back a while now, naw? Sound like yer puttin' it off.'

'Aye, ah suppose so.'

'Convenient that he's in there?'

'Aye. Probably.'

'We've got that in common, then,' she says. I'm still not sure if it's said in that *ach, ye know what he's like* type of way. The perceived threat level has reduced. She smiles. It doesn't last long.

'Look, we've got the first game ae the season on Saturday. Damian can come wi' me if he wants. He can sit close tae the dugout if he'd like that. Maybe meet some ae the players?'

She says nothing at first. Then: 'Ray makes ye aw these promises. Charms the pants off ye ... literally.' She's still thinking about *him*; the centre of our tiny shared universe. 'New beginnings, an' that. The same script every time, an' ah actually think he believes it himself. But he cannae stop the cycle. The bookies, the cards, the booze, the debts, the violence. Back inside. He's addicted tae the chaos.' Her voice softens. She still cares for him, it's clear. I'm suddenly disappointed in her, although the tenderness quickly passes.

'Ah cannae handle it anymore. Look at me.' She stops. And I do. 'Ah've had enough chaos. Aw ah want is some peace an' quiet.'

I get up. I fear she'll cry and blame me for it. I think she already knows I'm not like him. I shout bye to Damian – who ignores me – and turn to head back to Higgy's.

—My new uncle is leaving. He's a tall man. I thought I didn't like tall men. He works at the football team. Maybe he will take the boards down so I can watch again.

'Danny,' she shouts. I turn. 'Pick him up after his lunch on Saturday,' she says. 'Don't be late. Don't dare fucken let him down.'

'I won't,' I say. I reach into my pocket and walk the few steps back to her. I hand her Paul Gascoigne.

'Keep it,' she says. 'It'll mean more if you give him it.'

Friday morning. Of the written press, the *Ayrshire Post*, *Cumnock Chronicle* and *Kilmarnock Standard* are here. West Sound radio are coming later. Invitations have been sent widely. I shamelessly trailed my back story in the hope that they would take notice and show interest. My palms are sweating, and my mouth is drier than the Sahara, but these things must be done. The committee insists.

'Mr Garvey...'

'Danny, please.'

'Okay, Danny.' It's the *Cumnock Chronicle*'s lad. He looks keen as mustard. He can't be much more than sixteen, but he speaks with the deep, confident air of a middle-aged man. It's disconcerting. 'How does it feel to be back here ... where it all started for you?'

'It's good,' I respond. 'It feels like...' They know I'm going to say it. They want me to say it; '...comin' home.'

'Lugar at home tomorrow. Big test for ye.'

'Got tae start somewhere,' I say. The clichés rattle around my head, trying to find their way out: *Eleven ae them against eleven ae us. Need tae keep it tight at the back for the first quarter. Might be a game ae two halves.* Fans despise hearing these comments in post- or pre-match interviews, but I defy anyone to answer differently when faced with the same inanity week after week. Still, I've invited them in, and surprisingly, given our lowly status, they came. This is their game. I need to play it their way.

'They're a decent team. Big striker who puts himself about a bit. It'll be a tough game,' I say, doing the right thing in complimenting them.

'What's the mood about the club, Danny ... given the bribery accusations last season?'

'It's better than ah expected. The preseason friendlies have been fine an' we're rarin' tae go.' I glance down at my notepad trying not to make it obvious. 'The committee weren't aware ae any aspect of what was goin' on until it was too late.' A statement given to me by my new boss.

'That right?' sneers the man from the *Standard*, unconvinced. I didn't catch his name earlier.

'A lot's changed since ye pulled on the strip though, eh?' ponders the *Post*.

'That's true,' I say. 'Take That have split up, so have Charles and Diana...' They laugh. 'Reassurin' tae see that Celtic are still rubbish though.' There are four journalists here. Three feign mock outrage. Should be enough for a headline.

'Bit rich, eh?' says the veteran from the *Standard*. 'Takin' pot shots at another club ... state yours is in,' he taunts.

'Eh? It was a bloody joke, pal. Ah think Celtic are big enough an' ugly enough tae look after themselves.'

'Ah'm no' yer pal, son,' he says.

'Evidently,' I reply. There's an awkward silence. The other media lightweights shuffle uncomfortably.

'Your brother's in the jail again, isn't he? Nearly killed a guy.' The air goes out of the room, like a grumpy old bastard over the fence putting a knife through your new Adidas Europa football. 'Ye been tae see him yet?'

Rather than show them the door, I face it out. 'Naw. No' sure he'll be any use tae us ... the socks don't fit ower the electronic tags.'

'Aye, funny,' says the *Standard's* man. 'Think ye're gonnae need that sense ae humour this season.'

A fury suddenly rises in me. Like a thermometer dipped in boiling water. I'm not a violent person, I never have been. But I imagine dropping him to his knees with a metal bar across the back of the legs and then him folding onto his back like a broken deckchair and me straddling him, full weight on the chest and I'm bringing the bar down on his bloody face again and again and again and...

The door opens but no-one seems to notice it except me.

Breathe in ... *one* ... out ... *two* ... in ... *three* ... out. I get to *ten* and the pressure has lessened.

It's the young woman from the night of the interview. She closes the door behind her and stands silently watching.

'What's your name again?' I ask the *Standard's* man. He's almost certainly one of those angry old hacks who never has a hangover on his own time.

'How about ye just pick up the *Standard* any given Thursday. My name'll be under the piece on the back page.' He gets up. 'Nice tae finally meet ye, son.'

Okay, that's it for today, says the young woman, forcefully.

Without even a glance towards her, they all stand and file out.

'Hi, ah'm Danny,' I say, even though she already knows.

I know, she replies. *I'm Anne. Anne Macdonald.* There's a familiarity to her; to the way she says her surname. *I look after the contracts.*

The phone rings. It's Higgy, to find out how the press briefing went. I turn to the window as I start to speak, and when I turn back, Anne Macdonald has gone. My breathing is back to normal.

By the time I come out of the building the *Standard*'s man has left, but the others are still in the car park. They are equally nonplussed.

'The fuck was that aw about, Danny?' asks the *Post*'s man. Is he, too, sensing a bigger story? An opportunity to get promoted off the back pages and to nearer the front?

'Nae idea,' I stutter. They aren't convinced. 'Sorry, lads. Ah need tae go,' I say. I'm rattled and they know it. A visit to see Raymond is now unavoidable.

The night before the first competitive game of the season. I'm in the house watching *Top of the Pops*. I saw little of it while up north. It feels odd for it to be broadcast on a Friday. No idea when that happened. When I was younger, I made an appointment with it on Thursday nights. Looked forward to it from Sunday night, when I was lying in the bath listening to the chart rundown. Talked about it endlessly at school on Fridays. That and the football; the twin bookends of my weekly existence. Higgy thinks it is garbage, but then he always did. I reluctantly concede that tonight's show hasn't been the greatest in the programme's long history. Peter Andre, an Australian kid with a ridiculously muscled stomach, a criminally tepid Gary Barlow single called 'Forever Love', and someone called Sean Maguire – whom Higgy tells me is a soap-opera actor – are the real low points. Adding the two boring lads from U2 doing an updated 'Theme from Mission

Impossible' and it's a show that you'd happily invite Jehovah's Witnesses into your living room just to avoid. It's about as far as it's possible to get from Bowie's 'Starman' in 1972, or the Happy Mondays and The Stone Roses debuting on the same show in 1989. Tonight's episode is not one to be taped and repeatedly re-watched.

Higgy's had enough. Eventually, he switches channel. We watch the start of an American TV show: *Friends* – ironically, since neither of us has any. Higgy loves this programme. He's in his mid-fifties. The main characters are mid-twenties. He lives alone, excepting my current residence. The friends seem to live in two flats, right across the hall from each other. There's one with a ridiculously annoying voice and hyena laugh that the others – the *cool* others – merely tolerate. *She's no' in it that often*, he informs me. That being so, I struggle to see how he identifies so strongly with it.

'It's funny,' he says. 'Feels like a comfort blanket bein' wrapped around ye for half an hour at the end ae the week.' Escapism. I found it in music and the books of George Orwell and Barry Hines. Higgy finds it in fictional pals like Joey and Chandler and their vicarious enjoyment of *Baywatch*. Each to his own.

I open a book. His programme finishes.

'That's a strange hobby ye've picked up,' he says, looking at the cover.

'It's no' about *actual* trainspotting, dopey.'

He looks none the wiser and gulps his beer.

'Thought more about the starting line-up?' he asks.

'Aye.' But I'm keeping it to myself right now. Best to wait to see if they all turn up. Training has been better attended than I anticipated. The drills are developing well, and the younger ones are showing more and more promise. And with Harry Doyle cracking the whip, a more positive attitude is developing.

'When ye next seein' Raymond?' This catches him off guard.

'How?' He means *why*.

'Just askin'.'

'Ye thinkin' ae goin'? Ah'll come wi' ye, if ye like. Be a wee day out for us.'

'When's the next visitin'?'

'Eh, next Wednesday, ah'm sure.'

'Ah'll see. Maybe.'

Higgy has been telling me to wait – to hold off seeing, or speaking to, my brother – since I came back almost three months ago. He suggested waiting until the season has started. He visits regularly himself. Doesn't want Raymond thinking no-one cares. It's always been inevitable that I'll go, but I've been in no rush. Delaying it has given me only the slightest feeling of control, however. Just a little. Raymond might not be snapping fingers like he once did, but the effect is the same as it's always been. An audience with King Raymond. The king in exile.

'The guy from the *Standard* was a bit weird,' I say to Higgy.

'Aye?'

'Aye. A pretty fucken strange encounter, all round, that yin.'

'What wis his name?'

'Dunno. Didn't get it, an' he wasn't for givin' it up. Surprised they even showed up.'

'Don't think ah invited him. Did you?' I ask him.

'Naw. Em … naw, why would ah dae that?'

'Aye, aw'right. Nae need tae get so defensive,' I tell him. Higgy gets up from his armchair.

'Ye heard ae a woman called Macdonald?' I ask him.

'Common name. But then there are loads ae farmers about here.' He laughs at his own joke. 'Naw. Who's she?'

'Dunno. She was in at my interview, an' she just showed up earlier at The Barn.'

'Probably somebody fae Kidds. The chairman's got loads ae folk schemin' away in the background. Auditors an' lawyers an' that.'

'Said she looked after the contracts.'

'Well, there ye go then,' he concludes. 'Ah'm just gonnae catch the last orders at the pub.' He gets his coat, a bunnet and heads out.

∩

I'm rereading the words written in the first Barshaw Bridge FC programme for season 1996–97. It's eight pages long. Every word composed by me. Something I can get wrapped up in. A mission I've been on. Folded and stapled, it looks like an independent music fanzine, cobbled together by bored bedsit teenagers passing the time until their adult lives begin. But I regard it with pride. It's more than words and images printed on four sides of light-red A4 paper. It's an embodiment of history; an acknowledgement that an important moment took place. I used to have lots of football programmes, swapped and collected between football team-mates. Raymond sold them all, the cunt.

The cover image is an action shot of Sean O'Halloran. There's an introductory column. An opportunity to properly welcome in the promising dawn of a new season. To ingratiate myself with the handful who regularly follow the home games. If we have fewer supporters than players tomorrow, we're in real trouble, but we need to start somewhere.

'From the Archives...' is a feature highlighting famous games from previous eras. There is a book in my office with newspaper clippings and hand-written summaries going back nearly thirty years. It looks like Higgy's handwriting for the most part.

I've cheated for the first one, selecting a famous result in club history. A win against all the odds.

April 1973
Irvine Meadow 2 (Johnstone, Morris)
Barshaw Bridge FC 3 (Mordue 2, Telford)
Attendance: 3,357

I enjoyed the time spent in the library in Cumnock, researching the historical facts. I tore some content from old publications when the librarian wasn't looking. It reminded me of better times in Aberdeen when the sound of silence was a comfort. With the hairs on the back of my neck raised, I assembled an account of what must've been an outstanding match for the small number of travelling Barshaw Bridge supporters. Irvine Meadow would go on to win the Scottish Junior Cup that year.

The back page has the squad names, and to one side, a player Q&A. For the opening match of the season, it features Paddy Gilhooly, the returning club captain. I hope these features will make the players seem a bit more connected to the supporters. Make them feel part of the shared ambition.

The rest of my prototype programme comprises specific adverts for local shops and businesses. And more general advertisements for cigarettes and alcohol. The Oasis song of that name will be our run-out music for the first game of this new season.

I've compiled a list of music to be played through the PA system before the match, and at half time. Anything, in fact, to indicate a new, youthful approach. A willingness to consign last season to the dustbin. To give us an outsider's fighting chance.

I put the printed stock back in the cardboard box. If somebody had told me, six months ago, that this was my future, I'd have considered them mad. It's funny how things turn out.

∩

A different route for the morning run on the day of the first match. There's no thought process at work. No superstitious basis for it. It's just a random decision that draws me into streets I can barely remember having been down before. Although if we win, I won't alter it until we lose.

My breath makes instant clouds in front of me. It's colder than it's been since I returned to the village. Crows caw from hidden locations. A dog barks in the distance. I put the headphones on and click the Walkman. 'Bill is Dead'. It's from the best Fall LP in more than ten years. Since *The Wonderful and Frightening World of...*

These are the finest times of my life. And, weirdly, it's beginning to feel like it. I can't put my finger on it. For the first time in a long time, I'm looking forward to things. To seeing Damo. And Nancy. There's purpose. And with Raymond and Libby both largely absent, there's calm. The old lad from the *Standard* apart, being back here feels like finding a favourite pair of jeans, lost for years. They still fit, and there's even a twenty in the pocket. It's a surprising revelation.

I start visualising the season ahead as a cartoon strip: I'm Roy Race, star player of the famous Melchester Rovers, until our career ended when we lost a foot in a helicopter crash. But we're back, Roy and me, as player-manager ... a new left foot grafted on thanks to innovative, ground-breaking laser-assisted surgery. 'Real *Roy of the Rovers* stuff', writes the *Kilmarnock Standard*, as we – Roy and me – score a last-minute penalty to win the Ayrshire Cup. And just as the imaginary ball hits the back of the imaginary net, I turn an ankle on a kerb.

I limp down an incline. Semi-detached houses line either side, like a guard of honour for a retiring player. There's a hammerhead at the bottom. A high fence with several holes in it, some newer houses beyond it and the woods beyond them. I hirple down the street knowing that I'll have to turn and jog back up once the pain subsides a bit.

A door opens. The last house on the left. An old woman walks slowly to the end of a path that's surrounded by wild overgrown weeds.

'Oh hullo, there,' she says as she peers across the street through milk-bottle glasses. 'Any post today?'

'Ah'm no' the postman, missus,' I reply, smiling. I walk over to her.

'Up awfy early then.'

'Ach. Aye ... ah'm just...' Then it dawns on me. Like a dense fog lifting. I'm back there. It's like the sudden, stinging sharpness of a leather belt coming down on my tiny outstretched hands.

Aul' Jock Reid ... he's no' right in the heid. His wife's a hoor, an' his daughter's deid.

The house. The one on the news when I was a child. The one she was taken from. The woods over the fence where her mother was found hanged. This is Jock Reid's house. This is Jock Reid's wife.

'Ye couldn't pick the milk up for me, son?' she asks. 'Just since yer passin'.'

'Eh ... aye. Of course.' Suddenly I'm trembling. I bend down and pick up the bottles.

She turns and walks towards her house rather than take them from me. I have no choice but to follow her through the unkempt, thigh-high landscape to her front door.

'Thanks son,' she says. A warm smile follows.

My hands shake as I hand her the bottles one by one. I worry she can see it. Probably not. Can she sense it? Is she aware of my heart pounding?

'If I had a few caramels, I'd give ye them,' she says. 'A wee reward, ye know?'

'It's fine, missus...' I leave this open. She doesn't fill in the ending. *Reid* is etched into the rusty metal plate. It's her. There's no doubt.

I tell her I must go. She says 'thanks', and 'yer a nice lad'. I look back at the house from the top of her road. And suddenly, recollections come rushing into my head like I've just been injected with a hallucinatory drug. I recall the vans and the diggers and the white tents in the garden. And then there's Higgy and Deek Henderson standing in front of me in the road. They both believed she was there, convinced she was buried in the ground around the house. The definition is becoming sharper. More focused. She was in my class, little Louise. Little Louise-Anne. There were only thirteen of us. Her name was after mine in the register and I remember our teacher reading mine out and I put my hand up and then that terrible silence and she looked up and remembered and she burst into tears and we were all sent home because no-one else was there to look after us.

It could've been me. It should've been me.

Aul' Jock Reid ... he's no' right in the heid. His wife's a hoor, an' his daughter's deid.

Poor Jock Reid. Poor Danny fucking Garvey...

Just a fortnight before the end of the 1983 league season, Barshaw Bridge had their biggest game in a decade. An Ayrshire Cup semi-final draw at home against Auchinleck Talbot. I was sixteen and in the midst of my exams. I'd been training with the Bridge that whole season. Turning down offers and requests from various professional clubs Raymond had deemed unworthy. We were – in his words – waiting for the right opportunity to knock.

Deek Henderson, Barshaw's manager, had given me my debut a month or so earlier. A week prior to this, he called me to his office where – drunk – he locked the door, dropped his pants and asked me to wank him off.

I did. I liked Deek. He wasn't a shouter; not at me at least. He'd been patient with me in training. He encouraged me. Told me I was very special. A special talent. I wanted to play for Barshaw Bridge. To make Raymond and Higgy proud. To make my manager happy. I just wanted to play. It seemed like a fair swap; a hand job for a first-team jersey. I masturbated twice daily at that age. I was good at it. One more wouldn't matter. I just assumed the whole team had gone through this initiation. This one-off show of personal commitment and determination.

Deek Henderson cried when I'd finished. I felt sorry for him and then disgusted by him. Sitting there on the edge of his desk. Tracksuit bottoms at his ankles. Tears running down his face. His own spunk all over his thighs. He pleaded with me to keep it between us. That others wouldn't understand.

But I told Raymond.

Then I blocked it out. I just wanted to play. I figured Raymond would know what to do for the best.

I played in seven games before the semi-final; six in the league. I did well. We won four of those matches. I scored a hat-trick in one game; from midfield. I started against the mighty Talbot. Almost one thousand supporters jammed themselves into our tiny ground that Saturday in May 1983. We struggled in the first half, but kept the score to zero, and limited them to a handful of chances. In the second half though, Talbot had a man sent off for raking his studs down my left leg, having been booked for an almost identical challenge on Scotty Sellars in the first half. We would never have a better chance of reaching a final. With fifteen minutes left, and me on the verge of cramp, the ball spilled out from a corner. I was on the edge of the Talbot box. I could hear Deek Henderson shouting, 'Shoot, Danny. Fucken shoot, son!' but I didn't. I weaved around the first two defenders, put the ball through the legs of a third, and then casually lifted it over their keeper.

Barshaw Bridge FC 1 – 0 Auchinleck Talbot
(Garvey, 77)

That night, Raymond took me to six pubs. I was drunk by the time we'd left the second. We didn't go home. I woke up in a remote, smelly house on the edge of Cumnock. I had a blinding headache. I had been sick all over myself. I looked for Raymond. He was in a back room in bed with a red-haired woman old enough to be our mother.

He got up, and we left without the woman waking. Raymond took the keys to an old Mini that was parked along the dark lane.

I don't know who the car belonged to. It wasn't yet six o'clock on that Sunday morning and there was not a sound to be heard.

'Here, you drive, superstar,' Raymond said.

'Fuck off,' I said, shivering.

'Ah'm serious,' he said. 'C'mon. Nae cunt's about. Ye deserve it. Plus, ah've been on the Charlie.'

'Aye, an' ah'm no' even seventeen,' I protested.

'Who's gonnae see ye out here? The fucken scarecrows? Ya wee chicken, ye. Get in an' drive!'

'Naw. Bugger off.'

'Dae it,' his tone shifting to anger. 'Or ah'll tell every cunt ye wanked off Deek fucken Henderson tae get intae the first team.'

Louise-Anne Macdonald was all anyone could talk about when I was a child. The local speculation about what had happened to her. Higgy and Deek Henderson and their total conviction that her grampa was responsible. And I was jealous of her; of the attention she got. Everybody feeling sorry for her, when the possibility remained that she was in a better place. That whoever had her now cared for her more than *he* had. Even if he hadn't done away with her, he'd fucking let her go. He'd let her out of his sight. He'd been too fucking wrapped up in his own selfish thoughts. Too bothered about his papers, or whatever was on the telly. Or playing that stupid fucking piano. These were the things that preoccupied me for years, when I wasn't playing football. Right up to the night of the Talbot semi-final.

Two days after that last match for Barshaw Bridge, I was on my way to Aberdeen.

My earlier optimism has evaporated. The chance meeting with the old woman has shaken me, forcing me to remember the reasons I came back here. She has no idea who I am. I barely know, myself. A dull ache in my head is building.

Higgy has gone out. His traditional prematch pint and fry-up at The King's being touted as *his* superstition. His house is quiet. Last-minute preparations before I go and pick up the boy. I come out of the bathroom and an insistent noise breaks the silence.

The club's mobile phone is ringing. I didn't recognise its tone since it's the first time I've heard it ring. It takes me a while to locate. I put it in a drawer the night it was given to me.

'Hullo?' I answer timidly, as if I was the recipient of the first-ever telephone call.

'Gaffer,' a deep voice replies.

'Who's this?'

'It's me, boss ... Jaz.' It takes me a while. 'Jaz Sinclair,' says Jaz, perhaps acknowledging we haven't spoken much since preseason training resumed a month ago.

'What's up?' I ask, knowing something is.

'Ah'm out for the game. The day, ah mean.' I leave a space for him to fill. Partly because I'm uncomfortable speaking on the tiny grey thing in my hand. Partly because the brief conversation with Jock Reid's widow is still distracting me. And partly because I despise it when players call off matches on the day of the game.

'Ah've got the skitters,' says Jaz. Hard to tell if he's trying to avoid the detail. 'Been up aw night. Fuck all left in me.' He sounds desperate. 'Ma arse has been pumpin' out thick filthy water ... s'been like drainin' the oil fae a fucken car's engine.'

As he pleads, I glance at my notes. He knew he wasn't starting anyway. I picked the team at Thursday's training. Higgy thought it was a mistake to tell them. He might've been right.

'Fine. Are ye comin' though ... tae support the team?' I ask.

He hesitates.

'Okay,' I say. 'Double trainin' sessions next week then.'

Jaz Sinclair seems to take this as a win, albeit one he's had to work for. It's highly unlikely he wouldn't be able to play, but a severe hangover is more likely to be the prompt for the call. He wishes us luck and hangs up, as I search for the button that would've allowed me to end the call first.

I hear the ringing sound again, but I'm heading out the front door, and the phone remains in the drawer it was returned to.

🔈

'Afternoon ... is Damian ready?'

'Are you Danny? *Raymond's* brother?'

'Yeah, I ... em, is Nancy about?'

'Naw. She's at work.'

'Oh. Aw'right then.'

The woman folds her arms.

'Did she mention me takin' the wee man tae the fitba?'

'She did.'

She's sizing me up. I guess this is Nancy's mother. It's less the physical resemblance, more the impenetrable suspicion. She looks me up and down. The emphasis placed on my brother's name betrays her opinion of him. She'll assume I'm cut from the same cloth.

'Damo!' she yells, without turning to direct her voice into the house, where the boy must be. We stand watching each other for what feels like ten wordless minutes before the boy appears. He is wearing the spaceman's helmet. The visor is open.

—*Mum told me my new uncle was coming. She told me he was a nice man. That he wouldn't have a beard on. And that he would take me to watch football.*

'Aw'right, pal?' I ask him. He nudges his way past the older woman. He doesn't look at me at all.

—*I don't like talking to people I don't know.*

'Bye, Gran,' he whispers, confirming my suspicion.

'Bye, son,' she replies, her eyes never leaving mine. 'You do what yer uncle tells ye, okay?' The boy nods. I put out my hand to take his. He ignores it.

—I don't like people I don't know touching me.

'He doesn't like to be touched,' his gran informs me.

'Ah … right. Okay,' I say.

'Damian … *Damo*. Ah got ye somethin'. Want tae see it?' I ask him.

He nods. I hand him a small package, wrapped in a tissue. He looks at his gran, who raises an eyebrow. Damo takes it, unwraps the tissue. He doesn't speak, smile or look at me. He reaches into his jacket and pulls out a small plastic bag. He puts the tiny figure of Paul Gascoigne that I've just given him into the bag.

'Paul Gascoigne. Ye know him?' I ask. He nods again.

—Laudrup, Ravanelli, Shearer, Juninho, McManaman, Red-knapp, Schmeichel, Beckham, Gullit, Zola, Vialli … Gascoigne.

'Get him back here five o'clock latest, right? He has tae have his tea at five.'

'Ah will. An' thanks,' I say. She watches us until we are out of sight.

Damo walks purposefully. All my attempts to talk to him fall on his apparently deaf ears. I ask him if he's excited about today's match against Lugar Boswell Thistle. If he's looking forward to going to a new school. If he likes music. I look down and into the visor. His lips are moving in silent chant.

—Laudrup, Ravanelli, Shearer, Juninho, McManaman, Red-knapp, Schmeichel, Beckham, Gascoigne, Gullit, Zola, Vialli.

'Aw'right, wee man?' Higgy greets us at the gate. 'Didnae think his ma would let him.'

'Why no'?' I say.

'Ach, just ... y'know?'

'Actually, ah don't.' It's a small step for the boy in the space helmet, but apparently a giant leap for the band of damaged adults around him. We leave it at that.

''Mon, son,' says Higgy. 'Want a sausage roll?'

Damo nods and follows Higgy over to the rusting van with the steam billowing out of its bolted-on metal flue.

—I like sausage. I like rolls. Mum brings me rolls home from work. Sometimes they're still hot. I want to watch football. I'm good at watching football.

The match-day programmes are in the box at the makeshift turn-stiles. I paid for them myself to be given out freely on this opening day of the season. It's an hour before kick-off. The players from both teams are appearing in gangs from cars parked up like the start of a rally. The nets are up. The referee is already out inspecting a pitch that I doubt will have looked much better. The sun is shining, and a shiver runs down my spine.

I watch my players head for their pegs and hang their jackets up. There's no allocation but even though we are now using last season's away dressing room, a natural order emerges. Forwards and midfielders together nearest the door. Defenders and the keeper grouped over to the left. The bench runs around three sides, interrupted only by the route into the toilet and the showers. I stand at the blank wall, acknowledging the mumbled 'Boss', that comes from the majority.

I count them. Forty-five minutes to go and I have thirteen. Harry Doyle is out pacing the car park. There will be hell to pay for the three who remain AWOL. I go outside and call him back to take the warm-up drills. I hear him ushering those already stripped out onto the pitch. A car splutters through the open gate and stops next to me.

'Sorry, gaffer,' says Stevie Smith, the driver. 'Fucken puncture, man!' I look down at the thin replacement wheel.

'Fair enough,' I say. 'Get a shift on though.' The defender and his passengers, Fraser Boland and Luke Lorimer, all sprint into the cabin.

'Right, everybody ready?'

'Fucken bang on,' says the captain.

I've handed over the team lines. My team's studs have been inspected. We're ready.

'Everybody know their positions?' They nod collectively. 'Win the one-on-ones, keep it tight at the back ... don't get dragged out ae position if they start movin' about.' It seems like the list of trudged-out clichés every coach from Boys' Brigade teams to international-level exhorts in the minutes before kick-off. The minutes when players aren't really listening. Those seconds when they are in their own space, anticipating the game ahead. The match going their way. A match-winning performance. All the training-ground routines coming together and coalescing around a formation that fits each player perfectly. Eradicating any thoughts of loss or fears of serious injury.

'Who's yer favourite player, Damo?' I hear Higgy ask the boy from over my left shoulder.

—*Laudrup, Ravanelli, Shearer, Juninho, McManaman, Redknapp, Schmeichel, Beckham, Gascoigne, Gullit, Zola, Vialli.*

'Gascoigne,' he whispers.

The crowd – I've counted fifty-seven heads – seems impressed by our positive start. Only one negative shout so far – 'McIntosh, yer a fat cunt!' – which received a 'Tell yer ma tae stop feedin' me buttered scones when ah'm ridin' her up the arse then,' from the keeper. Apart from that, quiet encouragement.

Predictably, this changes when we concede. Ten minutes from half-time, our discipline slips. A nothing ball over the top from the opposing left back. Their striker easily outpaces Gilhooly and slots it under Tony McIntosh.

—*One-nil to Lugar. McIntosh, yer a fat cunt!*

'Maybe a change, Boss?' says Harry Doyle. I don't answer, and he automatically sends the subs up the line to warm up.

Strawhorn is hauled down on the edge of the box. He gets the free kick, but not before a deserved yellow for head-butting his Lugar marker. A yellow that would've been a red had the ref been closer to the play. My players fight over who's taking it. Strawhorn grabs it. Gilhooly grabs him. The ref threatens more cards. 'Fucken state ae these jokers,' says my opposite number, just loud enough for me to hear; laughing at us.

—*Strawhorn has never scored a goal in a first half.*

'Aw'right, Damo? Ye want some crisps or somethin', son?' Higgy's voice distracts me from the action. I'd almost forgotten the boy was here.

'Hey, Damian. Everythin' okay?' I ask. I go over to him during the break in play as the referee takes more of our names.

'Strawhorn has never scored a free kick,' he says quietly, through the open visor. I smirk at the boy's prescience. This statistic isn't about to change.

'A first time for everythin',' says a hopeful Barshaw punter.

His optimism will be misplaced. I don't need the conviction of a ten-year-old in a space helmet. Strawhorn is raging. There will be no composure. No skilful, subtle bending of the ball around Lugar's substantial wall.

A fifteen-yard run-up for a shot that's only twenty yards from goal. With a six-man wall of their heftiest lined up eight yards away at most. Predictably, my striker tries to bludgeon the ball, presumably hoping to take a defender's head off in the process. It sails high over the bar. The ball is still rising as the ref signals for half-time.

—*Strawhorn has never scored a goal in a first half. We are losing one-nil.*

'Need tae send that fucken wean up in his spaceship tae get the baw back … fae the moon!' shouts a Lugar fan. A handful of others laugh loudly. They give Strawhorn the 'wanker' sign. His head is swarming in a red mist. Before Gilhooly can grab him, he veers off towards the small group and launches his forehead right into the first face; a teenager, no more than fifteen. Blood spurts from a split nose. Players who were already in the changing rooms rush back out. I grab my nephew. He screams at me. I let him go as someone barges my back.

—*Don't touch me. I don't like people touching me.*

It takes longer to calm Damo down than to put out the terracing firestorm. The bloodied teenager is attended by the Lugar management and their magic sponge. The ref and his linesmen act like a synchronised wrestling tag-team. They pull shirts. They yell obscenities and threats and gradually it dissipates.

—*My new uncle punched a man. My new uncle was screaming and shouting 'cunt' at the man. Cunt isn't a nice word. My new uncle seems like a nice man. But he shouted 'cunt' a lot. And punched a man.*

Eventually, the teams are separated, back behind the plywood. Strawhorn has been sent off. He grabs his clothes and will listen to no-one, least of all me. He'll be reported. He – with me accompanying him – will have to attend a disciplinary hearing at Hampden. It'll be a ban, and probably a long one. It will also be a police matter, if the opposition report the assault on one of their young fans.

The ref opens the door just as I am trying to reorganise our tactics for the second half. I notice the skin has been scraped from my knuckles. I wipe the blood from them on my tracksuit bottoms and put my hands in my pockets.

'Lads, an extra ten minutes,' he suggests. His voice is deep. His stature helping to maintain control. He has seen it all before. 'Any more fucken shite out there, an' ah'm abandonin' the game, right?' He directs this to me. I nod. 'You're in enough fucken trouble here, don't force me tae add tae it.'

'Cheers, Ref,' I say meekly. 'Appreciate it.' I don't know what my team think. About the ref. About their departed, fuck-witted team-mate. About me.

'Look, ye'se were doin' fine up tae losin' that bloody goal.' Harry Doyle assumes control. 'We kept our shape, we moved the baw well. Strawhorn wis the only yin no' contributin'. We've got forty-five minutes tae get back intae it. This shower are rubbish. Bloody *rubbish*. We're no' fucken beat here, no' by a long shot!' I watch the team. See a slim modicum of belief reinflate them. Harry Doyle has the man-management skills I lack.

'Boss?' he says, handing back the reins.

I stumble. Look around the claustrophobic room. The steam from perspiration on the cold blockwork. The harsh fluorescent light. I am dazed. The door opens.

'Right lads, let's go,' shouts the ref, before closing the door again.

I look back at them, my team. They are all watching me. Waiting for wisdom. They haven't given up. Not yet. I look at the boy. Even his face seems expectant through his open visor.

'Stevie ... son, you're comin' off.' I glance at an empty space. 'Where's Billy Gilmour?'

'He's in *there* ... havin' a shite! He's really superstitious,' says Denny Peters. Gilmour returns. He blushes as everyone stares.

'Billy, you're on for Stevie,' I tell him.

The studs rattle their angry war cry on the concrete, making the uncoordinated music of an experimental post-punk band. Gilhooly punches a ceiling tile above him. More damage to fix, but if that's what it takes, who cares? Young Billy Gilmour anxiously leans over Damo. He kisses the boy's space helmet three times. The boy recedes. Higgy shouldn't have brought him in here. He probably thought it was safer than being out there with him, in the middle of an aggravated crowd, regardless of how small it is.

I stand on the touchline. I feel the eyes of the committee burning into my back. They'll be starting to count the cost of their mistake. At least nine points adrift at the foot of the league table, and much harder games to come.

—*Lugar are a big team. They have old, fat men. An old, fat man has scored a goal. The referee said no goal. He waved his long arms about. Most goals are scored in the sixty-seventh minute.*

'Denny!' I call the youngster back. 'You're goin' on for Huck Finnegan. Ah want ye tae play in the middle. Linking wi' Billy, supportin' Sean. Tell Boland tae drop back a bit. Midfield diamond.' I make the change. Against the bulk of the Lugar men, most of my team now look like their sons.

—*Most goals are scored in the sixty-seventh minute.*

'Sixty-seventh minute,' shouts Damo.

'Aye, son,' says Higgy. 'It's about that now.'

'Most goals are scored in the sixty-seventh minute,' the boy says, loud enough for all around to hear him. It's the loudest I've ever heard him speak. And I get lost in the thought that he may well be right. Going into the last quarter, with a game still tight, a change being made on the hour. It either unsettles the team who's winning, if they fail to adjust, or the new player coming on fails to adjust to the pace and pattern of the game. Either way, the ten minutes after...

'GOAL! Ya fucken wee beauty, ye!' Higgy dives past me. Onto his knees, on the pitch. I missed it going in. 'Damo, ah bloody love ye, son. Sixty-seven minutes!'

—*Most goals are scored in the sixty-seventh minute.*

'What a move, Danny. Just like the other night. Straight fae the trainin' ground.' Harry Doyle is hugging Higgy. The players are hugging each other. Lugar players swamp the ref, claiming offside. From the middle of a red-and-white huddle, Billy Gilmour emerges. Still holding the ball he's just retrieved from the Lugar net. He points to Damo, and shouts, 'That's for you, wee man!'

—*That's for me. Wee man.*

I turn. Billy the Kidd and his Committed Three are smiling. Thumbs raised like a phalanx of satisfied emperors. Anne Macdonald has appeared, standing just behind them. She is applauding. I wave, but she doesn't return the gesture.

Gilmour calls for the ball. He receives it from Denny Peters. A split second later, Gilmour is on his back.

'That's it, fucken *do* that wee cunt!' yells the Lugar manager to his left back.

'Hey, enough ae that, for fuck sake!' I shout over.

'Who ae you talkin' tae? Ah'll fucken snap you in half, pencil neck!' And the lino steps in to separate us.

'Seriously?' asks the ref of us. 'No' been enough bloody boxin' aw'ready the day?'

Satisfied, he turns his back on us. Their manager motions silently to the effect that he'll see me later.

'Push it short,' I hear Billy Gilmour say to his captain.

'Get up the field,' comes the reply.

'Go on, short.' The youngster's confidence is impressive. Gilhooly looks over. I nod back. The free kick gets taken short. I can see the goal coming. I can see the five or six moves ahead. It's like the ball is at my feet and I'm making all the decisions for Billy Gilmour. He swerves past a defender and hits a peach of a shot.

'GOAL!' shouts Higgy. His joy is obvious to all. Twenty or so in the crowd behind us are jumping up and down, hugging each other. It's like we've just won a cup final.

'Get it right up ye'se, ya fucken jaggy bastards,' shouts Harry Doyle, in front of the Lugar contingent.

I try to pull him away, with Lugar men threatening all forms of violence. The corresponding away fixture will be intimidatingly brutal, but that's a worry for another day.

The final whistle blows.

Barshaw Bridge 2–1 Lugar Boswell Thistle
(Gilmour 2)

There are no handshakes, only scuffles. It is amazing that the players and coaching staff make it back to the changing rooms without further punches being thrown.

Tony McIntosh makes a beeline for the Barshaw home supporters.

'Still think ah'm a fat cunt, then?' I hear him shout at one.

'Ach, fucken gie's peace,' is the muted reply.

'Thanks for that, an' sorry about the trouble,' I say to the ref as I hand him and his assistants their money. 'Fifteen quid seems a thin cut for a game like that.'

'Cheers, son. Ah enjoyed that. Like a bit ae passion, y'know? Close match, but ye'se did well second half,' he admits.

'Aye. Touch an' go, but ah think we just shaded it.'

'Ah'll need tae write up yer front man, Strawhorn.'

'Ah know.'

'My opinion? Ye don't need him. Ye'se played better when he went off. These youngsters are a guid blend. Stick wi' them, ye'll dae fine this year.'

I thank him again, and he leaves sharply. An experienced official who knows to get out of a contentious situation as soon as he can and once the money's been handed over.

Half an hour later, the Lugar contingent are also leaving. They aren't accepting the customary offer of a pie and a pint from their hosts at The King's Arms. Their anger may have dissipated but not to the extent that permits any well-wishing for the season ahead.

'Fuck off, ya stupid cunt,' says their manager, as I make one last attempt at a handshake. 'Just fucken wait tae we get ye'se back at our place,' he sneers, spitting phlegm onto a lush Kidd's carpet on his way out to the car park.

I open the door. There's a silence, but smiles are emerging on everyone's faces. The smiles uniformly grow, and a stamping sound accompanies the 'Barshaw Bridge, Barshaw Bridge, Barshaw Bridge' song, which grows in volume until everyone is on their feet, arms around each other, jumping up and down on the spot. Team spirit; if you can't develop it, you're fucked, but if you can capture it, nurture it and retain it, you have a chance.

I think we might have a chance.

—*Barshaw Bridge, Barshaw Bridge, Barshaw Bridge. That's for me. Wee man.*

The ground only clears around six o'clock. I know I'm in trouble when I see Nancy striding up the hill. Her mother is trying to keep pace but has fallen thirty yards behind.

'Enjoy that, Damo?' I ask him as we sit on a step at the edge of the pitch. I ask before the storm hits and I don't get the chance. He doesn't answer. The nets are down. The players have left, heading to The King's Arms with a few quids' worth of win bonus that Billy the Kidd has bunged them. He'd brought his new distributor to the game. Probably why Anne Macdonald made the briefest of appearances. A win, especially in controversial circumstances, opens wallets. Higgy is locking up. Harry Doyle is helping him.

—*Enjoy that, Damo? I have my tea at five o'clock.*

'Wee Billy's convinced you helped us win, pal.'

—*I helped us win. Five o'clock. Barshaw Bridge. Barshaw Bridge. Barshaw Bridge. My new uncle hit a fat man. He said cunt nine times and fat bastard twice.*

Thankfully, Nancy waits until she reaches us.

'For Christ's sake, Danny. What were ye told? Five o'clock, right?' I nod. 'He needs bloody routine. Ah thought ye appreciated that!'

'Ah'm sorry, really. Ah am. He's a great kid an'...'

'What dae you know, eh?' It's hard to tell who she's angry at. I'm not certain it's me.

'Ah told you tae get him back by five.' Nancy's mum has joined us. She's wheezing, but it must seem to her like a fag is the solution. 'Were ye just no' listenin', or deliberately ignorin' me?' she says between elongated puffs.

I sit with the tiny astronaut beside me, looking up into the sun as the two angry silhouettes in front of us shift their weight from one foot to the other, as if winding themselves up to vent.

'Are you listenin' tae me, son?' asks the mother.

I'm trying to stifle a laugh at the absurdity of it.

'C'mon, Damo,' says Doreen, drawing me a glare that might turn flesh to stone if she'd held it longer.

—*I helped us win. Five o'clock. Ya fat bastard.*

'I helped us to win,' says Damo, quietly.
    'Whit's that, son?' his mum asks him.
    'That's right, pal. Ye did.'
    'She's no' talkin' tae you,' her mum points out. 'Ah told ye no' tae trust another yin ae they bloody Garveys. State yer in is because ae them. Did ah no' tell ye it would...'
    'Aye. Ye did, mam. Ye *do*. Aw the time.'
    Nancy's mum sighs. I take some little pleasure that she's now here, sat on the naughty terracing. Same as me.
    'Look, Nancy...'
    'Don't *look* us, son!'
    'Mam ... thanks. But ah can handle this.'
    'Dinnae let this yin walk aw ower ye, like his br—'
    'Mam!' More forceful this time.
    And the older woman steps back, hands out, mid-shrug. Her head tilted to the side, *don't come runnin' tae me*-style.
    'I helped us win,' says Damo, again. He's laying his tiny football men out in a line.

—*Schmeichel, Laudrup, Ravanelli, Shearer, Juninho, McManaman, Redknapp, Beckham, Gascoigne, Gullit, Zola, Vialli.*

'That'd be some team, eh, Damo?' I say, and through the open visor, I see him. He's smiling. This strange crooked smirk.
    'Schmeichel, Laudrup, Ravanelli, Shearer, Juninho, McManaman, Redknapp, Beckham, Gascoigne, Gullit, Zola, Vialli,' he mutters.
    'Might need a couple ae defenders though,' I tell him.
    'Most goals are scored in the sixty-seventh minute,' he says.

'Aye.' I laugh. 'Ye were right about that tae, son,' I reply.

'Barshaw have only won four times after losing the first goal and a man sent off,' adds Damo.

'Jesus, is that right?' I say. 'You're like a wee Statto.'

'A wee Statto,' he repeats.

'C'mon, son, ye need tae get yer tea.' Nancy's mum, deep into her second cigarette, steps forward. The aggression has reduced. Content, perhaps that their boy isn't distressed.

'Comin' tae the pub, Danny?' Higgy shouts over from the door to The Barn. 'Ah, Nancy,' he adds, seeing them with me, and, 'Ye aw'right there, Doreen? Long-time, hen.'

Doreen looks at him with thinly veiled disgust. Doesn't reply. Higgy is a Garvey by default. No fraternising with the enemy allowed.

'Higgy,' Nancy acknowledges by way of politeness.

Her mother glares. 'Ah'm takin' him down for his tea. You can hang about here if ye like but ah've got things tae dae.' Doreen holds out a hand to beckon Damo.

The boy gathers up his men and puts them in their plastic bag. 'I helped us win,' he says to me. Looking right at me, for the first time.

'Couldnae have done it without ye, buddy,' I say, standing as he does.

'See ye'se later,' says Higgy. The door locks behind him.

—*I helped us win. Five o'clock. Ah'll fucken snap you in half, pencil neck.*

'Pencil neck,' says Damo, to his gran. And I laugh as I realise what he means.

—*Fat cunt.*

'What did he say there,' asks Nancy.

'Just something their manager said to me,' I say. 'He was fine, honestly. Ah see what ye meant about him lovin' the fitba.' And suddenly, it's just the two of us. Me and the mother of my brother's son.

'Ye have tae understand, Damo's ... he's no' like other wee boys,' she says, hesitantly. She sits where her son was minutes earlier.

I retake my seat beside her. Staring out at an empty green field, the sun disappearing gradually behind the church spire; the main punctuation mark in the village. Its long shadow points at us. Almost reaching our feet.

'Ah get that. You mentioned it before,' I say quietly. 'I appreciate how fragile he is.'

'He isn't fragile,' says Nancy. 'He can be really...' She tails off.

'Tell me,' I say.

'Every day's a challenge. Ah don't know what type of kid he's goin' tae be from one day tae the next.'

'How d'ye mean?'

'He can be ... He's sometimes violent – towards us. A right meltdown, y'know? Ah'm constantly worryin' about the kind ae future he'll have. The kind that *ah'll* have.'

'He seems really calm an' quiet,' I say, unhelpfully, as it turns out.

'Based on what? The ten bloody minutes ye've spent wi' him since ye've been here?'

'Ah'm sorry.'

'Aye, so am I,' she says, standing.

I've let her down. 'Listen, don't go, Nancy. Please. Ah want tae try an' help if ah can.'

'Why?' she says. It takes me by surprise, because I don't really know why. 'You don't owe me anythin'. It's no' your issue that his dad's locked up.'

'But still, he's family. You're f—'

'I'm no' *your* family, so if that's the pitch, just drop it. You owe us nothin', Danny.'

My interest in her isn't about remediation.

We don't speak again until the village clock strikes seven. But she didn't leave. She stayed. She sat down.

'Who d'ye think rings that bell?' I ask.

'What?'

'The church bell ... it rings every hour, but ah've never seen anyone goin' in, or leavin'. So, who makes it ring?'

'Christ knows,' says Nancy, before laughing at the absurdity of the question. 'Ye know, ah've lived here for over ten years an' ah've never given that a minute's thought,' she says. She looks like a different person when she smiles. 'An' now ah'll no' be able tae think ae anythin' else ... ever again.' I laugh at this. 'So, thanks Danny Garvey ... bloody thanks for that. As if this place doesn't drive ye mad enough!'

'We could break in. Find out the answer tae the dominant question ae the age. Nick some lead off the roof while we're there ... make it worth the effort?'

'Aye ... that'd be a good look, eh? A coupla thirty-year-olds shinnyin' up they auld drainpipes tae crack open a church.'

'Hey, ah'll *thirty* ye. Twenty-nine if ye don't mind!'

'Tough paper round wis it?'

'Cheeky bitch.'

She laughs and it warms the air around us. It's staggering how quickly I've become comfortable in her company.

'Where were ye workin' earlier?' I ask.

'The baker's,' she replies.

'Ye like it?'

'Hate it,' she replies, quick as a flash. 'Ah love bakin' but ah can't stand the way the shop's run. Ernie's a nice enough guy, but there's nae ambition at all. He's too lazy. The shop's barely survivin'.'

'How long ye been there?'

'Since 1985. Eleven years. Jesus ... a third ae my life!' She sighs. 'It's become a habit. Too scared tae chuck it, an' hunt for somethin' better, y'know?'

'Aye.' It mirrors my own employment. When I finally did make a move, it was backwards. Here. Arguably three steps backwards. 'When did ye first meet Raymond?'

Nancy smirks at this. I'm not sure how to take it. 'When ah first met your brother, he wasn't house-trained.' She laughs. 'Me an' Mam moved here in 1984. From Cumbernauld. Ah was eighteen at the time. My dad was a right bastard. Permanently drunk. Permanently violent wi' it. He'd lift his fist tae mam for no reason. Rangers got beat ... wallop. Thatcher's on telly ... wallop. Dinner no' ready ... wallop. First time he did it tae me, Mam hit him back. An' ended up in hospital. Ah phoned the police. They gave her fifty quid an' the address ae a women's refuge in Ayrshire. Six months later, we're here. She got a council house an' a job servin' school dinners. We've never seen him since.'

'Jesus, ah'm sorry.' I'm saying that a lot.

'Raymond was the first customer ah served on my first day.' She smiles sweetly at the memory. 'A doughnut, if ah remember rightly.'

'Aye, yer no' wrong there.' We stand in sync. 'Listen, ye got time for a quick drink? At The King's?'

'Ah should really get back,' she says. 'Mam's gettin' too old for any ae Damo's tantrums.'

'Ye sure? He seemed fine when he left.'

'His life runs tae a schedule, Danny. If he doesn't get his dinner at five, that'll unsettle him.'

'How about ye look in then, on the way past? If he's aw'right, come for one, if no', well maybe another time.'

She nods. I can tell it's reluctant, but it doesn't matter.

'Woah ... all hail the conquerin' fucken hero!' A round of applause follows this as I walk into The King's. Most of the team are still there, and several others who I spotted at the game.

'Aw'right, boss?' says Paddy Gilhooly, warmly.

'Aye, Panda, cheers. Well played th'day,' I respond.

'An' who's this?' asks Davie Russell. 'Introduce us, well!'

'Ah, this is, em … ma broth—…' I stumble.

'Ah'm Nancy. Pleased tae me ye,' says Nancy. Saving me like McIntosh blocking an unexpected toe poke.

'Whit can ah get ye'se?' asks Alf, his joviality prompted, no doubt, by the unexpected work his till is having to put in.

'A Coke for me, please … an' a…?'

'…Gin an' lemonade, please,' says Nancy.

Higgy wanders over from the pool table, where he's playing Harry Doyle.

'Whatta fucken game, son, eh? Telt ye, ye were doin' the right thing comin' back here, din't ah?' He's a bit pissed. 'Aw'right, hen. Sorry about yer maw, earlier an' that. The wee fella played a blinder, a fucken blinder. Oops, sorry. Mind ma language, love.'

'It's fine, Higgy. Ah'm used tae worse.'

'Here ye'se go,' says Alf. 'Aw the best for the season ahead, son.' His previous recalcitrance transformed in the way that only a football win can prompt. Everyone loves everyone else in the aftermath of a successful ninety minutes.

Even Nancy can see the triumphal effect that it has. It's too soon to say if Damo has been calmed by it, and I'm certainly not going to advance my amateur theory. But it seems obvious that the boy is pacified by the game. Even when chaos is breaking out around him, there's something about the pitch, the players, the bloody statistics of this daft wee village team that magnetises and placates him. I reach into my wallet.

Alf puts up a hand. It briefly resembles a Nazi salute. 'On the house, son,' he says, before adding, 'Unless ye'se lose on Wednesday night … then it's a fiver owed!'

We sit in the only quiet corner left in the lounge. There's widespread chatter and it's all good-natured. Billy Gilmour is slumped over a table with several empty glasses on it. He too won't have to put his hand in a pocket all night. Sean O'Halloran sits next to him, yawning. Denny Peters emerges from the toilets. He glances over, catching sight of me. Like a child caught doing something he shouldn't have been. I nod my approval.

'Kinda music do ye like?' I ask Nancy.

'The Pogues,' she says, taking me completely by surprise.

'Aye?'

'How, what did ye think ah was goin' tae say? The Spice Girls?'

'Well...'

'Ah saw The Pogues when they played at the Grand Hall in Kilmarnock. Raymond got us the tickets. Ah wis five months pregnant at the time,' she says. 'The calm before the storm.'

I put the money in. Punch the numbers. An accordion, and then Shane: *'One summer evening drunk to hell, I stood there nearly lifeless.'*

'I bloody love this,' she says. 'The line about Ray an' Philomena singing of my elusive dream. Jeez, is that no' just the saddest thing you've ever heard?' She stares at my face. I too have brown eyes, and it's like she's trying to see right through them. To what lies behind.

'Haw, it's Danny fucken Garvey!' A shout from the front door. Familiar. Unwelcome. 'Budge up, son.' It's Dennis Deans, half-cut and louder than he has any need to be. 'Ye've mind ae Charlie here, eh?' C90-head nods. Eyes almost closed. Too drunk to speak. A mere sixty minutes from renal failure, by the look of him. As he attempts to sit, Charlie's arse misses the chair and he collapses in slow motion onto the floor.

'S'aw'right, Alfie boy,' reassures Dennis. 'Nae hassle, like. We're aw pals here, big man, ken what ah mean? Charlie! *Charlie* boy ... wake up, man!' Charlie gets propped up in a corner, out of the way of the paying punters. A jacket thrown over him.

'Make sure ye take the cunt wi' ye, when yer goin',' says Alf, as if he was an unwanted umbrella.

'Aye, aye, aye,' says Dennis, waving him down.

'Happened tae yer haun?' He's looking at the bandages that

Harry Doyle put on my hand after the match. 'Thought it was yer brother that wis the boxer.'

'Ach, grazed it against a...' He's not listening.

'So, who's yer lassie, then?' he asks. 'Sure ah've seen ye afore though. Mibbe dancin' up the Bobby Jones?'

'Ah work in the baker's,' says Nancy politely.

'Servin'?' asks Dennis, with a confused look on his face. 'Ah'm in there aw the time tae. Ne'er seen ye.'

'Ah'm through the back, mostly. The preparation,' she confirms.

'Wear a hairnet?' asks Dennis, as if it's the only thing he can think of to say. Before Nancy can respond, he's off on a different route. 'So, when ye'se comin' round then?'

'Eh?'

'A bit ae grub, an' that. 'Member? Ye said so. Ali remembers ye. Says ye were a gardener or somethin'.' The pace of his delivery is rapid.

'Whit?' I ask, unsure where this is all headed.

'Ye had dirty green fingers, she says. Huvnae a fucken clue what she's oan about half the time, ken?' He says this to Nancy. 'Ah'm fucken gaspin'. Spaced-out. Necked an Eccy earlier.' I notice Dennis's foot tapping constantly, like it's waiting impatiently for a dancefloor to arrive. 'Sweatin' like a rapist, so's ah am.'

The pub's door opens. A man sticks his head through it. 'Den? Where the fuck are ye?'

Dennis turns. 'Let's fucken go, son. Rocco's waitin'.' Dennis turns back to me. He picks up my glass and drains the rest of my non-alcoholic drink in one go. 'Wan ah owe ye,' he says. 'An' mind, ah need a date for ye'se comin' round. You an' yer girlfriend here. Bring some strawberry tarts, if ye'se want.' He gets up and leaves, forgetting his unconscious colleague.

'Dennis! *Dennis!*' shouts Alf. 'Fuck sake, that's twice in a fort-night,' he protests. 'This cunt's goin' in the bottle bank out the back.'

'Thanks,'

'What for?'

'Askin' me tae come out. It's been a while.'

'It was just a wee drink,' I say. 'Ah don't have pals here. Don't really want any either, but be good if we were friends, ah think.' It's an unexpected turn, I must admit.

'Good for who?' She's teasing me.

'Ach, me,' I tell her. 'Ah'd really like tae help out wi' the wee man. Let him come tae trainin', as well as the games an' that.'

'Let's take it a step at a time, okay?'

'Aye. Of course,' I say.

Nancy looks up. A curtain twitches behind an upstairs window inside her house. 'She just worries, y'know? It was hard goin' wi' Raymond. He wasn't always a bad guy, yer brother. Just ... unreliable.' Her use of the past tense is telling.

'Aye, he's certainly that.'

'G'night, then.'

'Aye, ah'll see ye.'

She walks up the path, unlocks her front door and disappears into the darkness behind it. The upstairs light goes off. I turn and head down the hill. Back to Higgy's. It's been a good day. The reasons for hanging around are multiplying. I'll go and buy some gardening equipment tomorrow morning. I'll go and see Raymond on Wednesday; the afternoon before the season's first cup-tie against the holders, Glenafton Athletic.

⌃

'Strugglin'?'

'Aye, son. Ah'm rough.' Higgy's up, looking like an inflatable Bobby Charlton. He gingerly eases himself into his chair. He winces. As if the sound of the fly buzzing around is like having his head buried in the bass speakers at an AC/DC gig.

'Too auld for it,' I suggest.

'Ye might be right there, Danny Boy.' He coughs phlegm into his hand. 'Still, a win like that has tae be celebrated.' He staggers past me to the sink. He rinses the thick, yellowy shite off his hand. It takes a good few turns of the tap to make it go away.

'Fry-up?' he asks.

'Naw, ah'm good,' I say, watching the same hand reach into his bread bin.

'So, whit you up tae th'day?'

''Member Auld Jock Reid?'

'Christ, how could ah forget? How could *you* forget?'

'Ah didnae forget, ah'm just...' I don't know how to finish this line. For years, I couldn't stop thinking about Jock Reid. About what we'd done to him. 'Ah saw his wife the other day. Bumped intae her. Ah'm goin' round tae help her out.'

'By dain' what?' He seems stunned. It's hard to know why.

'The garden. The gutters tae maybe. Ah don't know. Anythin' that needs done probably. Why?'

'Listen, son, ye need to be careful if yer gettin' back intae aw that.'

'Aw what? What are ye talkin' about?'

Aul' Jock Reid ... he's no' right in the heid. His wife's a hoor, an' his daughter's deid.

I didn't see Jock Reid after the day of the piano. Not for another five years or so. It was like he'd just vanished. The taunting stopped because there was no-one for us to taunt. But I thought about him a lot. Wrote notes about him. Composed a short story about him in English class. And then suddenly, one frosty morning early in 1981, he was out in the village street. I saw him as I was delivering the papers. He was walking awkwardly, and with a cane. He looked as disorientated as he had back then, years earlier, in the makeshift dump.

'Are ye aw'right, mister?' I asked him.

'Fuck off. Wee prick,' he grumbled. He kept muttering something. *Leave me alone! Please leave me alone,* it sounded like.

I should've left him. Libby was in the car waiting. She wound down the window and shouted for me to get a move on.

'Just a minute,' I yelled back. 'Let me help ye, Mr Reid.'

'Get tae buggery,' he replied. And then he turned to me and said, 'What have ye done wi' her? Tell me, ya wee bastard ... Ah cannae fucken stand it,' and there were tears running down his face.

I immediately felt terrible for all the goading and the hateful chanting and for everything he'd been through and I put the 'papers down and I leaned towards him to take his arm. Maybe to help him home. Libby shouted, 'Get away fae him.' And I'm not sure if she meant me or the old man, but I turned to her with arms outstretched, and as I did, Auld Jock Reid brought the cane down forcefully on the back of my head. My hand went up. My blood was running through my fingers. Thick, and matting my hair. He swung it again and a loud crack suggested a broken middle finger. And I was on my knees, howling. And Libby was running towards us. And she launched into both of us, but it was the old man who was downed.

I remember that awful moaning. I couldn't see him, just one shoeless leg dangling from the small hedge Libby had pushed him over. A door opened. It was six in the morning and the noise was waking people.

The initial charges were dropped, although it took a lot to persuade Libby. Raymond wouldn't let it go. He wanted money for the inconvenience. He hadn't been involved at all. For months after it, though, Raymond just wouldn't let it go.

⌒

'Mrs Reid?' I'm speaking through the letterbox that bears her name.

'Yes?' she replies.

'Hi, it's Danny. Ah wis here before. Ah helped ye in wi' yer milk.'

'Oh. I remember. Is everythin' alright son?'

'Yeah, everythin's fine. Ah just wanted to see if ah could do yer garden.'

A lock turns, and the door slowly opens.

'Oh, hullo son, is everythin' okay?' she says, as if she'd immediately forgotten the previous exchange. 'What've got there?' She doesn't remember me from that night at the police station fourteen years ago. She might, if I told her my surname. But who would that profit?

'Ah brought some gardenin' stuff round. Thought ah could maybe tidy up a bit for ye.'

'Aw, son that's awfy nice but I can't afford tae pay for a gardener.'

'Ah'm no' lookin' for payment. Ah just want tae help.' She looks confused. 'Ah'm the new manager ae the junior team. It's just a part-time thing though. Ah'm lookin' tae fill my time a bit, an' help some folk out.'

'Oh son ... that's awfy kind ae ye. Are ye sure now?'

She leaves me to it, and I get going. The grass reaches my waist at the side of the house that faces south. Shears and a sickle are deployed early on. Three hours pass. The surface starts to resemble a hippy being forcibly shorn with bacon scissors. I'm staring at the rough terrain and images resurface. Wee Louise-Anne, playing in her garden. This garden. The gate's open and the wee dog runs out. And she runs out after it in her bare feet and away to the left and into the woods. The woman across the street was the last person to see her alive. I gaze over at the house. It's identical to this one. I wonder if the woman still lives there. If she still looks out and wonders if she could have been just a bit quicker to raise the alarm.

'Oh, that's lovely,' says Mrs Reid, when she sees the results of my effort. 'Yer doin' a grand job there, son,' she adds, dragging me back to the present. She's either going completely blind or just being overly grateful. 'Here's a wee drink for ye.'

She hands me a glass of lemonade. It's flat. Probably bought months ago. But I thank her, drink it and hand her back the glass.

'Have ye got any bin bags?' I ask. I've already filled the six I brought with me. Garden refuse mainly, but a shoe, four syringes, a dead rat and numerous used condoms were also in there, hidden in the undergrowth.

'Oh, aye ... I think so. In ye come,' she says, and I follow her. Through the dark, cold hall. Past the framed photographs of family, presumably; what must be a gallery of painful memories for her. We pass through a sitting room and I notice it, the piano. My heart almost stops. She sees me staring at it. I hear music, *his* music, coming from it.

Aul' Jock Reid ... he's no' right in the heid. His wife's a hoor, an' his daughter's deid.

'Do ye play, son?' She speaks and breaks the spell.

'Em ... eh, no. Sorry, no, ah don't.'

'I can't either,' she says. 'My late husband did. We got rid of it once, but he'd go searchin' for it when he wis in a bad way. They were difficult times back then. So we got it back here an' it seemed tae calm him down. I can't bear tae throw the auld thing out again. Jock loved it that much, ye see.'

I swallow hard. Despite myself, I'm edging closer to the wooden box. The same one I heard him play twenty years previously. I spot a small photograph that's partially concealed behind a vase.

She sees me looking closely at it. 'That's my Jock. Taken when he played for the local team.'

It's a picture in black and white, of a young man in a football strip. His hair is short, flat and he is smiling. His arms are folded, and his left leg is raised. There's a dark leather football under his boot.

'Ah remember the day that was taken ... just up the road there. Jock had won player ae the year. Ah didn't care much for the football,' she laughs. I turn to leave. 'An this is Jock wi' wee Lou, his granddaughter.' She shows the photograph. There's no hint of the tragedy behind it. A proud granda, balancing a dark-haired, laughing toddler on his knee. 'Her an' that wee Chatty Cathy doll. She went everywhere wi' it. Pullin' its cord constantly to make it talk. Drove us mad so it did.' She purses her lips.

When the little girl went missing, reporters and television crews descended on the village. I was too young to know why, but it was exciting. Libby shouted at me: 'That could've been you!' Her anger making it seem like it was somehow my fault. As years passed, I convinced myself that she'd said 'should've'.

And then sometimes, as a teenager, I wished it had been. I contemplated the odds of Louise-Anne having been lifted out of the existence she had, into one that was better, happier. And I envied her for the life I imagined she now had.

🔈

I just wanted to see her. I can't explain why.

'Is Nancy in?'

Her disappointed mother looks me up and down. Still evaluating me, perhaps. She turns, saying nothing. But pulling the front door closed. Through an inch-wide gap, I hear her shout from deep within the house. 'Somebody at the door,' she confirms. She knows my name, but presumably won't use it.

'Danny?' Nancy acknowledges, but with upward emphasis on the surprise at me being there. No clue given to whether it's a pleasant one or not.

'How are ye?' I ask. We're at eye level although I'm a step down.

'Fine. You?'

'Aye. Good.' I struggle with opening lines.

After an awkward silence, she says, 'Look, Danny, it's no' the best time just now, y'know?' I nod robotically, although I don't know. 'Mam's actin' up a bit.'

'Send her tae her room, then,' I suggest. Nancy looks at me strangely. 'Ah wis jokin',' I feel the need to add.

'Nancy!' The shout from the rear of the terraced house reverberates.

'Right!' Nancy replies. 'Ah'm comin'! Jesus Christ!' Nancy turns to me. 'Had a bit ae a barney, me an' her. Things are on edge.'

'Listen, ye fancy goin' for a walk, or somethin'?' I ask. 'Sure she'll let ye out for a wee while.'

'Depends what the somethin' is,' she replies. There's the faintest hint of a smile.

'Em ... ah dunno. A coffee, maybe?'

'Jesus ... on a Sunday, round here? You'll be lucky.'

'Aye. S'pose. Sorry.' *I just wanted to see her.*

She hesitates, unsure of what to say next.

'Look, ah'm out the back. Damo's puttin' up a tent,' she says. 'Ye could help him, if ye like?'

I sigh, and fear that she heard me, but it was from relief. Nothing negative.

'That'd be good. Aye.'

Nancy leads me through from front to back. Her mother glares at me. The feeling that their argument was about me is hard to dispel.

'Ignore the mess,' Nancy says, although I spot none; certainly not in comparison to the Steptoe's Yard of Higgy's accommodation.

'Hi Damo,' I say, waving through the back door.

The boy looks up. It's the first time I've seen him without the helmet on. Here, at home, where he feels safe. Where he needs no protective armour.

'He talked about ye last night,' Nancy says.

'That right?' I reply.

'No' he didnae,' says Doreen, dismissing her daughter.

'Let it go, Mam!'

'Couldnae get him tae sleep. Right out his routine, he was.'

'Okay, Mam,' says Nancy.

'Boy needs his routine, that's aw ah'm sayin'.'

'Mam!'

I go outside, to their back garden. Leaving them to their disagreement.

'It was a great game, eh, Damo?' I say.

The boy nods. He doesn't look up. 'A wee statto,' he says.

I laugh at this and then watch him, fascinated as he lays out the metal tent poles in exact order; the hooks all facing the same direction, like twenty glinting question marks lying in the grass.

'Want a cuppa?' asks Nancy from the kitchen.

'Eh, aye. Go on then.'

'What dae ye take?'

'Milk. Two sugars.'

'Strong colour?'

'Aye,' I reply, 'like American-tan tights,' and she laughs at the thought.

—*Schmeichel, Laudrup, Ravanelli, Shearer, Juninho, McManaman, Redknapp, Beckham, Gascoigne, Gullit, Zola, Vialli. My new uncle. He says bad words.*

Damo puts the canvas down and strolls over. He points at something to the left of me. We've been joined in the garden by his mum, with the teas. And by our suspicious chaperone.

'Schmeichel, Laudrup, Ravanelli, Shearer, Juninho, McManaman, Redknapp, Beckham, Gascoigne, Gullit, Zola, Vialli,' he says. I look left and he has them lined up along the windowsill. Left to right, blond goalie to Chelsea's bald Italian striker.

'What a team, eh?' I say.

'Need a defender,' Damo says, quiet and as monosyllabic as John Motson. I smile at him, but his expression never changes.

'Aye,' reaching into my pocket. 'Maybe this yin'll help out, then.' I hand him another figure; Rangers captain, Richard Gough. 'It's Richard Gough. He's a great defender, eh?'

'Christ ... what did ah tell ye?' says Doreen. She tuts. I'm puzzled. Nancy sighs.

Damo's hand reaches out, but Nancy's intercepts. 'Danny, stop buyin' him these things.' Nancy takes the figure before Damo can.

'Ah ... sorry, it's just a wee ...'

—*Need a defender.*

'Richard Gough,' says Damo.
   'Sendin' him signals. Confusin' the wean,' says Doreen loudly.
   'Look, ah appreciate ye takin' him yesterday, ah really do...' It's an officious tone. Coming from a different person than the one I was with last night.
   'Richard Gough!' Damo repeats, a little louder this time.
   'Look what ye've done now,' says Doreen. 'Ye've upset him. Just like yer brother ... bloody swannin' in...'

—*Need a defender!*

'Mum! Gie it a bloody rest, will ye? Christ's sake!'
   'Nancy...'
   'Richard Gough, Richard Gough, Richard Gough...' Damo is now shouting. Anger in his eyes. 'Richard Gough, Richard Gough, Richard Gough, Richard Gough!' Screaming it now.

—*I need a Richard Gough fuck defender! Gough. Defender. Fuck, fuck, fuck! Cunt! Cunt! Yer a fat cunt, McIntosh!*

'You need tae go,' insists Doreen. She's angry. With me for being there. With Nancy for letting me into their world.
   'Richard Gough, Richard Gough...' Damo picks up a tent pole and hits his mum with it.
   'Hey!' I shout at him.

—*Fuck. Fuck. Fuck. Cunt!*

'Don't shout at him,' screams Nancy.
   I take the pole away from the boy. Nancy wraps her arms tightly

around her son, who is now writing and yelling like he is possessed.

'Thanks for that!' says Doreen as I pass her. 'Thanks for nothing!'

I'm walking through their house towards the front door. Away from a commotion that I had unwittingly created.

I just wanted to see her. I can't explain why.

I am shaking. Angry, or ashamed? Hard to tell. I stumble over a fence. Tear my shirt on it. Cursing this village and the neurosis it represents. Down a back street and through a long, narrow unlit close. A short-cut away from where other people might be.

'You're Danny Garvey, int' ye?' A drunken, slurred voice from the other end of the darkness. I hesitate and begin to move back in the other direction. 'S'awright. Ah'll no' bite ye, son.' The man follows me; his voice quiet and pitiful. The face advances far enough into the light for me to see it. The ravaged, pock-marked surface a vague resemblance to someone I once knew. 'Ye don't know me, dae ye?' My head hurts. A battering might be a release.

'Ah … sorry. Naw. Ah don't.'

'Ah'm Scud. Scud Meikle,' he croaks. 'Ye dinnae have a coupla quid ye could spare?'

∩

The door opens. It shakes me out of my torpor. I've been sitting in the darkness in silence for over two hours. Nick Cave's *The Boatman's Call* is still turning, the aggravated needle grunting over the run-off grooves. I stopped crying an hour ago.

'Jesus Christ, Danny,' says Higgy. I've apparently given him a fright. 'Whit ye doin' here, yersel', in the darkness?' He'll see the scattered, crumpled tissues and think I've been wanking.

'Nothin',' I reply.

He sighs. 'Yer mam wis askin' for ye. Hopin' ye'd go up later this week,' he says.

I don't reply. He'll know something's wrong.

'Danny? What is it? Whit's up wi' ye, son? Is it Raymond?'

'Why did ye no' tell me aul' Jock Reid played for the Bridge?'

I had no close friends at primary school. No circle of shared acquaintances. And no-one I'd have brought back to Libby's house under any circumstances. Even my football team-mates were merely a supporting cast for a ninety-minute performance. And in the small village context, I was content with that. And when I left to go to a secondary in a much bigger catchment area, my confidence off the pitch couldn't match up to the level I could reach on it.

Perhaps it was inevitable I'd find someone like Scud Meikle to fill the gaps. I met Scud in 1979. I was twelve. He was a couple of years older. The shift in my relationship with Raymond began around that time.

That first conversation with Scud had gone somethin' like this:

'Fuck ae you lookin' at?'

I wasn't looking at anything, so I said nothing.

'Hey, ah'm fucken talkin' tae you, ya wee prick.'

I stayed silent, so he punched me. A dead leg was the result. I began to cry.

'Ya wee fucken wean,' he said, then leaned back in the seat, his work apparently done. Fifteen minutes passed.

'Ye got any sweets?' My leg wasn't dead anymore, but it still wouldn't be running away from this latest challenge. His tone was different now, less threatening, so I spoke to him.

'Just these Fruit-tellas,' I said.

'Fuck it, they'll dae.' He took the ones that were left in the wrapper.

'Ta.' He leaned in a bit. 'Don't think ah've seen you before. Whit's yer name?'

'Danny. Eh, Danny Garvey.'

'How auld are ye?'

'Twelve an' a half.'

'Are ye a Jungle Jim?' He could see that I had no clue what that meant. 'A Tim. A fucken *Cafflick*. Fuck sake, man.'

'Eh, naw.' I'd never been asked this question before. Never anticipated it being asked in a Protestant school.

A door under a large, ticking clock opened.

'Garvey. Get in here. Now.' Mr McMillan disappeared as quickly as he had appeared. I didn't move.

'Better go in there,' said Meikle. 'You've fucken had it, pal. He's a complete cunt.' He folded his arms and smiled at me. Mocking my fear. 'Meet me at the gates at half three. Ah've got somethin' tae show ye.'

Ah looked back at him and nodded. The door slammed behind me.

He showed me a belt that he had stolen from a teacher's desk. He made me hold out my hands as he used it. He told me to call him 'Scud'. Everybody else did, even his da.

Scud's family were from Cumnock. His house was close enough to walk to, but far enough from Barshaw that Raymond wouldn't easily find out. Scud ruled the little gang I became part of. He invented dares. Daft things like running at full pelt to reach the rope swing to cross the river – that one always saw me waist deep in the water. Springing out from behind the stone walls of the Barshaw Bridge, hoping that no traffic was approaching from the blind side. And repeatedly slinking up to Auld Jock Reid's house with a paper bag filled with Scud's fresh shite, to be set alight and left on the doorstep before chapping the old man's door and bolting out of sight.

Scud Meikle noticed me. He paid me attention.

I had known him less than six months when he attempted to jump over eight of us on his Raleigh Tomahawk. I was positioned at the end of the line. The rear wheel landed on my arm and broke it. I told Libby and Raymond I'd fallen off my own bike, being chased by bigger lads who'd subsequently stolen it. It was partly true. The bike did get stolen. It was just the circumstances surrounding the theft that were made up.

I couldn't play football for six weeks. Raymond suspected something unusual had happened, but I told him nothing. I didn't want him knowing anything about the secret life outside of our village that I now had.

Three weeks later, Scud Meikle tied me to the fencing around the old Barshaw dump. I hadn't sung the 'Aul' Jock Reid' song loudly enough, according to him. A young woman out walking her dog found me. I had my back to the metal. A bike padlock around my neck pinned me to the uprights. The fire brigade was called to cut through the chain. Scud's name was all over my cast – in more ways than one. I had no option but to tell Raymond how it happened. I exaggerated, naturally. I was prone to that back then.

The following day, my brother marched through the Cumnock woods dragging me behind him.

'One ae you fucken clowns called Scud?' he said.

A head appeared out of the den. 'Who wants tae know?'

'This the cunt?'

I nodded my head timidly.

Scud stared at me. 'Who's this fucken dweeb? Yer da?'

As he rose, my brother burst forward and down and stabbed him in the side with a kitchen knife he must've had concealed up his sleeve. It was a deep slash, but it didn't result in as much blood as I thought it would. The colour drained from Scud's face. A deeper shade of colour spread across his white T-shirt. He started making these strange moo-ing noises. Like a distressed cow stunned by the slaughterman's sticking blade. All the while, Raymond stood motionless and expressionless. But I have to admit I was excited by it ... that power, and the impact it could have.

I didn't visit Raymond for the twelve months he was in Polmont Young Offenders Institute. In fact, despite the seven years he has subsequently served, tomorrow will be the first time I've ever see him in detention.

Three

Nancy

The bus from Glasgow's Buchanan Street Station empties three-quarters of its passengers onto the pavement of a normal residential street in Riddrie. It has taken a journey travelling on three of them to get here. I understand why Nancy doesn't bring Damo. The building sense of dread is bad enough for me, although that may be more to do with seeing my brother for the first time in over a decade.

The determined band of prison visitors wait. We get our names approved and ticked. We wait some more. Gradually, the group thins out as the more experienced deal with the searches and questions with calm efficiency. It's a foreboding place, obviously, and its atmosphere makes me want to confess.

I'm the last to go through. I spend the final seconds wondering if I could just leave. Just disappear back through the public entrance. Would that attract more suspicion? Would they drag me back in and subject me to a more intimate examination? I have nothing to hide ... well, nothing physical. But I don't want to be here. I feel sick with anxiety.

I've no doubt Raymond doesn't want to be here either. He is serving nine years for grievous bodily harm. Almost four years ago, he waited in the dark shadows outside a Galston pub, followed an intoxicated man home, and as he staggered into the shadows, around the side of a windowless gable, attacked him. He battered his victim so badly that he was in an induced coma for six weeks.

A case of mistaken identity. The man wasn't the one who had

terrorised Libby, assaulting her in her own home. Raymond had reached out in desperation. Rocco Quinn agreed to testify that my brother hadn't been the initial aggressor. The lack of counter-argument meant Raymond's sentence was reduced from fourteen years. He remains in Quinn's debt.

I walk timorously through three guarded doorways, CCTV recording every move. And there he is. In a hall of regimented desks, looking like they've been set out for a school exam. He's sitting in the centre of the smoke-filled room. The centre of attention. Just as he always was. The nut around which every lever pivots. The key square in an expanded game of noughts and crosses.

'Well, here he is, boys ... the junior league Walter Smith!' Everyone has turned around. Looking at us. Studying my awkward reticence. 'Took ye? Fuck sake!' he shouts.

'Ah've been busy,' I say, quietly. Hoping the looks have stopped. That everyone has focused back on their own business.

'Yer late, tae,' he adds. 'Ye never used tae be late. Remember aw they times ye hassled everybody, shoutin' that ye couldnae be late ... or ye'd get dropped for the next game?' I look around. Some still stare. ''Member?'

'Aye. Ah remember.'

'So, what happened last month then?'

'Jesus, Raymond ... ah missed the bus, aw'right? Gonnae drop it, eh?'

'Fuck sake, Danny boy. I'm just rowin' yer tail, son,' Raymond says.

'How's things, then?' I ask.

'Fine. Same aul', same auld.'

'Can imagine.'

'Can ye? Can ye really?'

'Ah didnae mean it like that.'

'Ye seein' Mam regularly,' he asks, changing the direction, but not the attack.

'Aye,' I lie.

'Are ye fuck!' he replies. 'Higgy says ye've been twice.'

'Aye, well.'

'She's fucken dyin', ye know that, don't ye?'

'Well, obviously,' I spit back. 'But ah cannae fucken dae anythin' about that, can ah? Ah don't have a miracle cure.' These words, I regret them immediately. Thoughtless.

'Ye can gie her a bit ae comfort, though, in her last few weeks, ya selfish wee bastard!'

I look at my shoes. Shuffle uncomfortably in the plastic bucket seat I'm sat in. 'Look, maybe ah should come back another ti—'

'Fucken sit there,' Raymond instructs me. He rolls and then lights a fag. Hands me it, but I hold my hands up in protest. 'Chucked them?'

'Aye,' I say. 'Had tae make myself available tae play, just in case. So, ah gave them up.'

'When?'

'Two weeks ago.'

'Bloody hell ... better self-discipline than me. Hats off tae ye,' he says. He looks lean, likes he's been training hard for a bout. Or making sure he's ready for any spontaneous ones. His hair is shoulder length, greasy and lank. The beard is gone, a moustache remains. Eyes that are constantly planning an escape route. Robert Carlyle, as Francis Begbie, with Lennon-style specs, which he didn't need the last time I saw him.

'Heard the Lugar game wis a bit radio rental,' he says.

'Aye,' I say. 'A bit ae a baptism ae fire.'

'Lost yer temper, ah hear. Just like the auld days.'

'Eh ... naw, ah didnae,' I protest, as if we're back in our teenage years and I'm denying his accusations again.

He narrows his eyes and turns his head, like he's studying the results of a polygraph test.

He's the fucking liar, not me.

'Young kids bailed ye out though?'

'Aye.' Somehow, Higgy has managed to transmit this information to inside the prison walls despite the game only being played four days ago.

'Sound like ye were there,' I say.

'Still got ma sources.' He draws deeply and the roll-up almost disappears. After more awkward shuffling...

'Ye needin' anythin'?' I ask.

'Get us a few copies ae the *Loaded* magazines, eh? *Good work, fella!*' He cackles at this.

'Anythin' else?'

'Aye. As a matter ae fact...' He tails off, and then turns and snaps his fingers. A guard strolls over. 'Johnny Boy, any chance ae a loan ae a wee pencil an' a sheet ae yer pad?'

'Loan, Ray? That mean ah'll get them back?'

'Course ye will, son. Ah'm good for it.'

Both laugh and I recognise the charm offensive at work here. Raymond takes the paper and writes a date on it. As he does so, I decide to ask about the *Standard* journalist.

'You know anythin' about a guy called Sandy Buchanan?'

'Naw. How, who is he?'

'He covers the fitba for the *Standard*.'

'Never heard ae the cunt. How?'

'He's been fucken destroyin' us in the paper this last fortnight. Seems tae have a right grudge. First time ah met him, he mentioned you.'

His eyebrows raise. 'Sayin' whit, like?'

'Nothin' much. Just that ye'd put a guy in the hospital.'

'We'll that no' exactly news, is it? Whit's that got tae dae wi' junior fitba matches?'

'Dunno,' I say. I suspect he knows more than he is letting on. But then Raymond Garvey has lived his life by that code.

'Ah'd forget about the prick, if ah wis you. It's no' like you're Souness signin' Mo Johnston out fae under Celtic's nose. Yer the manager ae a dumplin' second division junior team fae the arse end ae naewhere.' If he means this as a comfort, it – like many of his attempts at positivity – misses the mark.

'It's the wean's birthday in a few weeks.' He hands me the paper, presumably to ensure I don't forget. 'Can ye get him somethin'? Fae me, like. Use yer imagination.'

'Aye. Sure,' I say. Half-hearted. 'Whit's yer budget?'

'Up tae you,' he says; code for *use your own money*. 'Ah'll square ye up when ah get out.'

'Aye. Right.'

'Ah will. When have ah ever let ye down before?' he challenges.

'How long've ye got?' I say.

'Hey, ya cheeky wee cunt!' he replies. Smiling, though. That cut-glass smile that reels you in before the teeth devour you.

'Naw, how long ye got left in here?' I ask. Fighting back. Wriggling free.

'No' too long,' he replies. 'Be out soon, accordin' tae the brief. Early release on compassionate grounds.' He laughs. 'Ah'll be able tae help ye at the Bridge.' Counterpunches.

'Ah think we're fine.'

'Dinnae look a gift horse, son.'

'Yer boy's growin' up fast,' I say. Shifting him onto different ground. Not safer, just different.

'Aye? Damo?'

'How many more weans have ye got?'

'None ... that ah'm payin' for, at any rate,' he says, laughing at a joke that just isn't funny anymore. 'Tough kid, that yin. Last time ah saw him on the outside, he tipped a can ae fucken beer ower my head. Nae warnin', or nothin'.'

'Seriously?'

'Aye. Mindin' ma own business. Up he comes. Starts screamin' at me. Before ah can get up tae him, ah'm wearin' a fucken lager shampoo.' He smirks. 'Damo ... he's no' normal, like.'

'Normal?' I say. 'What's normal? Like *you* "normal", ye mean?' I pose this quietly. He doesn't seem to read the inference.

'Aye. He's fucken mental!' He says this as if it was something to be proud of. Maybe he is.

'Wonder where he gets that fae,' I say, aiming to hurt, but he just deflects it.

A few minutes pass. Nothing is said. My brother passes them nodding and winking to others around him. A few return the signals as if it's a secret gag, known only to the inmates in grey.

'Have ye seen her, then?' he says, without prompt.

'Who?'

'My Nancy?' The "my" is unexpected. No point in lying though. Higgy has already seen to that.

'Aye. Ah took the boy tae the game on Saturday.'

'Aye? Whit d'ye think? Did she mention me?'

'What d'ye mean?'

'Nancy, Danny. Fuck sake, son. Keep up.' He lights another roll-up. Blows the smoke slowly out the side of his mouth. Draws again. Blows again. The prolonged action allows me the space to avoid answering. 'Listen, ah'm dead straight when ah'm outta here. Nae fucken danger. Ah've messed her an' the wee man about somethin' terrible. But that's aw gonnae stop, Danny boy. It's gonnae be a whole new me. Kickin' the fucken Charlie right intae touch this time. Ah mean it, nae temptations.'

He sounds determined but that's probably easier on the eve of a release than on the day of arrival. Raymond's had more new beginnings than Tommy Docherty's had football clubs. They all end the same way: struggling to come to terms with not having paid work, or with the relentless boredom of being in it. Drugs and booze and criminality filling the gap. He'll never be happy, and neither will those forced to be around him.

'Ah fucken love her. And the wean. Doreen though, ye met her?' I nod. 'Ah'd gladly fix that yin a fucken one-way ticket tae Siberia.' He hacks up a mouthful of phlegm and spits it into a paper hankie, which he puts back in his pocket.

The way he speaks about her though. When Nancy is the subject he's a different Raymond from the one I remember. I'm suddenly jealous of him and I can't work out why. It's a strange emotion. I haven't known her long but already it's obvious that the rest of her life will be wasted waiting for Raymond's miraculous conversion from small-time village ned with no prospects to someone with whom a reliable, loving, trusting relationship can be formed. And as for Damo, well Raymond's never been that good at looking after children. He fucking abandoned me after all. Twice.

'Ah'm goin' back tae the full trainin'. The discipline. Maybe get a few bouts sorted.'

'Aye?'

'Aye. Ah need tae settle down, son. This stretch has been fucken murder. Too many youngsters in here now. Aw desperate tae prove a point. Desperate tae take somebody down.'

'Has somethin' happened?' I'm not asking out of concern for him.

'Ach, nothin' ah cannae deal wi'. It's just...' He tails off. With a downward look, he appears immediately older and more vulnerable. His hair is thinning. After emerging from the Polmont year, Raymond was as hard as nails. The institution did that to him. He's talking now about challenges from wired young guys exactly like he was back in 1980.

'She's fucken braw, eh ... Nancy, ah mean?' His eyes light up as he returns to her. His new favourite subject.

'Christ, Raymond. What ah'm ah meant tae say tae that?'

'Whit? We always used tae compare burds!' he says. We didn't.

'You, wi' yon wee Alison Currie. Me wi' her maw!' He laughs at this.

'Fuck off,' I say. I feel my face reddening.

'Dinnae tell me ye've bumped intae her! She's wi' that plank, Denny Deans.'

'Naw. Ah haven't. Fucken hope it stays that way tae.'

'Mind ah paid her a tenner tae let ye fuck her anaw!' He can see the anger rising in me.

Nancy deserves so much better than this absolute waster. Everything's just a game to him. *I just wanted to see her. I can't explain why.*

'Scud Meikle's brother's in the squad,' I tell him. This puts him on his backside, like a fat defender I've just swivelled around.

'That right?' he replies. He takes a long draw of a new roll-up. He sits back in the seat. Legs spread. The body language says *what's that got tae dae wi' me?*

'Spotted Scud hangin' about tae.'

He doesn't immediately respond to this. He pauses. Looks around himself. He's been blindsided, I can tell. He starts a sudden shuffling of his feet and I sense his growing hostility.

I'm shaking inside as I say: 'An' ah went tae see Auld Jock Reid's widow.'

This grabs his attention. And action. The darts hitting the bullseye. The defining actions from our shared youth. The first two times he ended up inside. He grabs my sleeve and pulls me closer. Over Raymond's shoulder, the guard he called Johnny Boy has switched on his surveillance.

'Whit the fuck, Danny?'

I pull back, saying nothing.

He clears his throat. 'Stay fucken clear, right?' Down to a whisper, but the anger and the threat crystal clear.

I still say nothing. His eyes stay on me. Laser beams. Unsure of me, of what I'll do next.

'Everythin' aw'right here, lads?'

'It's fine, Johnny,' says Raymond. 'Just gie'in the boy here a wee Chinese burn. Aul' time's sake, ken?'

The guard looks at me, and nods before strolling on. Raymond has calmed himself.

'Ah'm helpin' her out. Doin' the garden, an' stuff.'

'Fuck sake ... ye've barely been tae visit yer dyin' mam, but ye've got time tae plant flowers an' cut hedges?'

'It's no' like that,' I tell him. 'Ah felt sorry for her. Everythin' she's been through. How could ye cope wi' aw that pain an' sorrow in yer life?'

'Look Danny, dinnae be growin' a conscience. No' after aw this time. Who would that benefit, eh?' he pleads. 'Ah mean, Christ's sake, it wis a fucken lifetime ago. We've aw suffered, specially me. An' it wis a bloody accident, pal. Ye know that?'

I look at my watch. I need to get out of this horrendous place. 'Listen, ah need tae go,' I say.

'Don't you fucken dare fuck up this release!'

'Ah'll see ye next time.'

'Ye've just fucken got here,' he protests.

'We've got the Glens at the Bridge tonight. Ayrshire Cup. Ah need tae get back.'

He sighs. He knows it'll have to wait. No more grabbing my hair and forcing his will anymore. Not while he's still in here. He calms down, at least for appearances sake.

'Right. Fair enough, then. Good tae see ye,' he says, and I don't know whether he means it, or whether there is thick sarcasm dripping from these four words.

'Watch yersel',' he asks. 'An' come back next week?'

'Aye. maybe,' I respond.

'Ah'm tellin' ye,' he whispers. 'Tell Nancy she's due a visit tae. An' mind an' see Mam, right?' he instructs.

'Aye. Right. See ye!' I hear him tap the table loudly as I walk away.

⌢

My head's swimming in a dank, murky swamp. Auld Jock Reid, my brother Raymond the prisoner, Scud Meikle, Libby, Damo, but mostly Nancy. All jostling for prominence in the impenetrable maze. The game passed by in a blur. We had no right to expect a win against the Glens, and we did better than many would've anticipated. A three-nil defeat is no disgrace. We kept our shape well, held it level until the last quarter, and only two brilliantly worked moves by Glenburn's speedy wingers undid us. The third goal trundled in with a minute to go, but by that time McIntosh had been taken off with a suspected broken jaw. He'd gone down at the feet of their striker but lifted his head too sharply. A knee went into the side of his face. Ten minutes of additional time came from us chairing him off the park to a waiting taxi bound for A&E, and then the ref scouring the penalty box for the five teeth he claimed to have lost in the incident.

I'm popping pills and nursing a raging headache. It's quiet and I'd assumed everyone had gone home, but no.

Danny?

I look up, surprised at a young female voice in my office.

Hi. It's Anne Macdonald. *The chairman wants you to accompany me on a PR initiative. Tomorrow morning. I'll pick you up at nine. Okay?*

'Eh … em, are ye sure? Me?'

Yes, Danny. You. And it's important, so dress properly. It's a meeting with a new sponsor. An independent bookmaker from Troon. He's interested in sport. So … best behaviour and bring out the good stories, got it?

I nod through the pain in my head. She leaves abruptly. I stand, intending to follow her, but I'm interrupted by a tapping at the window. I look up and wave at the man, bidding him come round to the entrance.

'Ye aw'right there, youngster?' I lift my fevered head from its position, held heavily by clammy hands. The man standing in my office doorway is Alan Rough, former manager of the Glens, and one of Scotland's greatest goalkeepers. He's wearing a black polo-neck sweater that makes his head resemble a coconut balanced in a fairground shy.

'Eh … aye.' I'm not sure what to say. Or why he's even here.

'Heard ye talkin' tae somebody, didnae want tae interrupt like.'

'Ach. Aye.' There's no-one here.

'Young boys played well. Hung in there an' gave us a good game,' he says.

'You still involved?' I ask.

'Naw,' he says. 'But ah still come an' watch when ah can.'

'Ah, right.' He doesn't seem to be here for anything else. But he isn't leaving. 'Sorry,' I say. 'Should've offered ye a drink, Alan.'

'Nah, yer fine, son. Ah'm drivin',' he says, performing a steering mime. 'Listen, ah'll get tae the point. Ah noticed ye didnae have a back-up keeper after yer number one went off.'

'Aye. Tough yin. Wee Lorimer isnae really a keeper,' I say, excusing my desperate instructions to him in the last ten minutes of the game.

'What'll ye do?' asks the former Scotland keeper.

'No' sure, yet,' I say. He could be asking this question of several aspects of my life. The answer would've been the same for all of them.

'Well, maybe ah could help,' he says.

I look at him. The perm's gone. He's kept himself trim, no doubt. But Alan Rough must be nearly fifty.

'Look, man ... ah really appreciate the offer, but McIntosh is on a tenner a week and travel expenses. Ah couldnae offer ye much more than that.'

'Naw ... no' me, ya daft bastard.' He laughs. I do too to offset my stupidity. 'This guy ... he's a pal. A relation, sort of,' he says. 'Had a tough time ae it. Brilliant keeper, though. Just wants tae get a regular game again.'

'Well...'

'He's an alcoholic,' Alan says. 'Played in the lower leagues about a decade ago. He's late thirties. Still springs like a fucken cat though.'

'Any good wi' crosses?'

'Born-again Christian,' says Roughie, laughing. I hadn't given the new goalkeeping crisis enough thought, but with Minishant away in three days' time, what've I got to lose.

'What's his name?'

'Josey Monsanto,' says Roughie.

'Continental,' I say.

Roughie smiles. 'Naw, he's fae Bargeddie.'

'Bit far tae travel, is it no'?'

'He just wants a game. Prepared tae make the sacrifices needed.'

'Okay, thanks. Can he get tae trainin' tomorrow night?'

'Ah'm sure he will. I'll get him tae phone ye.'

'Cheers Alan. Anythin' else ah should know?'

'He's a deacon in the church,' he says. 'So he might struggle wi' Sundays, but other than that, he's a good lad. Ah can vouch for him.'

We shake on it and vow to stay in touch.

An hour later, I lock up and I walk home slowly. Desperate to go back and talk to Nancy. To explain. But explain what? That I'm becoming more attracted to her? That Raymond still wants her? That he has a vision of them living as a normal family, in a normal house – probably Libby's after she's dead – him and his beautiful wife, and his uniquely gifted kid.

Or is it that I want these things?

How fucking mad would that make me sound to her?

'Want some fish fingers?' asks Higgy. He hasn't even checked that it's me. Then again, who else would it be?

'Naw,' I say, sullen and dismissive.

'Sup wi ye now?' He asks this like a dad growing bored with a truculent teenager.

'Nothin'. Never mind,' I reply.

'Boys did aw'right, ah thought,' he offers.

'Aye.'

'Dinnae be too hard on them, then.'

'Ah'm not bein'', I say. The sense of frustration inside me is growing. 'Look, Higgy, what dae you expect fae me in this job?'

'Ah just want ye tae be content for once in yer life,' he says, as if it's the simplest and most obvious goal there is. He shrugs. I know he means it. 'Go an' see yer mam,' he says. It's becoming a constant refrain. 'She needs ye.'

Anne is waiting for me at the bottom of the road. Her car is as distinctive as her: a sporty, purple, two-door Volkswagen Polo. It's five minutes past nine. I'm slightly late, but only due to the nerves that forced me to vomit twice. I open the door, and loud dance music from the bass-heavy speakers is making the car's interior vibrate.

'Mornin'', I say, with as much breeziness as I can muster. She looks around and nods. 'Sorry ah'm late,' I add. I slump back into a shaped leather seat that seems to reach around and cradle me.

It's fine, she says. *We're not due there until 11.00 am anyway.*

'So why are we leavin' so early?'

I just wanted to get to know you a bit better.

'There's no' that much tae know. A return trip tae The King's Arms would cover it.'

I want to understand how best to use you.

'*Use* me?'

Well, if you're going to be doing promotional duties for Kidd's Carpets, you're going to be doing them my way, understand?

'Em ... yeah. Listen, can ah turn the sound down? My head's hurtin' a bit.' I reach out for the volume fader, but she taps my hand.

My car, my rules. After a few minutes of making her point, she turns it down. The vice gripping my skull stops tightening.

'Who is that, anyway?'

Planet Funk, she replies. *'Chase the Sun'.*

'Ah. Okay,' I reply, none the wiser.

You like it?

'Naw. No' really. Just a bit mundane an' monotonous, y'know?' It's hard to think, never mind talk, with the music at such ear-splitting volume. Not that I've been, but this must be what it's like talking to someone in the Arches or the Sub Club in Glasgow.

You don't like music? she asks.

'Jesus ... without music, life would be a mistake.'

Ooh, very profound. And I feel a bit stupid for saying it. *So, what kind of music do you like?*

'Hmm ... dunno really. Quite eclectic, my tastes,' I say.

For example?

'The Smiths, Joy Division, The Fall...'

Ah, I see. Miserable indie guitar bands. Songs from the dark side? Eclectic. Yes. I get it. She smiles.

'Well, other stuff tae, but ye put me on the spot, that's aw.' The VW almost takes off over another hump. 'Jesus, could ye slow down a wee bit? Please?'

She takes her sun-shaded eyes away from the road to look at me and smirk. We continue at more than eighty in a sixty zone. She drives fast and recklessly, one hand on the wheel, the other resting on the gear stick. We're speeding over narrow country roads with hidden bends, flashing past a lumbering tractor like she's immortal. She's dressed in black, a short dress, tights and high-heeled shoes. Like a character from *L.A. Law,* and it's no surprise when she tells me that's her profession. It's a look as identifiable in its own way as the swaggering Liam Gallagher clones of Manchester.

I'm clutching on to the side of my seat like a child on a roller-coaster that I'm too small for.

You okay there? she enquires. I suspect she's enjoying my discomfort.

'Aye. No worries.' I'm beginning to feel glad I vomited earlier. 'Anne, can ah ask ye a question?'

Is it the one about where babies come from?

'Eh, naw.' I snigger nervously. Her polished assuredness un-nerves me. I've had too little experience of it, particularly with women of my own age. 'Ye seem a bit too ... professional tae be workin' for a wee carpet company.' She smiles. 'Dae ye know what ah mean?'

I suppose so. She finally turns the Ibiza soundtrack's relentless volume down. *I'm Billy Kidd's stepdaughter.*

While it explains a lot, it takes me by surprise.

My mum met Billy when I was off on a gap year, backpacking around Australia and Japan. I came home and they were married. Big surprise, she says. *I graduated from Strathclyde six years ago. Worked around the city, did some modelling ... agency work, and then I came back to join the company as a director two years ago.*

'Dae ye like him', I ask.

Yes. I do. Maybe not so much at first, but he's a kind man. A rough diamond.

'He never mentioned ye,' I say.

Why would he? I wasn't interviewing you. I'm not involved in the football side. I don't even like football. I prefer rugby.

'But ye were there that first night, an' he never even introduced ye.'

The football's his thing ... him and his pals at the club. It's his escape. I don't interfere. I give him advice, but he doesn't like it to be known that we're related. He thinks people will treat me differently if there's any suggestion of nepotism on his part.

'What's your thing?' I ask.

Holidays, work, food ... friends, clubbing, she responds without thinking. *'And you?'*

'Em, fitba an' music. That's about it, really.'

Ah ... Loaded Man, she says, sarcastically. *'Fitball's great ... an' Britpop's great ... an' big tits are great ... an' beer's great!'* A deep voice and a put-on accent, and she's taking the piss. She must have me mixed up with someone else.

'Ah don't drink,' I reply. 'An' ah don't buy magazines either. So, what's yer point, caller?'

She smiles ruefully at this. *Okay, then, are you Team Liam or Team Damon?*

'Em ... ah like both ae them. Does it have tae be a choice ... one or the other?'

She shakes her head.

She takes a corner at a speed that throws me sideways. The taut seat belt, the only thing preventing me from hitting the door. *For fuck's sake!* My shoulder almost pops out of its socket.

Ten minutes of mind-numbing music fills the gap where conversation was.

'So, are you fae Ayrshire too then?'

She adjusts the dial to allow me to hear her answer. *Originally, but we moved away when I was little. Up north. Ullapool,* she says, opening up more now, but still driving at a ridiculous speed. *I was adopted when I was six.*

This also takes me by surprise. There's no reason at all why it should. I just assumed her background would have been more stable, and unremarkable. I don't delve further though, for fear that the reasons for her adoption at that age are mired in some form of trauma or tragedy. I'm not sure I could cope with any more of either.

I have no idea where Ullapool is. 'They were a team on *It's a Knockout* once,' I say. She offers no acknowledgement. 'Dae ye like it ... workin' for yer da, ah mean?'

I don't work for him. I work with him, she says, forcefully. The volume increases. That's my punishment.

We pull up sharply at temporary traffic controls. A triangular sign warned of their location just over the brow of a hill, but Anne didn't slow the car. And she didn't flinch when she had to jam on the brakes either. The operator glares at me through the car's windscreen. With the music on and the windows up, we don't hear him shouting, 'Ya stupid cunt' at me, but it's an easy phrase to lip-read. He doesn't even look at Anne, yet she stares calmly ahead, even though he's almost on the car's bonnet, such is his rage. He brandishes the *Stop* face of his oversized lollipop at me until a car horn in the queue behind indicates its driver's frustration.

I look at Anne. She is totally unruffled. She revs the car. The operator turns the sign slowly. Before *Go* has fully appeared, we're off; redlining the dashboard counter. In the rear-view mirror, I watch the road worker kick out at something.

Anne smiles. *Live fast, die young,* she says, the smile bursting into a giggle.

'An' leave a good-lookin' corpse?' I ask, although slamming into anything at the speed she drives would put that part of the aspiration in jeopardy.

I'm constructing this life of achievement. Drawing it out of her. Piecing it together. Intimidated by her confidence. Digging for her happiness. She works hard, and parties hard. Enjoys her friends and their nights out, the food, their love of the Glasgow clubs: the Sub and the Buff, not the Old Firm, naturally. We're the same age, but opposites of each other.

'Dae ye have a boyfriend?' I ask her, during a mellower track. Her face is a mix of puzzlement at the questioning, and devilment at the boldness of it.

Why? Are you thinking of applying? She laughs when she notices me blushing.

'Thought this trip was for you tae get tae know me better?'

You've already told me everything I need to know, Danny.

⌂

We lose the first league game after the cup tie. It's a dreadful match, on Minishant's rutted piggery of a pitch, enlivened only by a muscular Doberman running onto the park. A full-sized shovel is needed to remove the enormous shites it leaves in three different locations. All attempts to entice it off the field fail. After a break in play of nearly fifteen minutes it drifts over to the touch-line, snarling at a linesman and chewing at the flag he drops in panic. Despite its size and the loudness of its bark, a brave Min-ishant centre half gets close enough to boot it right over a railing, where it subsequently attacks a supporter.

Minishant AFC 2-0 Barshaw Bridge.

Billy Gilmour asks me for an urgent post-match meeting. I panic, thinking he wants to pack it in. But instead, he pleads with me to speak to Damo's mum; to ask if the boy is allowed to come to all of our games, not just the home ones. Young Billy is convinced Damo is a lucky mascot. It's almost as if he can read my mind.

⌂

I'm at the library in Cumnock. Organising a timeline. Writing it all down. Connecting the fragments of Jock Reid's life like I was his biographer on a tight pre-Christmas publication deadline. It's a task I've thrown myself into. Since I found out about our shared past – that we both played for the Bridge; not the less gratifying parts – I feel like I owe him. There's that word again. This weird obligation that so many in Barshaw feel towards others, because of the things they have done to them – whether willingly or un-willingly. Jock Reid's resurrection might even be my salvation. If I can take some responsibility for the things that my brother did, then Nancy might see a better future with me than with Raymond. I've decided that Jock Reid will be the vehicle for my own renaissance.

Over the last month, my two principal sources have each painted part of the picture; his wife during tea breaks from my gardening stints, and Higgy, filling in the darker periods that framed the old man's suffering. Both responding politely to my inquisitiveness.

'Ah don't really know where he learned tae play piano,' Mrs
Reid tells me. 'He just always could, as far as ah can recall.'

'He wis a journalist. A good yin, tae. No' like these clowns now-
adays,' says Higgy. 'Ah've mind he even covered the Peter Manual
story. Won a few awards tae, if memory serves. Didnae help him
much when the tabloids came crawlin' all ower *him* though.'

'He was a right home bird, ye know. He was born in this house.
That's why it's always been so hard for me tae leave it, son.' She
tells me this as I flick through a box of old, torn sepia-tinted photographs that illustrate the moments of happiness and joy in their
young lives.

'He had this aul' motor. A vintage Rolls-Royce like somethin'
ye'd imagine Al Capone drivin'. Big wheels an' big sweepin' fenders
an' enormous headlamps. It wis an auld rustin' broken-down relic,
though,' says Higgy.

'He loved that car,' she says. 'That was his retirement dream ...
tae restore it an' go drivin' round the Highlands.' She laughs at the
thought. *There's more chance ae yer local team winnin' the Scottish
Cup,* she'd tell him.

'The motor never moved. An' he'd covered it in tarpaulin, tae.
When the wee yin went missin', the polis moved it an' dug up the
driveway an' the garden. Nosey bastards round here assumed it
wis because he'd done away wi' her.'

'We got rid of the car,' she says. 'After ... well, y'know...' I do,
because she told me. 'It was just too painful to look at.'

She must find it difficult, this revisiting of the past. Not, I
think, because she can't remember, but because she remembers
only too clearly. But she trusts me now. I'm a good listener. A con-
fidant. I sense that she likes talking about her husband and their
life together. Even the painful bits.

'We went fae sympathy tae suspicion tae accusation in less than
a fortnight. It wis absolutely horrible. Beth was our only child. She
wis Jock's pride an' joy. She wis a difficult birth. The cord got tied
around her neck an' her face wis blue when she came out of me,'

she says. 'Jock wis always ower-protective, right through her school days.' She glances up at me and an unusual look comes across her face. Like she's lost herself in the telling and only just realised that she should stop. 'I'm sorry,' she says. She looks away from me.

'Don't be,' I say. I'd make a good therapist. 'He's clearly a wonderful man,' I add, and she smiles, responding positively to me using the present tense. As if he's outside, pottering around in a greenhouse tending to his tomatoes.

Her head lifts again and she continues. 'Beth couldn't cope in the beginnin', after the wee yin disappeared. She wis a danger tae herself, an' Jock went tae pieces. The police were outside there for two months.' She has a photograph of little Louise-Anne with a small dog and it makes me shudder. She was in my primary-school class. She sat in the desk in front of me. I pulled her curly hair a few times. The names. *Our* names. That daily teacher song: *Abbott, Ainsley, Baird, Bruce, Davidson, Demarco, Forrest, Garvey ... Macdonald*. Macdonald. It makes me shudder. *Melville, Ross, Sinclair, Walkinshaw*. Our little band of thirteen. No-one sat in her seat ever again. Our teacher left it for her; waiting for her to come back. And there was always a pause in the song from the time when we returned to the class. A gap. A void. A silence. Missing.

She keeps speaking. It's like I've just surfaced from the depths of a deep pool and I can see her lips moving and I know she's talking to me but I can't hear properly, and it takes minutes for my muffled ears to clear to hear her say:

'He just lost his mind,' she says. 'He'd forget things, an' then he'd be wanderin' about the village at aw hours. Sometimes he'd get a bit ... aggressive, but it was just the frustration. The not knowin'.'

I don't remember leaving Mrs Reid's house. Don't recall how her painful monologue ended. Can't recollect if she asked me to leave or wanted me to stay. But I'm sitting at Higgy's table and he's filling in blanks, and memories that hid in the shadows are rushing out from the recesses and screaming at me.

'Ach, it was brutal … folk swarmin' about. Fae the papers. The telly. Vans an' dugs an' polis in white suits, diggin' up the Reids' garden. A woman across the road had mind ae seein' the wee yin gettin' skelped fae her granda that mornin'. She eventually telt the CID. Everybody fae the village had gie'd up searchin' an' the rumours started that she wis buried under that aul' bloody motor.' He pours himself a whisky and sits at my side. 'Ashamed tae say me an' Deek were up at the top ae the road, stood behind the tape. Watchin'. Waitin' for them tae bring her out.' He shakes his head. He picks up a photo from my file. The one showing Jock Reid in the Barshaw Bridge strip. 'Great player, by aw accounts.' He shakes his head. 'Poor aul' bastard.'

I swallow. It feels like I'm choking.

'Are ye aw'right, son?'

'What? Em … aye,' I reply.

'They never found her, wee Louise-Anne,' says Higgy.

I know this already, but he seems to think I don't. Either that or he's constructing an alternative version in which he omits that he and Deek Henderson were amongst Jock Reid's accusers. The voices in my head every night when I was trying to comprehend what had happened to my classmate belonged to them. They gave me someone to blame.

'An' then a year later … tae the day she went missin', Jock Reid's daughter gets found in the woods, hanging fae a low branch. Ah mean, how much bloody heartache can one man take, eh?'

Louise-Anne. *Louise-Anne Macdonald. A shoeless child on a swing*. Missing. Never found. I used to talk to her. While I hid under the Barshaw Bridge, waiting for them to find me. I spoke to her. She told me to go home.

'When aul' Jock hit ye wi' his cane, yon time, ah had to remind yer ma an' Raymond what he must've went through aw they years. The thought that she'd ran away because he'd leathered her for somethin' daft. An' that wis the last time he'd seen her. Ye ken whit weans can be like, Jesus. Drive ye tae distraction, so they can.'

I'm unable to speak. He's dredging up images that have lain submerged for years. I'm struggling to absorb the depths of this tragedy. Weighing up how I contributed to it years later.

'Raymond was for suin',' Higgy continues, referring to the aftermath of my beating with the cane. 'Even though it'd nothin' tae dae wi' him. Sometimes, ye've just got tae have a wee bit ae sympathy an' understandin', y'know?' He looks at me. Straight at me. It's a concerned look. His head tilted slightly, like a dog trying to work out the meaning of a command.

'Danny, son, ye maybe shouldnae delve too deep intae this again.' The *again* is confusing me.

And this may seem hard to believe. Unprompted, both Higgy and old Mrs Reid have spoken about the difference between loneliness and being alone. Higgy has spent much of his life alone. His choice, in the main. Mrs Reid – for other reasons – has been alone for decades, even when her husband was with her. Jock Reid, both maintain, had aloneness forced on him. Latterly, he seemed to find a certain insulated respite in that, according to his wife. Just before he died, the old man had found a way of coping, she told me. It couldn't be described as contentment, but it was a more meaningful existence. Unlike the days when we tormented him; when he wandered in a fog of pain and confusion, he went out walking early every morning. To be alone.

None of them were necessarily lonely though. Not in the sense that I have been since I left the village to go to the north-east. Or even before that, when my fragmented, complicated relationships in Barshaw left me isolated. Football has always been the only thing that's given me a sense of purpose. That's offered some degree of safety or security. On the pitch, as part of a collective. On the side-lines, as the orchestrator of that collective. But when the final whistle blew, there has only ever been me. Danny Garvey. *There's only one Danny fucking Garvey*. Belonging to no-one. Alone. And that's always been the root of the problem.

Loneliness is aloneness without choice. And it suddenly strikes me that I came back because I needed that solitude to be recognised. To choose not to be alone. To feel connected to something – someone – vital to my existence.

Barshaw Bridge 3-3 Largs Thistle
(Finnegan, O'Halloran 2)

Drongan 4-1 Barshaw Bridge
(Smith)

Cumnock Juniors 7-0 Barshaw Bridge

Barshaw Bridge 2-2 Ardeer Thistle
(Gilhooly, Bruce)

Three sombre weeks. Two home draws and an away defeat in the league. A miserable midweek hammering away at Cumnock in the cup. Josey Monsanto is proving to be more Andy Pandy than Andy Goram. He must have compromising photographs of Alan Rough, mid-perm. McIntosh's return can't come quickly enough.

Our play has been disjointed and desperate. Training is half-arsed. Apathy reigns. Harry Doyle can only do so much. The whole squad is looking to me for direction. Higgy tips me off that Billy the Kidd wants a quiet word. He feels my mind hasn't been on the job lately. He's pin-point accurate in his assessment.

I approach the next game with complete indifference. I tell Higgy about the Sunday at Nancy's house. And about Damo. It's a cover for the truth; that Jock Reid and his missing grand-daughter are occupying every waking thought. He warns me to get my head out of my arse. He tells me that too many people are depending on me.

Torrential driving rain reflects the mood. A Saturday afternoon home game. Touch and go if it'll be on at all. Winton Rovers are the visitors. They've made a reasonable start to the season. We don't even have a match-day programme today, because I haven't created one. I expect us to lose. I should be motivating my players. Analysing weaknesses that we can exploit. But I can't get them out of my head, these ghosts that haunt me.

'Look, son,' says Billy the Kidd, 'we never had any big expectations about this season, ye know that. But after the pre-season games, an' the Lugar win, ah thought we might be buildin' on that. Whit's goin' wrong, Danny?'

He won't sack me. We don't have any paying supporters calling for my head. The Troon bookie hasn't committed yet, so there's no sponsors making things so awkward for him that he must act. It's worse than that. Nobody gives a fuck. And he thinks that includes me. I ponder whether Anne Macdonald will be the one despatched to fire me, come the day.

'Had a bad run, Mr Kidd,' I tell him. 'Keeper gettin' injured affected the back line. We huvnae recovered fae that really.' He knows there's more to it than this. I consider adding nothing else. But the chairman is blocking the door to his office. Not aggressively so, just looking for some comfort. Something to cling to. Hope for the ninety minutes to come. *My* hope is for a waterlogged pitch and a ref with somewhere better to be.

'We're tryin' somethin' a wee bit different today,' I lie. It seems to calm him. 'A few things we worked at in trainin'.'

He smiles. 'Good stuff.' He edges away from the door. My appraisal is coming to an end. 'We're aw pullin' for ye, son. We know ye'll get it right.' The dreaded vote of confidence. When playing for greater stakes than this, a sacking invariably follows one. Billy the Kidd will be hoping I know the significance of it, that it's a warning. I want to care as much as I know I should. As much as I thought I did after the Lugar game. As much as my employer does. When I played, I could compartmentalise everything and focus solely on the game. That's far harder from the sidelines. As he opens the door to allow me to join my players, I resolve to do better.

'Right, listen up. Josey in goals...' McIntosh is back, but he hasn't trained yet. He's annoyed but I've always stuck by the rule that players who don't train don't play. 'A back three: Russell, Gilhooly, Smith. Midfield four ae Lorimer, Mickey Minns, O'Halloran and Dib Ramage.' The names are going on the board. 'Billy, Franco ... in the hole behind...' I see Huck Finnegan getting up off the bench. 'Dougie Wilson up front.' They all look surprised. None more so than Wilson himself. Finnegan says 'Whit?' It's certainly the change that I'd warned Billy the Kidd about. Although I only rehearsed it in my head in the subsequent walk along the corridor. No-one speaks. The shock is still settling. Dougie Wilson came from Glenafton but has so far showed little in training. Has barely spoken to anyone since signing.

Higgy opens the changing-room door. 'Can ah bring the wee fella in?' He has Damo with him. His visor's open. I'm so pleased to see him. I half expect Nancy to be behind them. But of course, she isn't.

'Hi, wee man,' I say.

'Aw, thank fuck!' says Billy Gilmour. He looks like he might cry.

'I'm here,' Damo says, with no emotion, and then, in a monotone: 'Thank fuck!'

It breaks the ice. Everyone laughs, except Damo, naturally. Even Huck Finnegan smiles.

'Better no' let yer ma hear that,' I say, 'or ah'll be in big trouble.'

'Big trouble,' says the boy.

'What happened,' I ask Higgy.

'Coupla days ago, ah took that Stretch Armstrong toy round that ye got him. Telt Nancy it wis fae Raymond for Damo's birthday. She wis askin' how it was goin'. Wi' you … here, an' that.' He stops himself, leaving me wondering if there was more. 'Just felt it wisnae fair for the wee man tae miss out oan the fitba while aw the grown-ups around him act like weans.' Evidently, I've told him more about the situation than I thought I had.

'Right boys … let's go. Hard workin', right fae the start! The three points are ours.' Harry Doyle is tempering his volume and cuts out the profanities. But everyone gets it. And somehow, suddenly, there's something; a shared ambition. A collective determination.

Billy Gilmour makes the entire team – plus substitutes – kiss Damo's helmet. As they do so I hear him say softly: 'Abbott, Ainsley, Baird, Bruce, Davidson, Demarco, Forrest, Garvey, Macdonald, Melville, Ross, Sinclair, Walkinshaw.' And I swear I nearly have a fucking heart attack.

'What d'you say?' Higgy looks at me and holds out his hands as if to say *why are you shouting at him?* And I didn't think I had but the whole dressing room is staring at me.

And then Damo says: 'Schmeichel, Gough, Laudrup, Ravanelli, Shearer, Juninho, McManaman, Redknapp, Beckham, Gascoigne, Gullit, Zola, Vialli.'

It's a turgid first quarter. Both teams struggle with the conditions when the ball goes out wide. Consequently, it has spent so much time in the air, NASA could've strapped a satellite to it. The hundred or so hardy souls who have braved the elements deserve better. Gradually, they get it. With ten minutes until half-time Gilmour forces a series of corners. A barely audible voice from behind me:

'Winton Rovers lost sixty-eight percent of goals from set pieces last season.'

I look around. It's Damo. I look at Higgy. He shrugs.

Another corner. Gilmour floats a lovely cross to the back post.

Russell heads it back across the goal. Dougie Wilson adjusts his position well to knock it in.

—Winton Rovers lost sixty-eight percent of goals from set pieces last season.

Half-time:

> *Barshaw Bridge 1-0 Winton Rovers*
> *(Wilson)*

'Fucken telt ye'se aw,' says Billy Gilmour, outstretched arms, a halved orange in his hands. 'That wean, swear tae God ... he's a lucky mascot, man!'

'I'm Mascot Man,' Damo whispers without looking up from his bagged squad of tiny players.

—Mascot Man, me.

'Just need to keep an eye on the rain,' says the ref, to me and my Winton Rovers opposite number. We trudge back out.

'Aye, no' sure we'll see this yin out, eh?' A hopeful prompt from the losing manager, but I'm not rising to it.

Five minutes into the second half, and we're two goals up. Another set piece. Dougie Wilson again. It'll look to my chairman that training-ground routines are the reason for this change in fortunes. But we haven't practised them. It's simply the spontaneous nature of the game.

There are ten minutes remaining. We're leading six-nil. And to exacerbate the unusual circumstances, the sun has come out. This game isn't getting abandoned now. 'Winton Rovers lost sixty-eight percent of goals from set pieces last season,' Damo repeats, and it strikes me that five of ours today will have increased that statistic.

I stare at Damo. I'm trying to penetrate his internal circuits; to understand this aptitude for analysing probabilities he must surely struggle to comprehend. He isn't even watching the game.

∩

I let Higgy take Damo home, ensuring that he's back before the previously designated 5.00 pm deadline. No point in fanning any embers that might still be burning.

'Well done, son,' says Billy the Kidd. 'See ye at The King's? Ah'm buyin.'

'Naw, ah'm gonnae head,' I reply. The Rovers team and management follow our chairman towards the pub for the restorative warmth of the soup and pies we've laid on for them.

'Well played, Danny,' says the ref. 'Ah did wonder about callin' it off,' he admits. 'The ball stuck quite a bit in the corners.'

'Aye. Ah know. Couldnae really have complained if ye had. Thanks though.' I hand him his money. 'Linos' are in there too.'

'Ach, let's keep schtum about that though, eh?' He winks. 'They two did bugger all out there anyway.'

He leaves. And then I'm alone. Just me and the seagulls flapping about in search of the last scraps of food before the diminishing light finally disappears. I sit in my office, watching them through the cracked window for more than an hour – until a rap on the front doors alerts me.

'Didnae think ye'd be here,' he says.

'Why?'

'Didnae think ye actually meant it.'

'Ah told ye ah'd be here, didn't ah?'

'There's loadsa folk've gie'd me promises ower the years. Doesnae mean they kept them.'

I'm taking a massive risk. Letting Scud Meikle into The Barn to clean himself in the showers, to sleep in my office every night; I doubt the chairman would understand the motivation behind my benevolence. My need to absolve myself of my guilt.

The bedraggled man comes in. The stench coming off him is terrible. Like someone who's lain in their own piss and shit and vomit for days. I've picked up some food and toiletries. I've looked out some of my clothes. When I hand them to him, he's like a child leaving the Christmas grotto at Fraser's, having just visited Santa. And then he cries, and I don't know what to say to him. So, I leave him to it, telling him not to come out of my office, and that I'll be back for him first thing in the morning.

I walk to Higgy's still lost in my ongoing preoccupations. But with fresh ideas about how I might honour them. It's amazing how a win changes my perspective. Football's ability to shut out the darkness. The pain behind my eyes lifts.

Higgy is still out when I reach his place. I find a note telling me there's some corned beef in the fridge, and to *go and see yer mam*.

Rather than putting on a record, I put on Higgy's TV. My new best friend. *Match of the Day* will be on shortly. I might learn something.

∩

'Fancy seein' you here.' The voice is upbeat. But I don't recognise it.

I'm on my knees and find myself looking up, the low-lying late-autumn sunshine around the body stood in front of me like an intense Ready Brek glow, making it difficult to determine the features.

'Gardenin', is it?'

I adjust position. The ruddy face of Sandy Buchanan, the *Standard* journalist, comes into focus. My sighs can, I'm sure, be heard at Kilmarnock Cross.

'Just helpin' out.'

'Part ae yer community outreach programme?' he sniggers.

'You're a bit far fae the white heat ae the action, are ye no'?'

'What d'ye mean?' he asks. It sounds like his feelings are hurt by the obvious sarcasm.

'Nothin'. Is it me yer after, then?'

'Naw, Brian Clough, as it happens, it isnae.'

I wait for his follow-on, but he walks past me. He rings the bell. He maintains his stare until he reaches the front door. I try to work my way behind it. To burrow in and understand what is driving him. How he seems to know more about me and – perhaps more directly – Raymond than I'd want him to. Sandy Buchanan has covered more of our games this season for his local newspaper than any other team. While the lingering stink of last season's shame might attract a casual interest, Barshaw Bridge is a tiny, second-division junior team fallen on hard times of its own making, penalised and consequently dropping down the divisions. We're hardly Glasgow Rangers.

'Can ah maybe help ye?'

He turns to face me. 'You the aul' woman's butler tae then?' he says, self-satisfied smirking in a way that would prompt my brother to deliver a swift fucking battering. The door opens.

'Yes?'

'Mrs Reid?'

'Yes.'

'My name's Buchanan. *Sandy* Buchanan. Ah wonder if ah might ask a couple ae questions about yer husband, Mr Jock Reid?'

She looks past him, towards me, for a sign, perhaps. As if I'm her advisor. I become aware of shaking my head. My attempts at telepathy fail.

'A lot ae questions about my Jock lately.' She smiles, but there's an edge to the way she phrases the words.

Buchanan leans in closer. I'm thirty feet or so away from them, pulling the last of the year's weeds out of the soil, so I can't hear what they say. But minutes later, Buchanan is inside the house, the door shut behind him. And my anxiety grows, sprialling out of me like uncontrollable vines. My paranoia creating scenarios in which new evidence has been found. A regional weekly newspaper now investigating an unsolved death, which will inevitably lead them to me. I think of Nancy; of how I'd be able to explain it away. And of Mrs Reid, the poor old woman I can see moving behind the net curtains. And then logic gets back in the driving seat and my heart rate returns to a more manageable level.

Buchanan remains in the house as I pack up. I put the tools back in Jock Reid's shed and leave with the refuse sacks full without letting them know I'm finished. If there is any accounting to be done, I'll know it soon enough. And it may even alleviate some of the weight I've been carrying.

Half an hour later, I'm outside the bakers.

—I see him. Outside the shop. Peering in. He's pretending to look at the cakes, but I see him. Looking for me. The cakes are just a cover. It's quite funny.

I pause outside, like I'm weighing the value of a cream doughnut against an empire biscuit. But I'm looking beyond the display. Past the man in the comical white hat and through to the back shop. I see her. She's there.

—Despite my earlier uncertainty, he's not at all like his brother. He feels safe, somehow. He's not painful on the eye. A wee bit like Noel Gallagher, but at least his eyebrows don't meet in the middle. He's shy and quiet and awkward, and I find it ... I don't know ... endearing somehow. The Raymond years were exciting at first, but the mental torment just became too much. It's just a diversion from the everyday, small-town monotony, I know that, but everyone craves a wee bit of favourable attention every now and again, don't they?

'A cream doughnut, an' an empire biscuit, please.'

'Sure thing, Danny,' says Ernie, the village baker. Without taking his eyes from me, he lobs the treats in a bag and twirls it around expertly to tighten the corners. I wonder how many thousands of times in his life he has done that. The Ronaldinho of the sugary-dough fraternity.

'She gets a break in about ten minutes, ye know.'

'Eh?'

'Nancy, son.' He nods towards the corner. 'Hing about ower there an' ah'll let her know ye're waitin' for her,' he says, winking at me; acknowledging my embarrassment.

—I'm curious about him. He doesn't seem at all like the difficult kid Raymond used to tell me about. Raymond always had a softness for his brother ... even in the midst of the pain that he said both had to endure. 'If I didn't look after him, who else would have?' Raymond would say. It was admirable, and the one thing that excused his other faults: Raymond was prepared to take the punishment for his brother, for something that wasn't his own doing, to give Danny a chance at a better life. I still find Raymond's unfailing loyalty to his family surprising and inspiring in equal measure. I'm not sure I'll be able to maintain the same standards.

He walks through the doorway that I've barely removed my gaze from since I was outside the shop. My breathing quickens like a fucking teenager at a school disco, waiting for a girl's pals to return with the thumbs up or down.

—It's a surprise, after the way I treated him at the house. I felt really terrible about that. He just showed up at a really bad time ... Mam nagging away at me. Picking at a scab that hasn't fully healed over, and then the blood and the pus starts weeping again, you know?

But I'm glad he's here. I'm pleased to see him. Apologising doesn't come easy for me, not after all those years attempting to defend his brother. Pleading for my mam to give him another chance. That the next time, it'd be different. Rent-a-fucking cliché, eh? 'Aw men are selfish bastards, especially when ye need tae depend on them ... wi'

the responsibility ae a wean. Happy enough tae be at the conception
... blah blah blah!' – Mam, speaking for the essence of female suffer-
ing just because it fitted her experience. Raymond was never like that,
I'd protest. 'No men are ever like that,' she'd say, all world-weary, '...
until they are.' And it kills me to concede that she was probably right.

I like him. I can admit it to myself now, if not to him. Damo likes
him too. I stand outside my son's bedroom door at night, listening to
him. Eavesdropping on his private conversations with Danny, the
Stretch Armstrong man.

'Ye've tae wait round the back,' says Ernie. Another wink. Maybe
he just has something in his eye. 'Here,' he adds. He pours coffee
into a plastic cup for me. A third wink. It's a twitch, not a hopeful
signal of my prospects. The two people stood behind me in the
queue also get winked at.

—We sit on the old bench at the back where Ernie sits at five in the
morning and smokes the dope he thinks nobody knows about.
Minutes pass, and I'm not sure if he's plucking up the courage to ask
me something. But if he dallies any longer, my break'll be over...

'Everythin' alright?' she asks.

'Aye. Things are fine. You?'

'All quiet on the Garvey front.' She laughs, thankfully. 'Damo
loves that doll ye got him.'

'It was from his da.' Thinking of Raymond's face when she
called it a doll.

'Aye,' she remarks. She knows the score.

'He's some boy,' I say, quickly adding, 'Damo, I mean,' lest there
is any doubt.

'Ah know who ye meant.' She smiles and it feels like the sun has
burst its way through the cloud cover.

'How's he gettin' on at his new school?'

'A bit up an' down, still,' she says. 'His teacher said the transition would always be difficult ... goin' fae one building tae another. But he's been unsettled for a couple ae weeks now.'

'Tell me again ... why did he have tae move school?' I broached this subject once before and got shot down like a man suggesting gun-control legislation to Charlton Heston. Now though, the terrain seems more agreeable.

'One ae the other parents made a complaint. Said that he should be in a special school.'

'On the basis ae what, exactly?' I ask.

She looks down. Plays with a band that's around her wrist. Sighs deeply. 'He hit another kid wi' a rounders bat durin' the sports. Apparently, it wisnae the first time.' Suddenly, her face is masked with a sort of tired pain; like she's exhausted with the effort of relying on the judgement of others.

'Was he provoked?' I ask. I'd expect Damo to be the type of kid that always gets singled out. Picked on. Bullied for being a wee bit different. A bit strange. A bit of a loner. For having a dad in jail.

'He said that the boys took his football players off him.' She sighs again. 'They bloody fitba men!' As if they are a totem of all that's wrong in her life.

'I think they're his copin' mechanism,' I say. 'The things that keep him fae gettin' stressed.'

'You been readin' the same books as me?' she asks me. I laugh nervously.

While in the Cumnock Library, I stumbled on a couple of articles that described traits in children similar to the ones Damo seems to have. The need for strict routine, to repeat the script of his life; the relentless pedalling of that bike up and down the hill being an obvious example. The sequence in which he recounts the names of football players. His astonishing memory for facts and figures and statistics. His compulsive need for balanced order. No wonder Nancy dreads the unpredictable chaos that a returning Raymond would bring.

'Ah wisnae steppin' over the line,' I say. 'Been researchin' the history ae the club an' ah found somethin' that...'

'And?' she asks.

'And what?'

'Your conclusions, Professor Garvey?' She's still calm. Best not risk delving any deeper for now.

'Dunno, yet,' I say. 'Ah've only read the first chapter.'

She laughs. She briefly touches my knee. It seems natural and unforced, but I'm wary of reading too much significance into it.

'Ah better get back in. Ah've got the rolls tae make up.' She stands.

I do too. 'Listen Nancy, wi' the wee man comin' tae the games now, you not fancy doin' the food at The Barn?' There's a curious look on her face. 'In the van, ah mean. The pies an' the Bovril's an' teas, an' that. We cannae get anybody tae dae it regularly.' She smirks. 'Sorry. Ye know what ah mean.' What I mean is that I'd like to see her more often.

'Aye. Maybe. Ah'll speak tae Ernie. He's no' the most imaginative, but ah'll see what he thinks.' She leans over and kisses me on the cheek. It was unexpected.

—God. I just kissed him. I don't know why. It seemed like a natural thing to do, but then minutes pass. We don't speak. It's awkward, and I feel like a total idiot.

It's astonishing how calmed I feel just by being next to her.

'Any chance we could take Damo wi' us tomorrow? It's an away game against Saltcoats Victoria.'

Her lips purse. I look down for fear that she'll find my next comment ridiculous.

'Some ae the boys think he's the reason we're winnin'.'

She looks at me as if I'm wearing my jacket back to front. 'Ah'll think about it.'

It's as good as I'll get. For Billy Gilmour's sake, I'll keep my fingers crossed. Barshaw's young star player has already suggested kidnapping the boy in the helmet in order to keep the winning run going.

—I agree to him taking Damo to an away game. Not because I'm totally happy with the idea, but because I need to get away. Back inside to hide my mortification. Jesus Christ!

It's a journey of more than an hour to Campbell Park, in Saltcoats. I'm in the back of Harry Doyle's car. Damo sits beside me. He's staring out the window. Expressionless. His bag of big-headed famous footballers has been bolstered by the recent additions of Roberto Baggio and Ryan Giggs. His mother has not objected to their purchase. Higgy's in the passenger seat reading the *Daily Record*. He reads it back-to-front. Mutters aloud about Rangers being odds-on for nine league titles in a row, and of how boringly predictable the Premier Division has become as a result of their dominance.

'Laudrup, though ... what a player he is!'

Harry Doyle nods silently. I wonder if it's in agreement or a sign of the state of the uneven roads through Kilmarnock.

'What a player he is,' says Damo, from the back seat.

'That's right, son. You tell 'em!' Higgy laughs. He moves onto the continuing coverage of the recent royal divorce.

During the enlightening journey, I also find out that today's opponents were founded in 1889. That they are nicknamed The Seasiders. I'm told that the club reached the quarter-final stage of the Scottish Junior Cup twice in the 1970s. The home legs both attracted more than three thousand supporters; numbers that most of the senior clubs in Scotland would now be envious of.

'How the hell does he know aw this,' says our astonished driver.

'Nae idea,' I reply.

'Ah'll tell ye one thing, though,' says Higgy. 'If Damo says it, ye ken it's true. Ye can take it tae the bloody bank, in't that right, son?'

'The bloody bank,' Damo whispers. Higgy laughs. Harry nods.

Saltcoats Victoria lose more goals from penalties that any other team in the league. Another Damo stat, but one that I'm very interested in. They have – according to Higgy who watched them recently – a backline of veteran defenders; slow and ponderous. Good in the air, but exposed on the deck, especially if, like today, the turf is firm and wintery, and the ball won't stick on it. The two centre backs are working their way down the divisions; one formerly with Cowdenbeath, the other a cup-winning captain of Beith Juniors from a decade earlier. But now they are in the Ayrshire Second Division; their team languishing just below us. Only Hurlford United have had a worse first quarter.

We've arrived early. Josey Monsanto is here. I spot the plastic Jesus on the dashboard of a gold Avenger. The holy goalie has retained his place, even though McIntosh is back, wearing a boxer's gumshield and looking like a stone or two has been shed. To my surprise, he has remained patient and even seems to have struck up a friendship with his rival for the number-one jersey.

The Campbell Park facilities are pitifully poor. The Barn, by comparison, is luxurious.

This club seems to be on its knees. I'm shown into the dressing-room area. There is no referee's room; just a big plastic sheet in front of a doorless electricity-meter cupboard. A circuit board adjacent looks like Victor Frankenstein might have used it to stimulate life in the eighteenth century. A solitary chair sits against the back of the cupboard, for the official's use. I lean over to flick on the light to the main space.

'Ah, for fuck's sake don't touch that switch … ye'll kill yersel,' the groundsman screams. He holds a wooden clothes pole that's longer than him and – while shielding his face – whacks the switch. The lights come on, flickering. 'Mind yersel' in there now, son.'

He leaves me to it. I haul the bag containing the strips in and start laying them out on a variety of dirty surfaces that look like contents of a skip has been dragged inside. The team show up in dribs and drabs, get changed quickly and head out for the warm-up. They return and I read the team lines and reinforce our tactics from Thursday night's training session: fast-moving, one-touch passing, ball on the deck and looking for the gaps in behind them, and the most advanced four all interchanging so their defenders don't know who to pick up. At Billy Gilmour's insistence, everyone touches the space helmet. And for almost the first time today, I see Damo smile.

From the first five minutes on, Saltcoats Vics look like a team desperate for the season to end. Two-thirds of them play like their careers already have. We're three-nil up after only twenty minutes. Two of our goals are scored from penalties awarded after our nippy forwards, Gilmour and Peters, are tripped by tackles so late they could've been timetabled by British Rail. Gilmour takes them, such is the sky-high level of his confidence. The first half ends with an injury to the far-side linesman. Some kids on a balcony overlooking the pitch have shot him in the arse with a pellet fired from an air rifle. He doesn't return, and we agree to a Saltcoats coach running the line to finish the game.

We score twice more, and I make substitutions, including McIntosh going on for Monsanto with twenty minutes left. He doesn't touch the ball once and spends most of the time leaning on a post. During the last ten minutes, I glance backwards and see him urinating against it.

Gilmour scores his hat-trick with the last kick of the ball. I reckon the ref stops it early, but no-one is complaining. Gilmour asks the Vics boss if he can keep the ball.

'Dae whit ye like, son. Ah don't fucken care anymore!' I hear him morosely reply.

We go back to the pub with the Vics lads. Sausage rolls and Bovril, in an atmosphere that resembles a wake. Damo has an orange juice as Gilmour tries – and fails – to teach him to play pool.

'Thanks, an' aw the best for the rest ae the season,' I say to my opposite number as we leave.

'Doubt we'll see it out, son,' he replies, and I know his spirit is broken. His determination to keep a team on the park, despite the losses, the facilities, the dwindling interest. The club has been around longer than many in Scottish football. He's now contemplating it folding on his watch. There's little sadder.

Saltcoats Victoria 0–6 Barshaw Bridge
(Peters, Gilmour 3 (2 pens), O'Halloran, Russell)

We're up to seventh in the league table.

∩

The leaves have clogged the drainpipes. Compressed into them so the gutters are overflowing at almost every junction.

'Are ye sure yer okay there, son?' Mrs Reid mouths dramatically through her bedroom window, unaware that I could hear her via the open top hopper if she simply spoke a little louder.

'Aye. No worries,' I reply. And she looks up as if stunned that the sound can reach her through the double-glazing.

I'm clinging to a rickety metal ladder in torrential driving rain, wondering what depths my desire for atonement might ultimately reach. When will enough be enough? Perhaps I already know the answer to this, and it won't be when the old woman knows the truth. It'll be when Nancy does. These acts of charity, deposits in the merit bank to offset the extent of my eventual bankruptcy.

I tie up the dozen or so sodden bags and leave them on the public side of the hedge. I don't drive, and I won't. But having to rely on one of Harry Doyle's lads with his work's van to complete the task makes me wish I was more independent.

'Here ye are, son,' shouts Mrs Reid. It's a cup of tea. She's standing in the shelter of her front door, holding the cup as if she expected I might take it with me. I trudge back to the door.

'Ah, thanks, Mrs Reid, but ah need tae go. Plus, ah'm filthy here. Yer carpets, an' that.'

'Ye sure? Och well, next time,' she says.

'Bye, Mrs Reid.'

'Oh ... wait. Ah nearly forgot.' She turns, leaving the door open, the wind blowing some wet leaves that I didn't capture into the hallway. 'Thought ye might be interested in this ... what with you being the team manager now.' She hands me a shoe box. 'Just some things from Jock's football years. I was lookin' for them for that man from the *Kilmarnock Standard*. Maybe *you* could loan them to him? Make sure ah get them back?'

I'm back in the library in Cumnock. Lately it's felt like more of a home to me than Higgy's place. I wrapped the box in my coat to protect it. I'm soaked to the skin after waiting for a bus that was delayed by flooding at Mauchline. The heating is on full, and I imagine that people see steam rising from me.

The box is a revelation. There's a Scotland Schools cap inside it, very like my own, only frayed and worn, and from three decades earlier than when I got my chance. There are clippings from several national newspapers, not just the local or regional ones that I occasionally featured in. And then there are some articles that Jock Reid wrote. Football stories, mainly.

One grabs my attention. It recounts the death of an elderly football fan at a cup derby between Auchinleck Talbot and Cumnock Juniors. The tense, tight match had gone into extra time. The old man suffered a heart attack just behind the home team's dugout. Several committee members carried him into the club's building. Finding the team changing rooms locked, they placed the man in the ref's bath, phoned an ambulance and then rushed back out to see their team score a last-minute winner. The man died.

Jock Reid's account for a national newspaper focuses more on the all-consuming passion for the junior game than on the questionable decision-making of the men involved. He stops short of suggesting that they knew he was already dead, but it's the underlying suggestion. Quotes from the man's family seem to exonerate their actions: 'It's what he would've wanted.' Not a matter of life and death; more important than that, eh?

I'm bringing him back to life. He's becoming fully formed. Flesh and blood again. His writing is sensitive but funny; empathetic, yet aware of the ludicrous logic of obsession. I'm lost in it, until the small plastic thing in my pocket rings and interrupts the silence, drawing withering looks from those around me.

'Danny, where the hell are ye, son?'

'Ah'm down at Cumnock, Higgy. Why? What's up?'

'Shh!' A man chastises me.

'It's yer ma, son. Ye really need tae see her. She's awfy poorly now.'

I whisper that I'll look in on the way home, then hang up.

It rings again. The librarian shushes me. Then, before I can cut short the call – Tony McIntosh, seeking a meeting – she starts towards me.

'Excuse me. Mr Garvey?' The librarian surprises me by knowing my name, and because she doesn't berate me. 'You were enquiring about a book the other week? We managed to get a copy.' She smiles, pleased with her endeavour. She beckons me and I follow her. She reaches below the worktop and shows it to me.

'Ah. Thanks,' I say. 'When is it due back?'

'A month from now,' she says, giving the inaugural date stamp to a book entitled *Obsessive Children: a Sociospychiatric Study* by P.L. Adams. I take it from her like it's the Holy Grail.

I head back to Barshaw, the box of Jock Reid memorabilia supplemented by some photocopied articles on the abduction of his granddaughter, the death of his daughter and a tiny column from the *Chronicle* detailing his own demise in 1983. All of it accessed via the library's revolutionary internet system. A whole bank of information on virtually any given subject under the sun. Right at my fucking fingertips. Hours pass like seconds, and I find it unbelievably addictive.

I've explained its extraordinary power to Higgy, who struggles to comprehend it. I'm not entirely sure I do myself. I imagine my schooldays would have been a wholly different proposition with such immediate access to unfiltered knowledge. Like a vast encyclopaedia that lives somewhere out in space. But it's hard not to fear what might happen to this library if nobody needs to read a book. If they only need to click a button.

I miss my stop, so deep am I in complex explanations of child behaviour that is very similar to what I've witnessed from Damo, and the more challenging aspects his mother has expanded on. When I finally get back, Higgy is out; up at Libby's, no doubt. He's barely here anymore. I want to read more. To get closer to Damo. To *feel* closer to Nancy. When I finally decide to make some toast, it's 9.45 pm. I'll go and see Libby another day.

⌂

'Danny, get up!'

I've slept in. There will be no morning run this Saturday. I have another sales event for Kidd's Carpets at 11.00 am that I need to attend. An hour at most, and on my own this time, since the boss's step-daughter is off somewhere with her boyfriend Joe. But since it's a part of my job description and Billy the Kidd supplements my wages by considering me a part-time employee of his carpets firm, I must be there. I can tell Higgy is not here giving me a wake-up call for that, though.

He stands at the foot of the bed in the upstairs room I've only recently moved my meagre belongings into. I lasted just over five months on the sofa. Constantly reminding myself that I wasn't staying, only passing through. But the growing piles of notes and textbooks and wall charts needed somewhere to go. We'd irritate each other, Higgy and me, especially in the days after a defeat. So I moved my stuff upstairs. To the pokey attic room I regularly occupied as a child. Flitting to and fro, back then, to accommodate

Libby's unpredictable houseguests and the spontaneous parties she held for them. Raymond shared a similar existence, although from just before his sixteenth birthday, I can't recall him staying anywhere other than here in Higgy's house. Unless he was being detained. Perhaps understandable that neither of us holds on to a recognisable concept of home.

'Get up!' Higgy's anger shocks me out of a dwam. A rude awakening from the best sleep I've had since I came back from Arbroath. 'Go an' see yer mam! Ah'm no' askin' ye ... ah'm bloody tellin' ye! She's got weeks. Ah doubt she'll see Christmas. What the hell's the matter wi' ye?'

And I'm forced to ponder this, the question at the root of everything. I don't know the answer. My team are finally playing consistently good football. The club itself is more buoyant than it has been for years. Everyone is pulling their weight. We're bringing in adequate money from a range of fund-raising initiatives that I've instigated. As far as a demonstrable commitment to the part-time job I took on, no-one can argue about the evidence. We're climbing the league, lower mid-table now; a miracle given the shackles of the points deduction.

I'm working hard at my strange relationship with Damo, Nancy and, God help me, Doreen. And I'm trying to repair some of the damage that I caused Jock Reid's widow. For fuck's sake, what more does Higgy want from me?

And then – as the door shakes from the force with which he slams it – it hits me, lying there in Higgy's cold attic room. Libby is a dereliction that I can't repair. I spent years in the cold north defiantly refusing to give in to regret, as if to do so would allow my mistakes to rush in through badly built levees, drowning me. I used injury and the reflective, contemplative time it offered me as a catalyst to becoming a better, more informed person. I came back to fix things. To address the failures. To absolve myself of a guilt that was engulfing me. I can't do any of these things with Libby. Because she can't be fixed.

Higgy is downstairs. Fuming at what he presumes is my indifference. He composes himself. Thinks about the words, and their order.

'She needs a bit ae time wi' ye, son. It's no' excusin' the past ... an' it's no' drawin' a veil over it either. But she's yer mam, Danny. Don't punish her anymore. At least ye've got the chance tae say goodbye properly.' He gets his coat. 'Ah'm goin' for a quick pint. An' then tae the bookies.' His voice breaks. He's in pain. 'Ah'll pick up the wee fella, an' see ye later up at the park.' He leaves before I can answer.

I watch him walk down the path into the teeth of a bitter November wind. Through the window, I watch him wipe his eyes with his hand.

We're at The Barn again, the last in a run of three games in a row. The first of them, a satisfying 5-3 win against Muirkirk Juniors. A pulsating match watched by close to two hundred people. Young Gilmour continued his scoring run with a brace. A Queen of the South scout was watching him. We followed that with a narrow single-goal victory against Craigmark Burntonians; a game notable only for a double penalty save by Tony McIntosh after the referee ordered the initial kick to be retaken for Gilhooly's encroachment. In keeping with the instantly forgettable nature of the match, we claimed the points as a result of an own goal.

Today's game is an Ayrshire Cup tie against Annbank United. It's a big game for two reasons. A win puts us into the quarters. Both teams sit equal in the league on points, having played the same number of games. Harry Doyle predicts it will be *nip an' tuck*. We need to take our chances, he stresses. But it's also Nancy's first match dispensing Ernie's hot food from the van. She's here, but Damo isn't. I find myself in the ludicrous situation of waiting for a ten-year-old boy in a space helmet to appear before giving the final team-talk. As if something in the boy's stored bank of statistics might give us the edge we need.

Fifteen minutes until kick-off and Higgy hasn't shown. It's possible he's punishing me. He'll know I didn't go to Libby's house. Or rather, I didn't go in. Her carers informed me at the doorstep that she was sleeping, having had quite an unsettled night. They would let her know I'd visited though. It was enough for me. I was relieved.

The rain is falling steadily but the turf seems to be holding firm.

We look lost in the first half. The pitch feels enormous. We're not moving quickly enough to shut down space. It's no surprise when they finally score. A shot from outside the box. McIntosh is rooted to the spot. The ball's in the net.

Annbank celebrate, and my keeper mouths apologetically to me that he saw it late. Another thing he sees late, as everyone else waits for the restart, is a right cross from behind him, connecting with his jaw.

'Where the fuck wis you last night, ya dirty bastard?' A woman. An extremely loud and angry one. Pushing a pram right into the middle of his muddy goalmouth.

'Carole,' he yells.

'Don't fucken *Carole* me, you! Where were ye?' She's screaming for all to hear.

The ball's back on the centre spot but no-one's watching it. Everyone's eyes are trained on the domestic disturbance. A handbag is out. It's being wielded skilfully. McIntosh hits the deck.

'Jesus Christ, should ah send her off?' asks the ref. He's at the touchline to ask us for guidance.

'Good luck wi' that, son,' sneers Harry Doyle.

'Where were ye, eh? Ah'll *tell* ye where ye were!'

'What wis the point in her askin' him, then?' says a supporter standing behind us.

'Ye were back at hers, weren't ye? That dirty midden.'

McIntosh says nothing. Two hundred and fifty sniggering people watching him on his knees. In the mud.

'Ye'se aw havin' a good look, eh?' Tony's woman stares down the pitch; a *c'mon, ah'll take the fucken lot ae ye'se* open-legged stance that prompts the nearest players to take a few steps back.

One last swing to the jaw and she's off. Tony McIntosh has remained silent about his whereabouts. She's left him with the pram. I shout to Josey Monsanto to get stripped. As substitutions go, this one is unusual.

'Sorry boss,' says Tony, sheepishly struggling with the pram's wheels in the soft, wet turf. The look on his face betrays his reason for calling me, requesting a summit. As he passes me, I notice that the pram contains two babies.

'Aye,' I say. 'We'll discuss it at trainin'.'

The first half ends without further incident, but fifteen minutes after it should have.

We head into The Barn, soaked and still shocked from the pitch invasion. Tony McIntosh apologises to everyone as he takes off his strip. He offers little explanation. He dresses quickly, wishes us well. The pram is blocking the dressing-room door. No-one can get in or out. His babies are now wide awake and screaming.

'Don't worry, man. We've got this,' I hear Monsanto whisper to Tony as he manoeuvres the muddy wheels and leaves.

The team is about to head back out when Higgy comes in. He stares at me sternly. Billy Gilmour's mouth opens in advance of Damo squeezing past.

'Wee man!'

'And Gilmour scores!' says Damo, like a tiny Archie McPherson.

'Well, ah fucken just might now!'

'Hey you,' shouts Higgy. His anger at me hasn't dissipated. 'Mind yer language in front ae the wean.'

We're a different team in the second half. The McIntosh incident seems to have interrupted Annbank's rhythm. The rain stays off and we use the wings better, having pushed Peters further out left and Lorimer stretching the game to the right.

In sixty minutes, we get our reward; a ball falling kindly to Davie Russell who lashes it in from fully thirty yards.

Two more goals in quick succession, one from Gilmour and one from O'Halloran, give us a bit of breathing space. In a frenetic last ten minutes, the Annbank captain is sent off for protesting a disallowed goal. From my perspective, it looks like he had a point. He pushes the ref over, and the red card comes out. A lengthy ban is inevitable after he spits at the official as he's wrestled away by his team-mates. I leave a few minutes before the final whistle. I need time to prepare. Harry Doyle sees it out.

I'm shocked when I see her. There was little enough of her the last time, but she's faded to the point where continuing to breathe seems unfeasible for her. After hugging me, Higgy gets his coat, and although I tell him to stay, I can tell he's relieved at the opportunity to go. He's spending more and more time here with Libby. He needs a break.

I sit next to her bed. On the arm of a chair. There's even less space in the living room now than there was last time I was here. More expensive things that bleep. More wires. More bags of fluid hanging from poles suspended above her. A bag, quarter-full of dark-yellow stuff. A tube connecting it – thankfully concealed under the blankets – to her rotten insides. I gag at the thought of having to empty it. But a nurse from Marie Curie will be back in a few hours. She'll do it and save Libby from having to listen to my daft, nervous chat.

She's awake. A mask over her nose, which she strains to pull back when she sees me.

'Aw'right?' I ask, stupidly.

'Help me up a bit,' she croaks.

Mindful of the bag of watery shite, I gingerly try to lift her.

There is no weight at all. It's like lifting a medical skeleton. Little muscle or sinew, just bone. She must be in intolerable pain.

She winces. 'Yer team win, then?'

'Aye,' I reply. 'Struggled a bit in the first half, but we got right back in it after the break.' I sound like I'm being interviewed, post match.

'Glad yer enjoyin' it, son.' She coughs. A little bit of blood on her lip.

I wipe her mouth. She looks at me. It's a look that says: *no' long now, son.*

We don't speak for a time. I watch television and pretend that we're watching it together. Libby stares at the wall. I think of Higgy, sitting here contemplating whether a pillow over the face would end their suffering, or just hers.

'Are ye stayin' then?' she says.

'What, now? D'ye want me tae?'

'No. In Barshaw,' she says. She coughs again but this time, it's almost soundless. Every time she does must knock another ten minutes or so off what little she has left.

'Ah ... I don't know yet. Depends.'

She doesn't probe. She won't have the energy. I take her hand. She looks at me strangely. She doesn't say anything else, and I sit there for a couple of hours, holding her hand as she drifts in and out of consciousness, until my shift ends and I get relieved.

I first spot him coming out of the bookies. I think he sees me, but I head off in the opposite direction, hoping that he didn't. I catch a reflection in a van's wing mirror and can see him gaining on me. I can hear him calling. Difficult to ignore. I dive into Ernie's shop, and Nancy's there, behind the counter. She looks up and I'm certain I see her smile.

'Hi.'

'Hi yersel', she says. 'That'll be four pounds, fifty-nine, Mrs Dodds.'

'Right, hen. Here ye are.' Mrs Dodds hands over a note. Waits for the change, takes the bag, swivels deftly past me like Maradona dodging static defenders, and opens the door. A little bell rings as Dennis Deans bursts in past her.

'God's sake! Where's yer manners?' Mrs Dodds tuts at Dennis's lack of chivalry.

'Ah knew that wis you. Did ye no' hear me shoutin' ye?'

'Naw, sorry. Headphones, y'know?' I point to my ears. Only thing I can think of. It seems implausible, since I'm not currently wearing any, but he doesn't query it.

'Ah spotted ye last week tae, speedin' doon the street in that wee purple motor. Wavin' like a bastard, ah wis,' he says.

I'm about to remind him that I don't drive, that it couldn't have been me he waved at, but he cuts across me before I can.

'Right, ah've finally got ye, so none ae yer excuses this time, Danny. Party at ours. A week on Saturday. Ali's insistin' ye come.'

I look over at Nancy, eyes pleading. Searching for an excuse that gets me out of what would surely feature high on a lifetime list of favourite worst nightmares.

'Danny,' she says, throwing a rope to a drowning man. 'Ye said we were goin' out on Saturday. The Pictures? *Jerry Maguire*?' God bless her! 'Don't tell me ye've forgotten?'

My eyes signal a relieved thank-you. Dennis looks at her. There's a flash of recognition. It takes him a minute or two. He was high and hammered but the fragments are returning. He remembers her.

'Ach, it's you!' Dennis says. A broad smile bursts across his face. He can't recall a name, but that doesn't matter right now. *Danny Garvey and a plus-one;* even better than anticipated.

'You an' him, eh? Ah had a lumber lined up for ye tae, Danny boy, but hey, nae problem if ye've got yer own,' says a determined Dennis. 'Both ae ye'se are comin'!' Nancy stares at me. 'Here's the address.' He takes her pen and scribbles on a napkin. Dennis is de-lighted. Like Leadbelly's man, going round taking names, he has another two for his deal with the devil.

'See the two ae ye'se about seven, then, aye?' He leaves, excited and without any further details being given.

Nancy and I stare at each other until she finally says, 'What'll ah wear?' and I breathe again and we both laugh, and the prospect of this unavoidable night down in a lowly circle of hell suddenly becomes a lot more bearable.

—Raymond phoned. Mam answered and there were angry words before I got to the call. He sounded drunk, although that couldn't have been possible. He was raging that I hadn't been on the visitors' list for such a long time. That I'm deliberately avoiding him. Cutting him out. I've used Damo as an excuse for this, but he can see through me. He knows that's not it. I'm just worn out; exhausted with being a 'prison wife'. Debilitated by the constant reminders of it. I need a break from it; a night off from my life.

I get the phone call early on the Friday. The news isn't good. The last league game before Christmas is off. A relentless deluge of water has fallen in Kirkconnel since the start of the week. Kello Rovers have hit a mid-season slump, losing their last three games. We, on the other hand, are in the middle of a purple patch. Up to sixth in the table, only ten points behind the leaders, Troon. We're also in the semi-finals of the Ayrshire Cup. No-one wants the run of games to stop. But the winter's coming and it could be weeks, if not months, before we play again.

I'm warming to the small, grey cellular phone. It allows me to let the full squad and backroom team know they have a free Saturday within minutes of me knowing.

Higgy calls. He won't be back tonight. He's staying over again but he tells me Libby is doing a bit better. He puts it down to me visiting her, but I know that's just to prompt a quick return. A quiet Friday night, then. I hunt for the plastic Woolworths bag with its unopened purchases from earlier in the week. I leaf through my new LP sleeves and start making a list. The best way to say many of the things that I'm struggling to articulate.

It feels like I'm experiencing palpitations. But I know it's just nerves. There's a lot to be nervous about, to be fair. Unequivocally, this is a date. The previous times have just been two people – friends from a small village – out for a drink. But this is an appointment. A specific time and place to be, as a couple. *Danny and Nancy.* And at what is ostensibly a fucking school reunion. What was I thinking?

—I've been in ten different outfits over the course of this afternoon; all variations on the same theme of jeans and a blouse. Apart from one. The option that keeps drawing me back to it. I wore that short black dress with the tiny white polka dots on the last night Raymond and I were out together. The week before, I had a few spare pounds. Can't remember where from. But I decided to buy Raymond something for his birthday. I was in the chemist's shop paying for it and the woman asked if I needed something for my split lip. Raymond had given me it the night before. I was so embarrassed; I just left the aftershave. I bought the dress in the Oxfam shop next door instead.

We went out for his birthday, him all apologetic and desperate to make up. It didn't end well, he got drunk and loud and spiteful, and we argued over Damo. But I love the dress. It'd be nice for it to have a different association.

It takes me half an hour to walk from the bottom of her street to her front door, so many times do I half turn and almost vomit from an anxiety that feels like it is consuming me from the inside of my belly. My mouth is desert dry. My chest is tightening. I could do with a drink; a real one.

'Hi ... em, is Nancy in?'

'Ah'm sure ye know she is.' Doreen, the Inscrutable. She must practise these folded-arm, pursed-lip, withering stances in front of a full-length mirror. I can imagine the postman approaching the front door to be met with a *whit the fuck's it got tae dae wi' you?* when asking for her signature as a receipt for a parcel.

She keeps me waiting outside in the rain. My hair is wet. It doesn't suit me the way it seems to suit the irritating, geeky one from Higgy's favourite TV programme.

'Mam ... God's sake, ask him in!' Nancy shouts from upstairs.

Doreen turns her body to the side. Just enough for me to ease past her. She's making it abundantly clear that she doesn't approve of this dalliance.

In the living room, Damo is sitting on a stool facing the television set. He's less than three feet from the screen.

'Blobby, Blobby, Blobby, Blobby...' he says, over and over. He's watching *Noel's House Party*; one of his obsessions.

'Ye get nothin' out ae him at all when that's on,' Nancy has previously told me. Beyond a cursory, 'aw'right, wee man?' which he blanks, I say nothing.

Doreen stands at the door. Watching me like I'd nick the ornaments off the mantelpiece if she didn't. I'm just about to sit when I hear Nancy on the stairs. Doreen sighs, and makes sure I hear it.

'Don't start,' says Nancy from the other side. She comes in. Made-up, hair tied back and in heels and a tight black dress with wee white dots on it. She is transformed.

'When will ye be back?' shouts Doreen.

'Ah've got my key!' Nancy replies, without a backward glance.

—He's here. Out of the loose, baggy sports gear. He's wearing black

trainers, black jeans, a T-shirt with 'The Fall' written across it, and a black Harrington jacket. His hair's wet. He's not exactly the Diet Coke guy, but he's here. I wasn't convinced he would come. No turning back now.

'Ye look really nice.' Only four words but still they stumble and trip over themselves.

'Bloody hope so; it took long enough.' She laughs. Nervously, and I'm not sure what to say next.

'This'll probably be terrible,' I say. Her head dips a bit. 'Ah, ah don't mean bein' wi' you. Ah meant a night out at the Deans's.'

Fuck it ... I should say that I've thought of little else than a night like this for months. That I've rehearsed scenarios where Raymond is informed of our developing relationship. That I'm growing to care more and more about helping her son find a way of assimilating. But I don't. We walk on in the rain to the far edge of the village. Towards the newer, identikit estate houses that hint at the lives of materialistic aspiration being lived inside them. Tiny pitched-roofed canopies over front doors that open straight into a *lounge*, not a living room. Drive-ways that can take multiple cars. Inbuilt garages that many have converted to living rooms. Because the *lounge* isn't big enough for the average family. Dennis Deans and his upwardly mobile Stepford wife Alison, and their three children live in one of these houses.

—We're standing outside this stranger's front door, and I wonder why I'm here. Imagining what Raymond would say. Maybe that's the answer.

'We could always just...'

'Go home?'

'Aye.'

It comforts me that we're both thinking the same way. Fearful of what lies on the other side of this door. But more than that: we're apprehensive about what the future will hold when we walk back through it at the end of the night. We stand together, shel-tering under Nancy's tiny umbrella, her free hand gripping mine. I reach up, arm trembling, and almost suffer a heart attack when the door opens before my finger reaches the bell.

'Aw'right, Danny ... an'...'

'Nancy,' I tell Dennis.

His eyes are wide and alive. 'Nancy. Aye. In ye'se come then. Just gettin' started.'

Nancy shoots me one final look, and in we go.

The group are sitting in a circle; split by gender at either end of this cramped space. The house is like a furnace. The women are fanning themselves. When the men high-five each other, which they do regularly, they show the sweat stains in the armpits of their pastel-coloured, short-sleeved shirts. The mix of perfume, sweat, smoke and cheap aftershave is, in its own way, as stultifying as The Barn's changing rooms. Bowls of crisps, nuts and cheese footballs are liberally spread. This could well be it for the food. I begin to wish I'd eaten before I came out.

—Certainly not turning out to be the evening I was expecting. He was trembling earlier when I took his hand. I'm so nervous and, if anything, I'm relieved it won't involve the formality of a sit-down meal. It's obvious that we're both out of practice in social situations, but I'm still glad to get out of the house and away from Mam's hec-toring for a night.

The women shout 'hiya' in unison. The men nod warily at us as we walk through the door. Dennis points at them and rattles off, 'Wendy, Sharon, Amy, Edie, Lynne one, Liz, Marj, Lynne two an' Yvonne,' with rapid-fire delivery. All raise their hand when called. Alison isn't amongst them. My breathing is accelerating. One of these heaving women would've been my blind date had it not been for Nancy. This thought relaxes me.

'Billy, Bob, Jamesie, Disco, Shagger ... sorry, Shug, an' Nixon.'

Dennis is on something, I'm certain of it. He is totally wired. After introducing us, he takes our jackets. I look at Nancy and wish we were somewhere else.

We get seated. Separated and in with our herds. Dennis runs around, filling glasses, lighting cigarettes and telling terrible jokes. It's funny how people with no sense of humour will laugh at everything.

Queen's Greatest Hits rattles out of a tinny CD player. I wouldn't be surprised if it's the only CD Dennis owns. All join in when 'I Want To Break Free' comes on. Their theme song, apparently. When the song finishes, Dennis turns first the music, and then the big light off.

Nancy looks at me as if she suspects we are to be ritually fucked and then brutally slaughtered as sacrifices on the green, circular shag pile rug in the middle of the singing circle. And that this is the only reason we've been invited.

—Alison Deans is an Ann Summers' party planner. I don't think Danny has twigged that yet. Marj, the woman I'm sitting beside has whispered that we all need to keep the night a secret because it was against the organisation's rules to have men invited. But Alison's doing this on her own time, so to speak. And, since, in her words, 'we're aw into it…'

I see those in front of me looking up. Over my head, towards the top of the stairs behind me. Three of the women applaud. The men wolf-whistle. Nancy's mouth is open. It's Alison Deans, *née* Currie's big entrance.

'Outdone yersel' this time, Ali,' says one of the men.

I look round slowly. Alison Currie, the girl my brother paid to fuck me when I was fifteen, is descending the stairs. She is wearing a French maid's outfit, several sizes too small, and carrying a selection of dildos, one of which is about a foot long and has the words 'Black Stallion' inscribed in white down its length.

—*I'm sure the 'it' they're all into, is each other. I'm certain they are swingers.*

An excruciating hour in, we manage to transmit a signal to each other. We meet at the upstairs toilet. When the queue is only me and her, she mouths, *Let's get the fuck out of here.* From inside the toilet, we hear one of the men. He's either offering advice to another male or psyching himself up: 'Yer a fucken lion. A lion! Now get in there amongst the pack an' take what's yours!' He growls. The door opens and he exits alone.

We rummage around the upper floor. We locate our jackets in Alison and Dennis's bedroom. A blow-up sex doll lies under the coats on the bed. There are chains and whips and masks and butt-plugs concealed under it. Denny Deans' Den of Sin.

⌒

'Jesus ... did ye see that yin take the Stallion in her mouth?' says Nancy, eyes wide at the recollection.

'Oh, aye. The Lynne Two lassie. Two thirds ae it down her throat. Ah was gaggin' after the first two inches. Fucken hell, that wis mad!'

'Not as mad as the price ae it ... a hundred quid? For a big, black rubber knob?'

'An' that guy, Disco, wis it ... see when he had that harness on an' Alison Currie wis on his back, ridin' him?'

'What kinda name is Disco, anyway?'

We're laughing so hard; tears are running down our faces.

'Well, that's a story ah won't forget in a hurry ... the night I got taken tae an Ann Summers Party on a first date.'

Nancy has admitted that this was, ludicrous as it sounds, our first date. It was worth undergoing the embarrassment of having Alison Currie describe my first sexual experiences to a bunch of braying strangers to hear Nancy say these words.

'D'ye think they've even noticed we've slipped away?'

'Ah think they'll aw be shaggin' each other senseless by now ... so, naw.'

'Have tae say, it was pretty funny when they all started singin' "Oh Danny boy" after she persuaded ye tae stick a finger inside that rubber fanny.' Nancy laughs, coughs and then hiccups.

'Serves ye right,' I say.

The rain has stopped. The King's Arms looks busy. The last Saturday before Christmas Day and it seems like the whole village is jammed into the pub. Some have even been squeezed outside. There's no chance of us getting in so I don't even raise it as an option. We keep walking. We reach the end of Higgy's street. Nancy's house is down to the left. We're at a crossroads.

—I don't want to go home. Not yet anyway. It's only ten o'clock. And I feel very relaxed; four large wine glasses' worth.

'So ... d'ye want tae come back tae Higgy's for a coffee. He'll be at Libby's.' I only think about these words once I've said them. Back to mine. Nobody home.

'Aye. That'd be nice.'

We're inside. I put the kettle on, and, as a form of comfort blanket, some music. We've left the lights off. The only illumination comes from the sodium streetlights outside. Nancy slips off her shoes and pulls the band from her hair, letting it fall over her shoulders.

'Who's this? Sounds good,' she says.

'One Dove,' I reply. Bought with an Our Price voucher Higgy gave me for my birthday two months ago. I'd already scratched *her* name into the run-off grooves.

'She's got a lovely voice.'

'Aye. The whole record's great. Here ye are.' She takes the mug. I've overfilled it and some spills on her dress. 'Jeez, ah'm sorry. Fuck sake. Don't know what's wrong wi' me.'

'It's fine. Don't worry about it,' she tells me. 'Come here an' sit down next to me.'

My heart is racing. Alcohol is probably making her less inhibited, and it would've helped me too. I'm panicking about my breath. I ate too many of those fucking cheese football things. She edges closer to me on Higgy's sofa. She leans closer still. She caresses my face and slowly turns my chin so that she can kiss me on the mouth. Her lips are warm and full and soft and lubricated by the wine, and it feels like we could stay here forever, and nothing would ever hurt me, if she just prolongs this kiss.

She takes my hand and puts it on her thigh, inviting me to slide my fingers under the hem of her dress. My cock hardens as I do this. I slip my hand to the inside of her thigh and then up until it touches her pants. I massage her through the material. Her legs open slightly, and she breaks off from kissing me to let out a little moaning sound. The needle grunts suddenly and she laughs at the surprise interruption.

'Better turn the record over,' she suggests, and I'm relieved at the opportunity to stand. My left leg was shaking and I'm sure she could feel it.

—I don't know what I'm doing. It's been so long. It's a strange experience; like I'm standing on the edge of the room, watching these two people, one of whom looks like me, but isn't me.

I take time turning the disc over, hoping it will calm me. A beguiling, beautiful voice sings and I turn around. Nancy has taken her dress off. She slips her pants down. Breathing hard, I struggle with my belt.

—He's shy and awkward, and desperately wants to do the right thing. It's endearing that he cares so much. The other guys I've been with – not that there have been that many, and certainly not in

recent years – were only interested in themselves. In their own grati-
fication. That's a real fucking turn-off.

'Here. Let me,' she says, and she undresses me like I've suddenly
become incapable.

We stand together naked, the faint orange glowing on our skin.
My cock is hard and pressed flat against her belly.

She's got a light around her; that's love.

'Have ye got condoms, Danny?' she whispers.

I mumble a response. Not wanting her to think I bought them
presumptuously for tonight, and not wanting her to think I've
had them hanging about unused for years. The truth is I bought
them in the toilets at The King's when we went there together. I
don't tell her this.

She lies down on the sofa as I get one, unwrap it and roll it on.

'Come here,' she says softly, and I lower myself between her legs.
She guides me inside her, and, in that warmth, with senses
heightened, it feels like my entire life has been a preparation for
this one moment. Nothing else matters. No-one else will ever
matter as much again. Not if I can remain here, like this, with her.

⌂

It's still dark outside. I don't know how long we've been asleep.
Lying here on Higgy's couch. Curving into each other. A warm
blanket covering around us, our sweat mixing.

'Danny, ah better go.'

I wipe my mouth, and my eyes search for some indication of
the time. 'Okay.'

She puts on her clothes with her back to me as I watch her.

'Ah'll walk you round.'

'No. It's fine. Honestly.' She says this with a formality that seems
out of place. Then she kisses my face. Her tears fall on my cheek.

'Are ye okay?'

'Ah'm fine, Danny. It's just … ah need tae go.'

I get up, the blanket still around me.

'I got you this.' I hand it to her. It's wrapped crudely in brown paper. 'Don't open it until Christmas Day.'

She looks at me strangely. Wipes her cheek.

I watch her from the front door until she's beyond the end of the street. It's 5.00 am.

—I woke up disoriented. And I felt completely vulnerable. Exposed. Out of my depth. It's hard to explain, because I like him, but all I could think of was Raymond bursting in, abusing me, battering his brother. I suddenly felt crushing guilt and shame for having cheated on him. Whether I like it or not, Raymond and I are forever linked by our son. Anytime I've tried to conceive of a future where that fact doesn't drive every decision I make, my mam finds a way to remind me of it. It's not only Raymond who's serving a sentence.

I'd just woken up and Danny called me by a different name. Louise-Anne. *It completely shook me up. It seems we're both searching for something that we've lost. And then he gives me this wee box. Something for Christmas. Knowing my bloody luck, it'll be an engagement ring and he'll turn out to be as mad and irrational as the rest of his family. I just had to get out of the house.*

I wake soaked in sweat. No-one else contributing this time though; just my own. A dream has been responsible. A vivid, depressing one, rendered in industrial black and white. I'm walking through the village, holding a trophy, looking for someone … *anyone* … to celebrate with. There's no-one to be found. Shop doors are open but everywhere is empty of people. The church bells ring but its pews are abandoned.

Balls are scattered on the pitch at The Barn, but no-one is kicking them, and I wander around this uninhabited place and I'm thinking how great it is to be alone, to be free, but after a while I yearn to talk to someone, to share the success, to talk about this new-found joy but there's no-one there, so I go to Libby's because she must be home because she can't go anywhere else, but all I find at her house is an unmade hospital bed and a substantial supply of medication, and I realise that I'm all that's left here, all that remains; so I open the brown plastic bottles and I swallow the majority of them, washing them down with a bottle of Buckfast that I find under her bed, but I don't want to die here, in her house, so I head off to the bridge, to cower under it and to disappear into some fond memory of a legendary goal, but as I walk past The King's Arms, I hear someone sneezing, and I approach the doors and I push them open, and everyone I know is crammed into the pub, including Libby, propped up in a corner, wired to a drip, and Raymond shouts 'Surprise!', and I cry at this, and I can't stop crying, because I've just fucking killed myself and it's all been for nothing.

The last doctor I saw summarised his advice thus: 'Face your fears, watch what you drink, keep yourself active.' Remarkably simple ways to fend off the blackness. Overall, it's been effective. Today, all three of his directions will need to work in tandem.

For the second time today, I'm out running. It passes the time. But doesn't do it quickly enough. I run past Nancy's house. It's the middle of the afternoon and the curtains are closed. Like a state of mourning is being observed. It's raining heavily. The village roads are deserted. Everyone is probably indoors complaining about the queen interrupting their day but watching her do it regardless. The loud, aggression of *EastEnders* being replicated in homes where too much alcohol's been taken too early; too much borrowed money has evaporated – spent on disappointing food and disregarded presents. I have no sympathy for those in such situations. I haven't had a Christmas present since I was fifteen. It matters little to me. It's a false conceit. I've always disliked Christmas. People trying too hard to conceal the people they really are, and invariably failing.

But this year, it seems worse, somehow. The only thing I receive from anyone is a phone call. Not the one I was hoping for.

'Haw … how's it goin', mucker? Merry Christmas, an' that.'

I hate you, telephone thing; listening in…

I didn't recognise the number calling me. I'm not sure how Raymond got a hold of this mobile one of mine. Higgy hasn't been to the prison recently.

'Aye, em. Fine. Happy Christmas to you tae.'

'So, what's happenin'? How's Mam?' he asks.

'Nothin' really. Just here on ma tod. Watchin' shite telly,' I tell him.

I've been sucked into more and more 'shite telly' lately, with Higgy almost permanently berthed at Libby's, waiting for the inevitable. Amazing how addictive it becomes, just because it's there, talking to me. Offering the illusion of interest. It's a lazy habit I need to quit.

'She's no' good, Raymond. It'll be anytime now.' There's a long pause during which I can hear the metallic rumble of activity and the higher-than-normal spirits of Raymond's fellow inmates in the halls around him. He sighs. I know it'll be difficult for him. Constantly pushing to get out, and public-sector bureaucracy constantly delaying it.

'Ye aw'right?' I ask. I feel like I should.

'Aye. Suppose so,' he says. 'Just hoped she could hold on a bit longer. Ah've finally got the date, Danny.' He sounds unusually helpless.

'Aye? When?' He can probably detect the tremor in my voice.

'First week in January. Supervised release terms are murder, but fuck it, ah'm done wi' aw this shite.'

'Aye. Ye said.'

'An' ah fucken meant it, tae!' He's angry. Probably not at me though.

'Okay.'

'Fuck's up wi' you?'

'Nothin'. Just been a shite few days that's all,' I say. I'm not lying either.

'How?' he asks.

'Ach ... fitba's been off.' I haven't heard from Nancy since she left early on Sunday morning. Fuck the football; that's what's *really* getting under my skin.

'Dinnae fucken gab tae me about bored, son.' Then he laughs. 'Ach, it's actually been aw'right here lately. Ah'm in the kitchens, cookin' up the Christmas dinners an' that. Tryin' tae sort out the presents an' shit.'

'What d'ye mean?' I can't disguise the surprise in my voice.

'Hey, it's no' aw about gettin' it up the fucken arse in the showers, pal ... or the screws batterin' fuck outae the Stoat-the-baw's day after day. Aw good relations mostly. We did a fucken run yesterday, hunners ae us. Dressed as Santa, raisin' money tae send weans tae Lapland.'

'Fuck off!'

'Tellin' ye. Ah fucken fell though. Twisted ma ankle. It's absolute agony. Swelled up like a bastard balloon, it is. Ah've been askin' for the doctor, but it's hard tae get tae see him. Ye need tae book it, an' it takes five or six days, it's nae use,' he mutters.

I hear someone shout for Raymond to get a move on.

'Listen, ah need ye tae dae us a big favour. Can ye nip round an' let Nancy know?'

'Know what?'

'That ah'm gettin' out! Christ's sake, Danny. Stop fucken dreamin' for a minute, eh? Ah'd want her tae come an' pick us up. She's still got the wee motor ah got her in Ernie's garage. Tell her tae be here early on the fourth. Dinnae want tae be hingin' about a Glasgow suburb straight outae fucken jail, y'know?'

'Raymond ... ah dinnae really...'

'Look, it's a bit fucken awkward cos we had a big fall-out last time she was here. Ah know she still loves us, but ah need ye tae play the peacemaker for me.'

'Right. Fine,' I say, my heart sinking right down into my bowel.

'Oh aye ... an' can ye sort out a room back at Mam's house for us? See ye, bro.'

And with that he's gone. To enjoy the comradeship of others, a three-course Barlinnie Christmas dinner – plastic cutlery, plastic plates – and gifts of tobacco or bags of coffee that his fellow inmates have swapped with each other to manufacture some good-will. I'm left contemplating the misery of life with him back on the outside. Merry fucking Christmas!

The rain has intensified. The short distance from Higgy's place to Libby's house offers no shelter. I'm walking – not running, since I have no desire to get there quicker – into the teeth of it, and I'm soaked through by the time Higgy opens the door.

'Aw'right, son?' His face is blotched and red. I can see he's been crying. 'Happy Christmas.' He holds out a hand to shake mine.

'Aye, same tae you.'

'In ye come. Wisnae sure when ye'd show. Huvnae put the dinner on.'

I drop my jacket on the stairs. Water drips off it. I go through to the kitchen and dry my hair with a dish towel. Higgy follows me.

'How's she been?' I ask.

'Ach, y'know...' he says. I don't enquire further. 'Ye hungry?'

I shrug. There's a couple of cold meat pies lying out.

'No' that bothered, really,' I say.

'Aye, me neither,' he says.

Christmas Day and none of us in this house can eat, to celebrate what we are conditioned to believe is the happiest day of the year. It may well be if you are rich enough to have options – to have alternatives to the imprisonment of each other's company.

Libby is mumbling something incoherent. She's in a morphine haze these days, as opposed to the Valium and alcohol ones of my teenage years. Hard not to think of the times when she had different types of tubes forced down into her stomach to pump out a poison that was self-inflicted. No such easy remedies this time.

She has lifted the mask up onto her forehead. Her eyes are open, and they look clearer than they have for some time.

'Raymond ... get yer ma the papers, will ye, son. There's a good boy.' She's looking at me. It's disconcerting.

'She's away wi' the fairies, Danny,' says Higgy. 'Aw the time, now.'

'Aye, okay, Mam. Ah'll just get ye them,' I say.

Her hand has reached over to mine without me even noticing the movement. The feel of it unsettles me, as if she's already dead and I'm touching her skin for the last time before the coffin lid is screwed down.

'Ah'm convinced she's hangin' on. Clingin' tae life just tae see her boy one last time,' says Higgy. He won't be saying this to hurt me. Raymond was always 'her boy'. I never came close. I accepted it over a decade ago. And Higgy may well be right. She's already on borrowed time, according to the nursing staff.

I tell Higgy Raymond's release date, and he sobs.

'Ah bloody hell, they couldnae just let him go now? Where's their fucken compassion.'

'Paperwork, apparently,' I tell him. 'It's the holiday season. Naebody around tae sanction it any earlier.' I don't know if this is true or not. I don't really care either.

Higgy wipes his face, probably embarrassed at me seeing him crying. 'Dae ye want some tea, an' a bit ae roasted cheese?' It's an excuse to be on his own for a couple of minutes.

'Aye. Go on then. Thanks.' It'll be the first thing I've eaten today, since the handful of cornflakes that lined my stomach for the first of the two runs.

The telly is turned down low. To reinforce the sense of unreality, Del Boy and Rodney are dressed up as Batman and Robin, for some reason.

Libby turns her head. 'Danny, son ... yer mammy loves ye.' Faintly, but clearly heard. This rocks me. I can't be sure if it's the younger me, or the me now that she thinks she's talking to. 'Mind an' stick in at the school. Dae whit yer uncle Peter tells ye, okay? Ah've kept aw yer things here for ye. In yer box.'

Higgy comes back through at this point. Carrying a tray with mugs and a plate on it. And we're both crying. Libby's eyes are closed. Her breathing is calmer. She seems content.

We sit silently watching telly, unable to hear it. Eating a Christmas Day dinner of roasted cheese. It's ten o'clock at night, and it feels like all three of us are slowly dying.

Sitting on the bed, there are so many things about the room that I've never noticed before. I was rarely in it, even in the early seventies, when Raymond and I officially lived here. This room was his room. My room was *our* room. Nonetheless, little has changed. A board with a punching ball on a flexible stick. A broken lamp shade. A poster of AC/DC. The sharpness of the sloped ceiling either side of the projecting dormer window that now I have to twist my body to avoid. A chewed skirting board where a mouse – or something bigger – seems to have made an escape route back into the relative safety of the roof space. A cupboard behind the entrance to the room that I can't even recall having seen before.

The cupboard door is locked, but the key is dangling from a shoelace looped around the handle, inviting someone to investigate its contents. The majority of these are stacked newspapers. Quite why Libby felt compelled to keep something as immediately redundant as news is beyond me. There are some boxed toys, black polythene bags full of musty-smelling clothes and a rolled-up rug. In the back corner of the cupboard, hidden under the piled-up papers, I find a box. It's heavily taped. Turning it around and over I discover my name written on its base.

The box contains a history of my younger life. The one I left behind before Aberdeen. Newspaper clippings reporting football matches I played in. Football cards that I valued. Kenny Dalglish, Andy Gray, Pat Stanton. The Scottish Football League ladders with club tabs that I adjusted regularly throughout the seasons whilst listening to *Final Score*. Copies of *Shoot!* magazine that Raymond once told me Libby had binned. A soft, airless football I was allowed to keep for scoring a hat-trick in a Schools Cup final. My Scotland Schools caps. The Barshaw v Auchinleck match programme from the cup semi-final with my name in the team sheet circled in red ink. A sheaf of football programmes. My football programmes. The ones that I was certain Raymond had sold. And the green primary-school banner that used to be pinned to the ceiling above my bed. My banner, with my name on it. Going back further, a spidery drawing from primary one with a silver star and a big, blue biro tick. From before *she* disappeared.

Standing up, and pressing my wet face to the window, I see the roof of Nancy's house is visible in the distance over to the right. An upper bedroom light is on. I'm not sure if it's her room, but I spend a sleepless night sitting uncomfortably on a small, wooden chair, staring at it, convinced that it is.

My brother's coming home to be with her, and their son. The easiest thing for everybody would be for me to disappear back into the north-eastern haar from whence I've come.

＾

I was desperate. I phoned Anne Macdonald. She came over and we sat in her wee purple car at the bottom of the road, and I poured my heart out. Told her of my painful dilemma. She gives good advice, does Anne. She always has done.

I left a message with Doreen that I needed to see her daughter. Doreen said she'd pass it on, although her reluctance to do so couldn't be disguised. But she kept to her word. And now, here we are.

We haven't spoken since that night over a week ago. We're up at The Barn. Sitting on a damp bench that we've sat on before. Damo isn't away in the distance this time though, distracting us, going up and down the banking repeatedly on his bike. This is a conversation for grown-ups, with grown-up issues to be addressed.

'How've ye been?' I ask her.

'Fine,' she replies. There's no real conviction to the response and I don't know what to read into it.

'The wee man have a good time then?'

'Aye. He did. Helped that he didnae have to go tae the school the week before, I think.'

'Hmm.'

We're dancing around it, but she must be regretting staying with me that Saturday night. Otherwise, she'd have called. She'd have got in touch. But she didn't, and it can only be because avoiding it might make it go away.

'How's yer mam?'

'Ach, she's done,' I reply. 'Ah'm sure it's only waitin' for Raymond comin' home that's keepin' her goin'.' I notice her head drop at the mention of this, but I don't turn to face her. I'm worried that I'd embarrass myself if I did. 'Actually, that's why I wanted tae see ye. He phoned on Christmas Day. He's got his release date. He asked if ye would pick him up fae Barlinnie.'

She sighs. 'What's the date?'

'Fourth ae January. He thinks it'll be about three in the afternoon or that.' Minutes of silence pass and I don't know what to add. Happy New Year to us.

—He made this mix tape for me. When I opened it, it reminded me of school discos and snogging boys and the dreams of doing something with my life … nursing maybe. He wrote a wee message inside the cover that made me cry. It was the sweetest thing. He wrapped it up and gave it to me for Christmas and it was perfect. I didn't know most of the songs, but I've just about worn out the tape listening to

them. Looking for things in the lyrics ... messages in his song choices that tell me what to do with my life. How to move on from this static compromise it has become.

But I can't just snap my fingers. I cried listening to the songs because those dreams are gone. I'm barely thirty and the course is set. I cried to mourn the girl that returned for one night at that party before Christmas. I cried knowing that was the last I'd see of her. And also, because I felt like I had led Danny on. And that was unforgivable. He's naïve and impressionable and vulnerable, and I knew all that before I even met him.

'Danny...' She reaches out and touches my arm. 'Danny, that night we had ... it wis lovely. Really.' She turns and I'm still not looking at her. Still trying to conceal the pain I'm experiencing. 'Danny, look at me.' She's saying this softly and compassionately, and I know it's merely a prelude to letting me down. I've heard this tone so many times before. 'That Saturday was just a...' She doesn't finish. 'It was great tae no' have tae think about Damo's problems, or about ma mam on my back day an' night ... or that Raymond's comin' home now, an' he'll be expectin' us just tae pick up where we left off.' Home; that fundamental concept that I have no understanding of.

—God, this is so difficult. How could I have been so stupid?

'He's the one doin' the time, Nancy ... no' you!'

'Really? You think that's the case?' She isn't angry. Isn't aggrieved. It's worse than that, she is submissive. Suffocating. Exhausted from the effort.

'Why are ye settlin' for this ... this fucken brutal unhappiness?' That was a bit unfair, I concede.

—If Raymond and I had the opportunity to start again, to wipe the slate clean, to learn from our mistakes, without any compromises or collateral damage ... would I want that? Or is the masochistic

comfort we find in the familiar just too powerful? I loved him once.
Time will tell. I convinced myself that the practical constraints, such
as lack of money or somewhere better for me and Damo to go, were
the things holding me back, not Raymond. My mam stayed far too
long in an abusive relationship for those same reasons.

'What am ah supposed tae do here?' she says. 'Everywhere ah turn,
ah'm trapped.'

I have no answer. She knows it. She's merely hanging on in quiet
desperation.

'Ah loved the tape.' The subject has been changed. 'Those songs
are really, really beautiful. Thanks Danny. Ah really mean that,
but...' She tails off. It's a conclusion. She kisses my cheek. She
stands, the paper with a time, date and location on it is in her
hand. We're done.

⌒

The morning of Raymond's release and, miraculously, Libby is
still here. Lucidity has long since left the building. She merely
exists. A collection of automatic motor functions, running out
of fuel. Something deep inside her draws the breath in and then
forces it back out. The gentle, almost undetectable rise and fall
of her bony chest now the only physical indication of life.
Medical people are struggling to hide their astonishment. *She's a*
real fighter, they've been telling Higgy for over a month. I ac-
knowledge my detachment. I find her determination to cling to
life strange, especially if it's only the promise of Raymond coming
home that's sustaining her. From my perspective it's not a life
that's been particularly rewarding. Happiness always seemed
fleeting, just out of her grasp.

It's late afternoon. Another miserable wet day. We're at the
house. Waiting for him. The prodigal. The car draws up. The same
one Raymond proudly described when I visited him in prison. It's

been in a lock-up for over a year, Nancy told me. Its suspicious origin was one of the reasons she and Raymond had argued.

She gets out. Alone. I meet her at the door. My open arms and outstretched palms asking *where the fuck is he?*

'Danny, he wisnae there. He'd gone already.'

'This what yer settlin' for, Nancy?' I say; words of spite and intended to hurt.

She glares at me. She turns and leaves, and I wish I hadn't said them. I go back inside and break the news to Higgy.

It's 7.15 pm. A car door closes outside.

Higgy gazes through the slots in the blind. 'It's him,' he says. 'Rocco Quinn's just dropped him off.'

The door opens. Raymond comes in quietly. The beard's back. He gives me the death stare as if all of this is my fault. It's a look I've come to know well. I'm about to get a mouthful but he catches his breath when he sees his mother; tiny in an oversized bed. Tubes and wires and drips and cables and bags.

'Aw ... fuck, Mam!' He drops his bags and falls to his knees at the side of her bed. Wailing into the mattress. Holding her fragile hand. Kissing it. Higgy puts an arm on his head, brushing his long, lank hair to one side. I pick up my jacket. Looking back at them, in the dim light, they are like the dark, despairing figures in a Caravaggio painting. I leave them to it.

🔨

Libby died early the following morning. The time of death recorded by a local on-call doctor as 2.50 am, although Higgy said it was about an hour earlier. He's here now to tell me we should be cancelling today's match. It's the first game of the new year. We haven't played for over two weeks. I tell him that I wouldn't be able to get in touch with the management, the players, the officials at this late stage, but in truth, I want the game to go ahead. It's me that craves the distraction – not to have to sit with my brother, watching his fake grief and remorse grow out of all drunken, self-pitying proportion. The funeral will be bad enough.

We arrive at Lugar. The memories of our league opener have not faded. There is aggression in the air. The players and management of both clubs are forced to navigate a narrow lane to reach the clubhouse. Pushing, shoving, swearing, spitting; a portent of the ninety minutes ahead.

'Kick-off's goin' tae be delayed a wee bit, lads,' admits the ref as he comes in to check the studs. 'Fifteen … twenty minutes, tops,' he says. He offers no further explanation, and both teams seem even more aggravated.

Ten minutes in and an inconspicuous Smith tackle sees the entire Lugar team, and several of their management, hound the referee into awarding the softest of penalties, which they score from. I'm already writing this game off, merely hoping that we get out of it with no more injuries. We're in fourth place in the league. Our progress is already beyond Billy the Kidd's wildest expectations.

Half-time comes and there have been eleven bookings: six for the home team, and in an obvious attempt at self-preservation, five for us. Gilmour is kicked on the calf as he enters the changing room, and it makes my mind up to take him off. He isn't complaining. Andy Meikle, our least-used player this season, goes on in his place.

Mid-half, Lorimer can't continue. He's been head-butted.

'Haw, Ref … look at this cunt. Send this yin off!' shouts the aggressor. The ref turns to see deep-red blood streaming from Lorimer's mouth. 'The filthy wee bastard's just fucken eaten our right winger!' There's no action taken by the man in the middle.

With the reluctance of a tired child getting dragged around a DIY store, I get stripped. It is perhaps typical of the downward spiral of the last fortnight that I'd end up returning to reluctant action in this one.

I've been on the pitch for fifteen minutes and in that time, I've been elbowed in the face, spat at (twice) and had my balls squeezed painfully at a corner. Miraculously, we're still only one down, but then again there's little obvious interest in the ball; it's just another incidental victim caught up in the maelstrom.

With ten minutes remaining a penalty-box mix-up at the back sees the Lugar defenders crash into each other, taking out the advancing goalie in the process. The ball breaks to Andy Meikle. He swings a left at it, mishits it and it trundles under the keeper's diving body. Had Andy connected properly, the goalkeeper would almost certainly have blocked it.

Lugar Boswell Thistle 1-1 Barshaw Bridge
(Meikle)

Bedlam breaks out. The Lugar manager advances across the pitch towards me, bull-necked and veins bulging. I imagine Raymond in a tracksuit, smirking. My fists clench. Readying myself for a battering but determined to go down swinging. I get in one jab to the four of his, before the sirens sound. The police cars drive straight onto the pitch.

Match abandoned.

We are locked in the dressing room waiting for the cops to clear the scene.

Four

Raymond

Billy the Kidd is a decent man. Seven months after he first made it, the offer of the suit still stands. And some financial assistance with the funeral. He told me this during a phone call to commiserate about Libby, and to inform me that the club will be taking no disciplinary action against me, regardless of what the SFA ultimately decide. That was two days ago. Today, I'm standing in the suit. Raymond needs the other one. It is his after all.

The arrangements have been hastily cobbled together, as befits the dysfunction that gels us together. A brief service in the funeral parlour in Cumnock, conducted by a man we've hired for as little money as possible. Then a burial on the edge of Barshaw, because Raymond wants somewhere for Damo to visit. Her condition was terminal for nearly a year, but none of us thought to ask what she wanted for her death. Raymond has used this against Higgy and me. Opening salvos in the war of accountability.

—There's an anger building inside me. It's hard to explain to somebody who's never been inside. It needs a release and all the wanking in the world isn't going to put a lid on it. Prison's a fucking pressure cooker, man. It's why so many end up straight back in there. You get conditioned to it. Once you're out it's just too hard to adjust to normal people and normal stresses. It overwhelms you and the smallest, simplest, most insignificant thing can trigger a reaction.

We sit in the front row, but on opposite sides of the aisle. Raymond to one side, with Nancy, Doreen and Damo in the row behind him.

The boy looks scared. Scared of the beard. Higgy is alongside me on the other. We didn't plan for it to be this way. We were late. Everyone else was seated. There's ten of us here. Two of the Marie Curie Community nurses who looked after Libby, and Billy the Kidd and his wife, representing the club and the players. He nods respectfully towards me and reaches out a hand to a distraught Higgy.

I learn nothing new about my mother from the service. Unsurprising, since we provided the content. *She was a Barshaw woman, born and bred. Fond of a night out. Never married, but a happy person, generous and fiercely proud of her two boys, Raymond and Daniel, whom she brought up in her own image.* Higgy gets a mention in despatches. But we just didn't know how to properly capture his role in her life: Confidante? Counsellor? Concubine?

I hate you telephone thing; listening in.

It vibrates in my pocket. And then it rings. I don't know how to turn it down or off. Raymond is enraged. He leaps across and grabs it from me before I can see the name or number. Probably Anne Macdonald, the only one I have listed in the contacts, so frequent have our recent chats become. I mumble an apology to the minister and bow my head as if he was the Pope.

—Something's up. I can tell. Something much deeper. Way beyond this. I've always been able to tell with Danny. His moods, the dark periods that fucking swamp him, and then start drowning everybody else. The clues are the short, clipped answers. They precede the silence. And that's usually the calm before the fucking storm, man; the point where I usually end up taking a fall for him.

Damo spends the fifteen minutes of the service waving at me. His mother takes him out as 'All Things Bright and Beautiful' starts up, after he takes the opening bars as his cue to yell his name repeatedly at the top of his voice. The minister thanks the Marie Curie nurses, alerts us to their donation box at the entrance vestibule, and invites us to the committal service at Barshaw Cemetery.

We stand at the imposing wooden doors, the three of us, shaking the few hands there are to shake. I see my brother observe the one belonging to Billy the Kidd drop a fifty into the donation box. There's no way that'll make its way to its intended beneficiaries.

The formalities concluded, it's just the three of us and Nancy in the rain at the graveside. We don't speak. The temperature is rising. It seems inevitable that Raymond will explode at some time. I can only hope Nancy's not there when he does.

A taxi ferries Higgy and me back to The King's Arms. Nancy and Raymond take the car, with her driving. A lift isn't offered, nor is it requested. Space is what's needed here. But space isn't something a small village affords. There's one in the ground and one out of prison. Its population has evened itself out. But the village still feels suddenly unbearably claustrophobic.

—*Those silences; they'd last for weeks on end. Months, sometimes. You never ever knew what Danny was thinking. It got a bit fucking creepy, to be honest with you. Then when he did come out of it, he'd create his own version of whatever events had caused it. That wee lassie getting taken – that was the trigger. I was only about eleven or twelve myself, but I remember it like it was yesterday. Her name was everywhere – on posters, on the front pages of local papers. It was as if she was the centre of everybody's attention and Danny couldn't cope with it somehow. I remember just after it happened, he fucking vanished. Must've been for about two days. Christ, everybody thought they'd both been abducted. Turns out Danny's hiding under the bloody Barshaw Bridge. 'Ah want to be like Louise-Anne,' he says to Libby. She went daft at him. I fucking leathered him, and he didn't speak to anyone for about a year. I'm this close to doing it again.*

'Through the back there, lads,' says Alf. 'Sorry for yer loss. First drink's on the house.'

'Cheers, Alf,' I respond.

Higgy hasn't spoken a word in my presence since the day began. We go through to the small back room. Bench seating encircles the pool table that dominates the space. A dartboard hangs at the head of the table. You have to stand at one end of the table and throw the arrows over it. The baize is pock-marked and rutted as a result. Alf has put us in here because he knew our numbers would be low. No point infecting the rest of the pub with our grief.

—I'm angry. And, I think, with justification, that I asked Danny to do one fucking thing for me and he couldn't even get that right. There's fuck all sorted for her funeral. Nothing arranged that wasn't done at the last minute. She knew she was dying. So did they. For the best part of a fucking year, too. Higgy, I can understand to an extent … He's probably been in denial about the whole terminal diagnosis. But Danny? The whole point of getting him back here was to look after her in her last months. But you could count the times he saw her on the fingers of one hand. He's a selfish wee cunt. I don't care what he says to the contrary … that's the fucking truth of it. That bastard phone going off in the parlour put the tin lid on it. I was fit to be tied when that happened.

The spread is meagre. Two small trays of cold sausage rolls and white-bread ham sandwiches with curled-up hardening crusts. They won't be eaten. Scud Meikle will be grateful for them later. The sparseness of the reception for his dead mother is Raymond's route in.

'Fucken scandal, this,' he says. 'A last supper? Fuck sake!'

'Raymond,' says Nancy.

I look up when she says it. She looks at me. Higgy is oblivious to it all.

'Whit?' Raymond replies. 'It's a fucken disgrace, this.' He spits, and I get a whiff of his whisky breath. I could condone my brother's grief and need for drunken oblivion if it was genuine.

But it isn't. 'You two cunts ... eh? Couldnae have fucken honoured her better than this?' The rage is surging through him. There will be violence. Fuck him, I hope there is. I hope there's enough that he breaches whatever restrictions he's under and the cunt's put back inside. I don't tell him this; of course I don't. But it's what I'm thinking. It's probably what we're all thinking.

'What d'ye mean by that?' I say. I'm scared but I'm determined not to sit here in silence.

'Dae ah need tae say it again, like?' His fists are balling. Nancy is trying to pull him back. Stopping him from getting up. 'Ah wis fucken banged up, in case you two pricks hadnae noticed. Bit fucken difficult tae sort out a funeral do fae inside Barlinnie. But you ... Jock fucken Stein ... you've got the time an' the money. Ye just didnae fucken care enough.' He reaches into a pocket and for a minute I imagine a gun coming out, the urgency of his release-day visit to Rocco Quinn's place finally explained. But he has a brown paper bag in his hand. He unscrews the quarter bottle and gulps it down, wiping a wet, scabby mouth on the sleeve of his suit jacket. Nancy's eyes plead with me to stay silent. To let him get this out. To let it blow over. But I can't.

'Fuck off, Raymond. Ye couldnae even head straight tae the house tae see her dyin'.'

'Whit d'you say tae me, ya wee cunt?' He's up now, boxer stance. Weight on the front foot.

'Away tae sort out business wi' Rocco Quinn, was it? That yer priority?'

'You gave her the wrong fucken pick-up time, ya stupid cunt! Ah had tae get a lift fae Rocco Quinn. How the fuck else was ah meant tae get back, eh?'

—*He's a devious little bastard. He always has been. He twists situations and, more often than not, I take the hit for it. But he's picked the wrong day for it this time.*

'Don't gie us the martyr shite, ah'm fucken sick ae hearin' it. My whole life ... *poor Raymond*. Poor Raymond, fuck all!' I say these words as calmly as I can. Hoping that he'll hit me.

'Boys ... *please*,' says Higgy. The sad old bastard is crying. His heart breaking.

Raymond leans in further and I'm forced onto my feet, back against the wall. Head against the dartboard.

'Ye got a point, son? Fucken come ahead wi' it, then!'

'Raymond, that's enough!' shouts Nancy.

'Everythin' that's happened tae you, ye've done tae yerself. Libby always covered it up. Could never accept that anythin' was actually your fault ... even when the house got done wi' her inside it. Aw down tae you!' That should do it.

He headbutts me. My nose bursts and the crimson spurts down my face, into my mouth, before spilling onto my white shirt. The pain is a release. Higgy is rocking back and forth now, wailing.

Nancy yells.

'Yer usin' her death tae get back at me, that it, ya heartless wee cunt?' He spits this at me. 'An' wi' everythin' you've got tae hide, tae!'

—I always promised my mam I'd never bring any of it up: the truth about the stabbing, him taunting that poor old cunt to the point of him being sectioned, then fucking hitting him with that bloody motor. Even when I went inside, I honoured that fucking promise. But she's gone now. Why am I still protecting him?

'Why the fuck should ah care ... she never cared about me!' I shout at him through swallows of blood. I'm goading him. He draws a boxer's arm back, but Nancy is clinging to it. Doing her best at restraint. He relaxes the arm. He adopts a different approach.

—All his life, I've done this. Looked out for him. Shielded him from

the wee cunts that bullied him. From the reckless things he did. From himself. From the truth. Well, no more, Danny boy, no fucking more!

'Yer right,' shouts Raymond, into my face. 'She never cared. She fucken hated ye.' His saliva hits my cheek. 'She wis raped an' you were the result. A constant fucken reminder ae the worst thing that ever happened tae her. Shoulda fucken aborted ye, but naw … that auld fucken clown there…'

He turns and spits at Higgy, who is making these strange moo-ing sounds. Just like the ones Scud Meikle made after my brother stabbed him. Not for the first time in my life, I'm speechless. I don't know what to say. I can feel the weight of the air descending. The room's getting smaller, like the ceiling and the walls are all slowly closing in, and they are going to keep going until they crush us all. Maybe it's what we deserve; this fucked-up collection of condemned souls.

—I didn't really mean this. But, hey, I'm not fucking perfect either. He just pushed me too far. He always has. He hasn't lost that uncanny fucking ability to wind me up to the point where I batter somebody. And I have to deal with all the consequences.

My drunken brother is interrupted by Alf, the pub landlord. He's holding a baseball bat.

'Get the fuck out, son … or it's the polis. Dinnae really think ye want that, eh?'

Raymond weighs this up. I'm sure part of him is thinking, *fuck it, freedom's fucken overrated anyway*. I sit here wishing he is.

He has a dart in his hand. I'm willing him to drive it into my skull. But he drops it. Nancy drags him away. Through the door and outside. I'm shaking my head, as if doing so will make all this go away.

The heavy air's being sucked up and out through the vents in the wall. I sense the room slowly returning to normal. And then it's suddenly quiet. I'm left with Peter Higgins. The man with all the answers. But I don't have any questions. I know from the crumpled shell in front of me that it's the truth. I silently stare at him – my saviour — shocked, contemptuous and, yes, maybe even a little relieved. I grew up believing my mother hated me for no reason. At least now I understand.

'It wisnae like that, son,' Higgy burbles through the tears and snot. He can't – or won't – look at me. 'Yer mam loved ye. She *did*. She wanted ye tae make a life away fae here, no' because she didnae want ye, Danny. But because she was ashamed ae herself, no' you.' He's pleading on behalf of the deceased, but I sense that these are his feelings, not hers.

'Yer a fucken snake, Higgy,' I yell. It stuns him and he looks up pained, as if jabbed by a cattle-prod. 'Did ye see a wee ready-made *Bisto* family there, eh? Libby, you an' yer two weans? Spotted yer chance, did ye? Couldnae compete wi' Eddie fucken McAvoy, but an anonymous fucken rapist ... that's a competition that even a borin' cunt like you could win! *Dinnae flush him doon the lavvy, hen. We'll keep him an' ah'll be his da!* Wis that it?' And at the end of this, I'm crying too. The rage within me is all-consuming.

This – like many things I've said to him throughout my life – was nasty and spiteful. I'm not a bad person. I don't lean towards cruelty the way my brother does. But I've damaged him. Higgy is a broken man. His words eventually coalesce into a torrent of unintelligible gibberish. And I leave him to it; the mourning and the malt, the whining and the whisky.

Anne Macdonald picks me up on the road out of Barshaw. It seems odd that she won't ever come to Higgy's house for me. She always makes me take the fifteen-minute walk.

She isn't on good form. I can immediately tell. Something seems to be on her mind. There's an edginess I haven't previously detected. Even her driving seems more measured. More careful. Like she's preoccupied. There's no music today, thankfully. Those impressive speakers are asleep. This near-constant run of head-aches may yet dissipate.

'Everythin' okay?' I ask.

Yeah. Why wouldn't it be?

'It's just … ye seem a bit tense.'

It's nothing, she replies. Then adds, *Nothing important.*

A few minutes pass, before she sighs and admits, *I fell out with Joe. Over nothing, really.*

'Oh. Right,' I say, not sure whether I should inquire further about something that's apparently nothing.

Joe, she has previously informed me, is her boyfriend. They met at a club in Glasgow. Mutual instant attraction, she claimed. Billy the Kidd loves him. Loves the connections that Joe's family offer. They are food distributors, supplying the best hotels and restaurants in Scotland.

Joe's father, it transpires, created the hugely beneficial opening with the Texas-based Lavery Hotel Group that our short-notice marketing trip today is helping to reinforce.

She turns her head. Her look invites the question.

'Want tae talk about it?' I offer. It'll be a distraction.

With you? This is said in surprise, not with any aggression. As if she thinks I wouldn't be interested. But I am. I have my own emotional battlefield. It'd be nice to focus on someone else's for a change.

'Well, aye. Why no'?'

She sighs again. Her professional demeanour is founded on am-bition, control and drive, of trusting her business instincts. Now, confronted with the unpredictability of a close relationship, she suddenly seems much younger. Unsure of herself. Something I can identify with.

We've reached this point – I've reached this point – where I need a bigger challenge. You were right about me not really fitting in with

Billy's company. He's working hard to elevate it, but when all's said and done, it's a small local business that doesn't really need full-time legal representation. And it's really difficult for a woman to be taken seriously in a closed business community when her father is her boss.

She leaves a gap. Offers me the opportunity to comment. But I don't. I'd rather listen. Understand.

I've had an offer. A big law firm in Edinburgh. My eyebrows rise. *It's a great opportunity for me. And the job is in an area of corporate law I specialise in.*

'Edinburgh's no' that far,' I remark, thinking I've understood the root of the issue with Joe, given that it isn't so far removed from my own.

The job's based in London. Full-time.

'Ah. I see. An' Joe isn't pleased about that?'

No. He isn't. Anne Macdonald pulls the car over into a lay-by at the top of the Electric Brae. We're not alone. Numerous other cars – mostly filled with excited kids – are experiencing this weird natural phenomenon. The optical illusion of seeming to move forwards when actually going backwards. A sensation we both recognise.

'Well, that's a big deal,' I say. 'That's no' fallin' out over nothin'.'

No. You're right, I don't suppose it is.

A gull lands on a waste bin next to the car. It stares us out, expecting us to drop food out of the window just like everyone else in the lay-by. It waits, defiantly.

We're at a crossroads, she says, and it could be said of almost everything in my complicated life. She's speaking for both of us. *We can't conduct a long-distance relationship. Life just isn't like that anymore. I'm having to choose between my career or him.*

'What would you feel if he'd been the one havin' tae go?'

She pauses, reflecting. Like it's a perspective she hasn't considered.

I'd want him to take the opportunity. I wouldn't want to be responsible for him giving up on his dreams. Settling for something less.

But it's different for him. He'll inherit his dad's business. He already
has all he wants. When I told him about the job offer, his reaction
was to ask me to marry him.

'Fuck sake,' I splutter. 'That sounds well thought-out!'

I then spend half an hour telling her about my own situation;
the heart-tugging similarities, if not the shared financial circumstances. But I suspect she isn't really listening. Isn't completely
paying attention. The gull shites on the windscreen.

She smiles, and then laughs.

She's made a good life for herself, has Louise-Anne Macdonald.
She has choices. She might not see that right now, in the midst of
this personal dilemma. But there's no doubt it's a better life than
she would've had. Stuck in Barshaw, existing. Unappreciated, just
like the rest of us. I'm pleased for her.

We arrive at the Texan billionaire's hotel. All talked out.
Neither of us in the right frame of mind for PR showboating.

And we leave in silence too. We don't speak on the journey back
to Barshaw. We don't talk about the meeting in a luxury hotel with
its new American owner and his representatives. We don't
mention the positive discussions about next season's club sponsorship. We don't make any reference to the wandering hands of
the Texan businessman's son – that touched her arse as the staged
photographs were being taken. And we don't say anything about
the fight I got into trying to defend her.

She wants there to be no mention of this. Ever. She drops me
off in Cumnock and drives away without any further acknowledgement.

The library is quieter than usual. I'm told that the opening hours
have been reduced. Local Authority funding has been redirected.
Edna, the librarian with whom I've developed a first-name-terms
relationship, is surprised I haven't read about it.

'Council cutbacks,' she says, middle-class politeness masking righteous anger. 'Nobody values peace an' quiet an' the time to reflect anymore. Books are becoming redundant, Danny, now they've got the internet.'

The library will close soon. Not just for the day. For good. Crawford Cramond, the councillor who once had eyes on The Barn, has decreed it. It'll finally be off the council's estates maintenance bill. It'll become a betting shop, or a fucking McDonalds, or a mobile-phone emporium. A response to society's acceptable addictions. She goes into a backroom to make tea for us. I get up and start ripping the final chapters out of hardback books in the biography section. It matters little now, I suspect. These unimportant stories of self-indulgence will get pulped. Nothing surer. And if people don't already know that Anne Frank died at the end, then they shouldn't be allowed near a library in the first place.

Beyond my sadness for Edna, and disdain for the hypocrisy of a few small-minded capitalist councillors, it matters little. My twin research projects that were born here are now all but complete.

Other things are also ending. We have a handful of league games left. If we lose them all, we'll still finish fifth. We're ninety minutes away from a regional cup final, and the committee have sanctioned decent bonus incentives. The club is suddenly awash with positivity, but I can't share the satisfaction with the person to whom it should mean the most.

These conflicting feelings. These fucking headaches. I'm suddenly ashamed of how I always blamed Libby for her indifference towards me. Higgy may have persuaded her not to abort me, but I've accused him of doing that for his own ends.

The day after the funeral, a note with my name on it was propped up against the salt cellar on Higgy's table. In it, he tried to explain. Libby had made Higgy promise never to tell me, but in a moment of weakness, months ago, he'd spilled it to Raymond during a prison visit. He was merely looking for guidance – did Raymond think Libby would want me to know before she passed away? The only surprise here was that my brother had kept this secret. Maybe only until the time when it could have maximum impact, though. Had the roles been reversed, I suppose it's what I'd have done too.

The box of my things in the upstairs bedroom was Libby's project. A hidden collection of achievements that encapsulated her pride in me and allowed her to bury the remorse she felt for having wished me gone before she had even met me. And the truth of the banner? Who can really tell? But I now suspect Raymond threw it out, blamed Libby and then took my pocket money from me in return for 'saving' it. Higgy's note concluded with him forgiving me for what I'd said to him in the back room of the pub, and pleading for my forgiveness in return.

Since Higgy reinforced Raymond's truth about Libby, I can't look him in the eye. He fucking betrayed me, after all. I couldn't forgive that. But weeks have passed and now, he's all I've got. I don't know what to do around him. Higgy's stopped coming to the games. Stopped being a part of the thing he loves most in the world. Stopped being in his own house when I'm there. He spends his time in The King's Arms. The one place he's unlikely to en-counter me – the ghost in the machine. Doreen brings Damo to our matches now. She sells the hot food from the van and Damo stands by me. I'm currently serving a ban for 'aggressive behaviour' during a recent game at Whitletts, so Harry Doyle has taken a more active role on the touchline. And it seems that I'm banned from seeing Nancy too. We're all just getting along by not getting on.

I'm ashamed of the things I've been put through. I'm ashamed of the person I am.

But Higgy and I are here now. His money is running low and the pub is no longer an option until giro day. We navigate his small house, avoiding each other as much as possible. I want to tell him that I'm sorry for his pain, and for making it worse. That I love him; that Libby was so very lucky to have him in her life. But I can't. I can only hope *she* told him this.

We draw three-all against Annbank in a blustery, rain-soaked evening match at The Barn. Billy Gilmour scores a hat-trick but gives the match ball to Damo. I haven't the heart to tell my young player that we'll need to get it back as the club budget doesn't stretch to brand-new footballs. But it does give me an excuse to speak to Nancy, if she'll see me. I leave it a couple of days, repeating the words I'll use like an actor heading for an audition that might change his future.

'Hi. Ah was hopin' ye'd have waited the other night.' In the dress rehearsals, *Ah've missed ye* was the opening gambit. In the moment, though, it didn't feel right.

'Danny, it's difficult, y'know?' There's no hostility. Just weariness.

'Aye. Ah get that. Have ye seen Raymond recently?' I ask her.

'No. He went off the rails a while back an' Damo was really upset. My mam threatened tae phone the police if he didnae go. He's away back tae Galston now.'

We're back sitting on the same bench. If we'd been teenagers, we might've carved our initials into it after the night at Alison Currie's house.

'That whole thing wi' Raymond ... ah should've acted differently,' she admits.

'Nancy—'

'No ... let me finish, Danny. Ah need tae say this.' She sighs deeply. There's a weight to get rid of. 'There's a deep connection, ah can't deny it. More than just Damo. For years ah felt that I was the only thing that could save Raymond fae himself. That if I abandoned him, he'd be finished. But there were too many excuses ... too many times pleadin' for forgiveness for some bloody stupid avoidable trouble he'd got himself intae. An' ah couldn't stand ma mam's holier-than-thou attitude. Ah know she meant well, but she was just desperate tae tell me that she'd been right about him all along.'

I lift her chin with my hand. She's crying. She wipes her tears.

'Raymond's like a drug. Excitin', an' a rush at first, but then ye know the more ye see him, the more ye know he's goin' tae leave you wi' nothin', an' probably even kill ye.'

I'm not here to talk about Raymond. I came to find a way back to Nancy. Her son is the route. He's all I've got to negotiate with.

'Listen, Nancy, ah didnae want tae overstep any marks, here, but ah've been lookin' up some things. About Damo's...' I stop myself from adding 'condition', although that's what I think it is. 'Some studies ae kids wi' similar behaviour patterns ... that are similar tae Damo's, ah mean.' I'm treading warily here. Aware of the very thin ice that I'm standing on. I wait for her to close the conversation down as she has done many times before. But she doesn't. She doesn't say anything. I'm being allowed to continue. 'There's tons ae these cases...'

'Ah, right ... he's a case now?' The ice cracks. One wrong move and I'm straight through it. Frozen out.

'Sorry. Ah didnae mean that.'

'Danny, ah was jokin'.' She relaxes. Puts a leg over the other and sits back, sipping her coffee.

'Ah found this study, up in the library at Cumnock. It was de-scribin' young kids that were considered tae be disruptive in their school classes or emotionally unstable in some way.'

She's listening and I'm unsure if this is information that she already knows. Or whether I'm breaking new ground.

'When was the first time ye can remember there bein' an issue wi' Damo?' I ask this too formally; like I'm an analyst in a lab, or a psychiatrist inviting her to recline on his sofa. But she answers.

'It began when he was about six. We got called tae school. Ah remember a silly young lassie, his teacher in primary two, callin' him wilfully nonconformist. Ah mean, for Christ's sake, he was a six-year old kid ... they're all like that at that age! Raymond was ragin', as ye'd imagine.'

'He was there?'

'Aye. It was just before he went inside. There was an argument wi' Mr Masson, the head teacher, an' Raymond pushed him over a desk. Masson called him retarded.'

'Damo? Or Raymond?' This makes her smile.

'Damo. Raymond just bloody flipped. Damo's in there, absolutely screamin', teachers come runnin'. Police called … the usual story. An' Raymond's already up on the assault charge. Just couldn't help himself. Damo's stuck in the middle of these three men all shoutin' an' swearin' an wrestlin' his dad out the school. Ah wis mortified. An' it took weeks for Damo tae get over it. Nightmares, wettin' the bed, screamin' for hours on end. You name it.' She wipes her eyes. I take her hand, as if I'm guiding her through the maze of her painful memories. 'Of course, a few months later an' Raymond's got the jail, an' everybody at school just gives up on him. Assumes it's aw tae be expected comin' fae a home wi' a parent in prison. For the last three years at that school, ah often felt ah was there just as much as Damo! There was always somethin' goin' on. Him gettin' teased or bullied. Ah remember one time this wee bastard tells Damo to show everybody what he does when he goes to the bathroom. Damo pulled down his trousers an' pants in the lunchroom an' tried to do a shit in the middle of the floor.'

'God sake,' I say, then: 'Kids forget things quickly, if they're occupied wi' other things.'

She corrects me. 'Children don't just forget trauma. It's always there, under the surface.'

'Can ah ask somethin'. Ye might think a bit … strange?'

She smiles. There's a bemused look on her face. She's so easy to talk to though. 'Well ye can try.'

'See the three guys? Did they all have beards?' She laughs.

'Funnily enough, they did.'

She nods intently for almost half an hour as I put forward my theory that Damo is autistic. She has heard of it but doesn't know exactly what it means.

'Ah read about this young lassie fae Australia. She wis the same age as Damo is now. She was gettin' bullied an' made intae an outcast fae these horrible wee preteen bitches. She was becomin' a social misfit,' I tell Nancy. 'The school performed these tests that revealed her tae be "retarded".'

Her eyes widen at this.

'She eventually dropped out ae the school. Her mother took her tae mental health agencies for help. The girl struggled tae make eye contact, tae speak tae people properly ... tae control the melt-downs. Nancy, this isnae somethin' he'll just grow out of. That's just one story though...' I hand her the manila folder. 'There's hundreds ae them, all followin' the same basic patterns. An' they're all now classed as "intellectually gifted". I think Damo's what's known in here as a "high-functioning autistic".' I explain this theory. 'Ye should hear him at the fitba. He knows everythin' about statistics ... games fae years ago. Scores, sendin' offs, every-thin'. It's like he only needs tae hear or see somethin' once an' then it's locked in here forever.' I point to my temple. I know she's ac-knowledged this as well. There's just hasn't been any support for her to push back against what she's been told. 'Football is his anchor. The only thing that keeps him sane. He needs tae be in a different place,' I tell her. 'Somewhere that'll support him, and you. No' just stickin' him in a corner an' brandin' him retarded.'

I walk her home. It's a beautiful day. Late winter-crisp and un-seasonably dry. Spring's just around the corner. The hopefulness of the season's conclusion being pre-empted, somehow.

'Ah'm probably goin' tae be leavin',' I say.

Nancy looks surprised. And maybe a bit disappointed, al-though maybe I'm misreading her. I've been guilty of that before.

'Aye? When?' she asks.

'After the final.'

'Where are ye goin'?'

'Ah don't know yet. Need tae get away fae here though. Back up north, maybe.'

'That sounds nice.'

I'm not sure what she means by that. Nice? That's a bit like special, isn't it? The indifference irritates me.

This is only the third time I've seen Nancy since the day of the funeral. Once, through the baker's window as I was running past. The second time, just last week when I picked up Damo to take him to our home game with Whitletts, which naturally we won. The awkwardness between us, Doreen like a custody supervisor ensuring there's no rule-breaking at the handing-over of the child. He's the only thing connecting all of us now; a shared desire not to take away the thing that he loves most.

I ask how *she* is. She answers matter-of-factly, by reaffirming that Raymond is staying in Galston. Despite everything, she's still putting him first. Before her own happiness. It explains why he and I haven't encountered each other. That's it. A collection of fragile, damaged adults unable to communicate with each other. Repeating the behaviour of their parents.

I catch the bus to Glasgow. Get the train out to Mount Florida. I arrive at the National Stadium an hour before the time of the SFA disciplinary hearing, having agreed to meet my chairman here. I wander around downstairs. I marvel at the gallery of legendary players who played on this world-famous pitch in front of truly staggering crowds, when football, not religion, was the opium of the people.

My phone rings. It's Anne Macdonald.

Danny?

'Aye?'

It's Anne. How are you?

'Ah'm fine. You okay though?'

She doesn't answer this. Instead: *I just wanted to call and say sorry for the way you were treated at the hotel the other day. That was unacceptable,* she says.

'It's aw'right. As long as you're okay.'

I'm fine. I'm used to it, but that doesn't make it alright. I was really touched by the way you looked out for me. Thank you.

'Touched'. Yes, that was the problem.

'Em … it was, ah … nothin'.'

And I've sorted it out with my stepfather. He fully understands. No need to raise it again.

'Okay.' I mouth a silent apology to a receptionist who has raised an eyebrow at me as if I'm conversing on the pitch during a minute's silence. I see her glancing over at the waiting Lugar representatives who, when I turn to face them, look similarly disturbed.

Billy the Kidd is set to land a massive carpet contract with the billionaire entrepreneur from America. Chuck J. Lavery – the tanned Texan cowboy whose son felt Anne Macdonald's arse before I skelped him a dull one – has bought one of the most prestigious golf courses on the west coast of Ayrshire, and the chairman's company will be redoing all the floor finishes for the clubhouse and its five-star hotel complex. But as Anne has said, I've heard nothing from Mr Kidd about the unfortunate incident. Forgotten; as if it never happened.

In a stroke of opportunistic genius, the hotel will be Barshaw Bridge's new sponsor for the 1997–98 season. But I won't be here to see it. Once the season's finished I'm off. I've made some calls. Alan Rough thinks he might have scored an opportunity for me through a mate of his in the Highlands. Billy the Kidd knows this. According to Anne, her stepfather now understands why I must go, and he won't stand in my way. He's already hinted that I should take some time off in the summer's close season. They don't want to disrupt the team before the final. I return to the front lobby in time to see Billy the Kidd come in with a man I recognise from last season's newspaper clippings as Wullie 'Aye' Gilchrist. Our chairman clearly wants an off-the-record chat before the hearing. He must've been hanging around the car park, waiting near the VIP parking spaces, God bless him.

Mr Gilchrist is the league secretary; Lord God Almighty in the Scottish Junior Football firmament. He's responsible for everything from fixtures to appointing the officials, to keeping all the player registration records. It's a fulsome role. Pivotal to the running of the game, and Wullie Gilchrist knows it. He is known in the game's inner circles as 'Aye, Claudius'; wielding an emperor's power and with a ruthless streak verging on eye-bulging madness.

'Follow,' he commands, and the group of us here for his judgement all rise and follow him upstairs. Weirdly, I didn't recognise my opposite number from Lugar; the one who landed four heavy skelps on my face. He's wearing a suit and a far calmer demeanour. He nods at me as we go into the big mahogany-lined committee room. Bizarrely, given the carnage that was unfolding, he and I were the only two individuals reported. I wasn't aware of this until we were leaving the Lugar Boswell ground under police escort; the ref in our vehicle and still in his kit since his clothes had been flushed down the home team's club toilets.

The jury is assembling. Five club secretaries – all of whom look stressed and exhausted – and Aye, Claudius. The panel, based on their verbal contributions to the proceedings, turn out to be a mix of the bright and fair, and the daft and dangerous. They have to demonstrate that indiscipline on and off the pitch won't be tolerated and that is easier when those bringing the game into disrepute aren't the Old Firm. The power to fine, to censure, to suspend. That power resides here, in this room.

These powerful men, have had the match reports and one from the police for over a month. They pore over the ref's written account, highlighting details such as: 'Mr Edmonds (the Lugar manager) entered the field of play. He gesticulated towards me in a threatening manner and called me "a useless wee poofy cunt".'

'Mr Garvey (the Barshaw player-manager) entered my dressing room at half-time and screamed, "You're fucken hopeless, Ref. My players are gettin' a fucken doin' out there an' you've lost yer whistle up yer bloody arse!" When asked to modify his language,

Mr Garvey then said, "Talk tae me like that again, an' ah've have ye fucken stabbed, ya cunt!"'

My face reddens. My blood pressure rises. But this situation needs calmness. Everyone is staring at me, including the Lugar lads. This can't be right. I don't ever act like that. I'm not an aggressive person. That's Raymond … he's the one with the hair-trigger temper. I don't recall saying that, I remark, but if I did then it was in the heat of the moment and I apologise.

The ref's notes go on to describe the ensuing chaos, focusing on the fate of the young nearside linesman, who was officiating at his first match and has since decided to call it quits.

'And I still haven't been reimbursed or had my clothes returned,' the ref's report concludes. At this, the Lugar chairman lays a Tesco carrier bag on the committee table. It has the referee's clothes in it; laundered and ironed. A white envelope with his fee in it accompanies the bag. It represents their plea for leniency.

'Could've been worse, ah suppose,' says Billy the Kidd as we descend the staircase to the car park. I suspect he's holding back. 'A fine's aw'right if it makes it go away.' I'll be paying it, in any case, not him.

His concern going into the meeting was that Aye Claudius was behind the severity of Barshaw's punishment last season, desperate to make an example of the club. Gilchrist has either forgotten that, or more likely, his dislike for Lugar is simply greater. Either way, they will be docked points from the start of the following season. As the home team, their fine is three times what ours is, and their manager will be banned until the end of the season. My only other censure is a blessing in disguise; a three-game playing suspension. *Halle-fucking-lujah*.

'Ye sure yer alright, son?' asks my chairman. Concern for my well-being is the opening line of every conversation between us lately. No-one wants the cup run to come off the rails, it seems.

'Em … aye. Just felt a bit light-headed, y'know?'

'Aye. It was awful warm in there. A lot ae hot air…' He tails off as our fellow defendants emerge from the building. Handshakes are exchanged. No grudges are held. By the time the pleasantries are concluded, the Carpet King is late for his next appointment.

'I'm fine. Honestly,' I reassure him.

We reach his car. He pauses and breathes in deeply. 'Listen, ah've had a phone call, Danny. Let's get a private chat, soon son, yes?' My phone then rings, interrupting him.

By the time I've looked at it and decided to ignore the call, he's in his car and heading off to a meeting.

⌒

It's the day of the cup semi-final. Barshaw Bridge v Beith Juniors. It's not a two-leg match, and we have home advantage. I suspect we'll need it. Beith – or The Mighty, as they're known – are riding high in division one. They'll bring a decent crowd. Good money for the club from tickets, the programmes and Nancy's hot food. We're being politely diplomatic with each other for Damo's sake, but there's still so much I want to say to her. It'll have to wait though. There's someone else I need to talk to first.

I'm out running. *It's Good To Be On The Road Back Home Again* in my ears. I no longer have the need to keep myself match fit, but the running has quickly become a head-clearing habit. I underestimated its value. It's later in the morning than I would've preferred. I waited until I heard Higgy going out before getting up. Avoidance coping; it's something I've understood more of during the long hours spent in the library.

A car pulls in to the kerb. With the headphones on, I don't hear its driver. But I am aware that it's crawling alongside me.

'Want a lift,' says Sandy Buchanan.

'Naw. Yer fine,' I reply.

'Look. Dive in, will ye? Ah've got some news ye might be interested in.'

The inside of his car is filthy, like he lives in it permanently.

There's a sleeping bag in the back and discarded fast-food cartons litter the passenger footwell.

'Sorry, about the mess, like,' he says. 'Split up wi' the wife, y'know? She gets the house ... ah get the eight-year-auld Vauxhall Nova.'

'Hmm. Sorry tae hear that,' I say, automatically. Although I couldn't care less.

'Fuck her. She was a cow, anyway.' He offers me a cigarette, which I decline. 'Ah, big cup game th'day, isn't it? Beith, aye?' He sucks the breath between his teeth. 'Tough yin. Ye'se'll probably get a pumpin'.'

'Is this yer pre-match interview, pal?'

'Hey ... nae need for that. Ah'm just sayin'.'

'Look, ah'm in a bit ae a hurry. Ye said ye had somethin' tae tell me.'

'Ah've had a tip. A source inside the polis. Told me a few months back, that they'd got this new lead on the wee Louise-Anne lassie that went missing twenty-odd years ago.'

I'm not sure how to respond to this. The name is like a stab. *Louise-Anne* ... The register song:

Abbott, Ainsley, Baird, Bruce, Davidson, Demarco, Forrest, Garvey ... then nothing. *Melville, Ross, Sinclair, Walkinshaw.*

The dark hair, pale skin ... on the front page for weeks. And then again when her mother killed herself. I shudder. I can remember the sound of her voice now. The way she squealed when her hair was pulled.

The absurdity of a local newspaper's sports reporter breaking an age-old child-murder-mystery story from inside a smelly Vauxhall Nova has rendered me temporarily speechless.

Eventually he says: 'Ah know you've been up there a lot, lately. The Reid place, ah mean.' It sounds like an accusation.

'So? What the fuck ye implying?'

'Naw, naw ... it's nothin' like that. Just thought ye'd want tae know. Maybe prepare the auld woman for the worst.' This is a bizarre turn of events. I was convinced the Cumnock Carl Bernstein had it in for me. We sit in silence. Him waiting for the nod that it's okay to continue.

'Look, mate. Can ah ask ye somethin'?' I say.

'Aye. Fire away, son.'

'All that fucken shit ye gave us at the start ae the season ... what the fuck was that aw about?'

'Ach. Aye ... sorry about that,' he admits. 'Ah thought ye'd be just like yer brother.'

'And? That's the reason we got aw that crap in the papers that we didnae deserve?'

'Well ... yer brother's a cunt.' Forthright and straight to the point. 'Ye'll get nae argument from me on that,' I say, establishing some common ground. 'He's a cunt, right enough.'

'But ah gradually realised you were different. Aw that useful stuff ye were doin' for the auld woman.'

'So, what is it wi' Raymond then?'

'That fella he nearly killed? He's our next-door neighbour ... or at least he was until the missus kicked us out. Lives on his own, an' could barely dae anythin' for himself when he finally got out the hospital. My Moira's in there, feedin' him, sortin' his washin', runnin' the messages. She's nearly fucken ten years aulder than him tae.' He shakes his head. I'm starting to put it together. 'She's spendin' more an' more time down there, an' well ... ye can guess the rest, eh?'

It seems that Sandy Buchanan now considers me to be a kindred spirit. Sharing a common enemy in my brother; the catalyst for our pain.

'Why were you in at Mrs Reid's then?' I ask.

'Ah'm a hack, for Christ sake. Ah was sniffin' about,' he admits. 'Ah knew this break might be comin' an' ah was after a head start, like.'

'So, what's the story?'

'*Mornin' glory.*' He laughs at his own joke. I don't. 'No' a fan?

Fair enough.' He drags a dog-eared notebook from his side pocket. 'This guy fae Girvan ... he's in the hospital. Dyin'. There's a priest there. Takes his final confession. The guy tells the priest that he'd accidentally killed a wee lassie that went missin' fae Barshaw in 1972. He was helpin' tae renovate a remote farmhouse on the edge ae the woods. He was reversin' a digger an' it hit somethin'. He got out an' there's the wean under its wheels. Dead. Rather than tell anybody, he puts the wean's body in the pit and fills it in wi' aw the hardcore in the bucket.'

Higgy had said this was considered a possibility, once they'd found nothing by excavating the Reids' garden and ransacked their house. That wee Louise-Anne had simply fallen down an old mine, or over the edge of the Barshaw quarry with the deep pond at the bottom. Or that she could be buried under the foundations of one of the new houses. Kids hung about on the building sites all the time in those days. I did it myself. It was an exciting, noisy adventure playground where the workies would give you a bite of their sandwich, or a hurl in the diggers. It wasn't such a leap that this could've been the explanation, was it? I mean, some of those cruel little bastards from around here could even have done it to her. Why the automatic assumption that she'd been murdered by her own grandfather? *That* made no fucking sense at all.

'For fuck's sake! Why did he no' just tell somebody it was an accident?' I feel the tears welling.

'My pal in the polis says the guy was already up on a gross indecency charge. Scared ae losin' his kids, apparently.'

'But no' that bothered about somebody else losin' theirs? Jesus fucken Christ!'

'Ah know. Unbelievable, right?' Sandy Buchanan's emotional detachment is depressing. It's just another job for him. 'He asks the priest tae tell the cops the truth if he dies. He snuffed it a month ago. They've looked at the dates. It aw checks out. He was workin' there at the farm when she disappeared.'

I'm struggling for breath. Like something is compressing my

chest and it won't stop until the ribcage stops resisting. I cruelly taunted Jock Reid for years and that was bad enough. And I was there when he died too. That was all so unnecessary, all of it. I worry that it will destroy Mrs Reid when she finds out, as she will soon. But how can I have any chance of a future with Nancy unless this slate has been cleared? Sandy Buchanan tells me the police now have warrants to demolish the garage sheds that were built back then, and to excavate the ground beneath them. I need to tell Mrs Reid before that happens. And I need to make my own confession to her about Raymond and me and the night her husband died.

He drops me at the house. Genuinely wishes us luck for the semi-final, saying he'll be there to cover it. But I can't focus. I can't get Jock Reid's suffering out of my mind. And what his daughter must've gone through. His granddaughter, her whole life ahead of her. All those years of mental torture at the hands of the tabloids, the local community, and a bunch of ignorant, bullying children; and of one in particular. And all because of an avoidable accident. For fuck's sake. All of it, for nothing.

⌂

Higgy hears me vomiting upstairs.

'Is that you? Danny? Are ye alright?' It's a half-hearted attempt; he must feel compelled to ask.

'Aye. It's me.'

I come out of the toilet and he's facing me. Unsure of what to say. We've gotten so used to clipped platitudes these last few weeks, on the odd occasion we meet in the kitchen or pass each other on the stairs, anything more is painful.

'Nerves?'

'No. Ah'm fine.' I need to maintain the illusion of control. 'Are ye comin'?'

'Ach, son ... ah dunno.'

'Higgy, fuck sake. It's the semi-final. Barshaw are *your* team, no'

222 DAVID F. ROSS

mine. Ah'm really, really sorry for everythin' ah said tae ye after the funeral. Ah wisnae thinkin' straight.'

'Ah know, son. Ah know.' He steps closer and hugs me, and I start to cry. I can't stop myself. 'We're worried about ye. Everybody is.'

'Fucken Raymond,' I say. 'Cares about bugger all but himself.'

Higgy sighs and lets me go. 'It's a cycle thing,' he says. 'A son without a da, becomes a da that cannae connect wi' his son. Becomes a son that bloody hates his da an' wishes he was dead. It's the hate that drives it. But ye have tae let it go, son.'

It feels like the biggest game of my life. It feels like we're playing for the very soul of Jock Reid. The incentives aren't financial ... at least not for me. The King's has closed for the game. Punters and villagers and business colleagues of committee members mix with away fans. The attendance must be close to a thousand. It's astonishing, and not quite believable when compared to where we were nine months ago.

My players are also up for it. All except Tony McIntosh, who arrives late, apologetic and smelling of booze. There's no bravado. Something is wrong with him, and he takes his demotion to the bench with what appears to be relief. It isn't like him to be so defeated. I recognise the darkness and tell him he's free to go home. But he stays.

We still have a couple of men out injured, but McIntosh apart, we're able to field what I consider to be our strongest team based on current form.

Before we head out, Higgy brings Damo in. The wee man shakes every player by the hand like he was royalty being introduced to them. The players are the only people he's happy to touch. The boy says 'good luck' in a rehearsed monotone. No smiles. It's a serious business.

Beith Juniors have the confident air of a team with a hand on the trophy already. We're the only club left in the cup from outside of the first division. This should be relatively straightforward for them. Other than remind them of these facts, I don't offer much of a team talk. The sessions and strategies were all worked out at training during the week. This is about rising above ourselves, individually and collectively.

The first quarter is tight. Beith know they're in a game and it has taken them by surprise. I note how much bigger their players seem to be. But not in a carthorse-type way. Big, powerful and nimble. Black-and-white stripes making them seem taller and slimmer. They are adapting to us. I watch their animated manager and listen to coded shouts that shift tactics and formation seamlessly. They are a good team, no doubt. But if we sit back and admire them, we'll get battered.

There's a break in play. A Beith man getting attention for what looks like a hamstring pull. It's looking like he'll have to go off. Paddy Gilhooly comes over.

'What's the plan, boss?'

'Push Davie Russell into midfield. Base of a diamond and pull Smith and Ramage in tighter.'

'4-4-2?'

'4-1-2-2-1.' I can see him trying to do the arithmetic in his head.

Harry Doyle jumps over with the pad. 'This is what we mean,' he says. 'We need tae stifle the midfield. They're movin' everything through they two lads in the centre. Switch about an' get them blocked. Got it?'

'Aye,' says the captain. He runs back, pulling the affected players to one side and reassigning them. The Beith sub is on. He looks like an identikit of the one who went off. Their squad is strong and there's loads of alternatives amongst them.

Five minutes later, we're a goal down. They work a lovely move down the left. A simple but effective cross, and the downward header is powerfully directed past Josey Monsanto's flailing left arm. Once again, I admire how quickly they adjusted to our changes and punished us.

My thoughts drift back to Jock Reid; imagining him in a red-and-white strip, dominating the midfield, marauding towards the Beith penalty box, unleashing a shot and ... PHEEP! The whistle.

'Penalty!' shouts Harry Doyle, and I rejoin the present tense.

'Fuck happened?' I ask him because, even though I was watching, I didn't see it.

'Wee Gilmour. Hit a shot fae the edge ae the box an' it came off an arm.'

By all accounts, we're extremely fortunate to be getting this penalty kick. The Beith contingent are giving the referee dog's abuse. Their manager appeals to me, but I just shrug. What does he expect me to do? Appeal to the ref to overturn it?

'Ah didnae see it,' I say, giving the age-old cliched response.

'Aye. Fucken convenient,' he replies. I leave it at that. Can't admit I was daydreaming.

There's a couple of bookings for dissent. To rub salt in the Beith wounds, Gilmour scores from the spot. It's virtually the last kick of the half. When the whistle goes, their keeper boots the ball high over The Barn's metal roof. I watch it trundle down the hill right into the village's main street. A youngster pops out from behind the church and disappears with it.

'In ye'se come. Quick,' shouts Harry Doyle. We've had a let-off, and we know it.

'Well played, boys. Tough going out there. They're a good team but we're still fucken in this,' I say, clapping my hands in encouragement. 'Forty-five minutes fae the final. Just keep that in yer mind. Every cunt around here writing ye'se off for six months, an' now look at us, eh? Fucken proud ae every single one ae ye'se!'

They haven't seen this emotion from me before. And they can't know the reasons for it. But it seems to galvanise them. Even Tony McIntosh has emerged from his shame and is yelling encouragement. We're so pumped up for this half, I almost anticipate the team doing a haka on the halfway line before the game gets back under way.

As we stand, Billy the Kidd sticks his head around the door. 'Great stuff, boys. See they bonuses for the final ... get us through this an' ah'm doublin' them!' He's also emotional. And pissed. But his heart's in the right place, and the team breaks out a chorus of 'Billy the Kidd'.

The second half passes me in a blur. Like being out for a long run and reaching a destination with no recollection of how I got there. My aching mind is somersaulting over hundreds of different obstacles.

In the end, I'm told how almost without touching the ball at all, Paddy Gilhooly made four Beith Juniors players look like four versions of Higgy. How he slid the ball calmly out to Dib Ramage on the right wing. How the ball – as it made its way effortlessly up the touchline, propelled by Dib's right foot, direct to Dougie Wilson's left, glinting like a diamond in the sun – seemed to know its destiny. How Billy Gilmour, our stand-out player in a team becoming far greater than the sum of its parts, casually rolled it into the path of the eventual goalscorer, Sean O'Halloran.

'Did ye see that, son? Danny! Fuck sake, we're in the bloody final!' Higgy hugs me, lifting me off the ground.

I am dazed. I spot Damo's arms up in the air. Nancy is running over towards her son, smiling broadly.

The Beith manager offers a hand. 'Well done, son. Gutted about the penalty but ye'se were the better team second half. Aw the best in the final.'

Our players are jubilant. Some of the younger fans are on the pitch, running around with them. I spot Tony McIntosh hugging Josey Monsanto.

Nancy winks at me. 'Ye did it, Danny. Ah'm really pleased for ye.' She takes Damo's hand and turns to walk away.

I start to walk after her, but I'm lifted sharply and before I know it, I'm on Gilhooly's soaking, sweaty shoulders. The rest of the team swamp him, and we tumble over. When I get back to my feet, Nancy has gone.

'What's up wi' ye? Must be fucken burstin' inside, naw?' Harry Doyle is bemused by my surface calmness.

'It's fine, Harry. A few things on my mind, like.' He looks disappointed. 'Ah'm delighted, mate. Really. But we've still got another ninety minutes. We've won nothin' yet.'

'Aye. Big, big progress, though son. Ah'll see ye down at The King's, wi' everybody else?'

'Thanks mate. Aw down tae you an' the team. Enjoy yer night.'

He nods and leaves me to pay the officials and clear up. I sit in the office after everyone's gone. Various scenarios emerge and then retreat. I contemplate using the tactics board to attempt to determine a way through the mire I'm in. Instead, I take the key and unlock the committee room. The drinks cupboard wedges open and I bring out Billy the Kidd's decanter. The whisky level is low, and I empty what remains of it into a glass. But I don't get to drink it.

When I go back through to my office, my brother Raymond is sitting in my chair.

—I don't know what he's told you about me. Although I can imagine it won't be good. My role in his life has always been that of an excuse. An excuse for his behaviour. Every time he gets caught doing something, he finds a way to implicate me. He used to run with other kids from the village, he would have been about eight or so. Anyway, I catch him out at the old dump. There's a wee group of them ... all taunting this poor old man. And our Danny is at the centre of it. The fucking ringleader, chanting this stupid song and throwing rocks at him. I chased the lot of them away and then went home and phoned the police to come and get the old man.

'What ye here for?' I ask him, as calmly as I can muster.

'Ah need a favour,' he says. He's hesitant. On the back foot. The control has shifted.

—I'm not proud of how the funeral turned out, you need to understand. I've got a temper ... never denied that. And, fuck me, does Danny know how to draw it out. It's got me into a lot of trouble over the years, but I want that to change. I don't want to be back inside. I want to be with Nancy and my boy. I can't do it myself. For once, I need my younger half-brother to help me. He owes me this.

'That right?' I say. I notice that I have a pen in my hand although I don't recall picking it up.

'Look, Danny, a lot ae shite's passed between us down the years. But ah need this. Ye owe me.' This feels like an interview. Him on the other side of my desk. In my office. And that perennial suggestion of obligation.

'Ah need stake money for a bout. One last thing an' then we're square, right?' he says, jabbing a finger in my chest. I hand over what I have, and a plan forms before quickly dying. Accusing him of its theft won't work. I need something else. He has what he came for, but I'm not letting him off that easily.

'I don't owe you anything now,' I say, trying my hardest to deliver it like Morrissey did. With the same certainty. The same conviction. He sniggers in disbelief. 'But we're still no' square.'

'Yer fucken jokin', son!' He leans forward. Eyes widening. 'Ah've fucken done time for ye twice, ya wee cunt!' Here it comes again, his true self. Myopically aggressive. He really should see someone about that temper. I shake my head, dismissively. He's losing everything. Nancy, his future – his fucking freedom if I have anything to do with it.

'You stabbed Scud Meikle, no' me...' I remain calm and assured. I'm proud of myself for this. But he doesn't let me finish. He's on his feet.

'Aye, ye've fucken conveniently rubbed out your part in that, eh? Comin' runnin' for me, tellin' me the cunt had broken yer arm an' nicked yer bike, an' that he'd stuck ye wi' a broken bottle. The big fucken gash in yer side, remember ... that one that ye fucken gave yerself!' His voice is getting louder. 'An' ye'll no' remember padlockin' yerself tae the fence that night either, eh?' He's prowling now. Slamming his fist into the wall. I just need to keep calm. Ignore the provocations. It's nearly over. 'An' when that aul' bastard Jock Reid died. Ye remember that day, Danny? Ye remember drivin' the car? You! No' me. You. Speedin' up. Aimin' the fucken thing at him? Ye managed tae erase aw that tae? Some fucken boy.'

And then I'm screaming: 'You fucken blamed me for her goin' missin'! You all did. It wisnae my fucking fault. It wisnae my fucking fault, Raymond!'

But he's gone. I'm alone. Yelling into the darkness. He wouldn't have listened anyway. He never did. No-one of them fucking cared enough to even feign interest. He got what he came for. If my plan works, we won't see him again.

He's always had a warped view of our upbringing. It's like staring into the looking glass with every incident involving my brother. He's deluded. Beyond help. The truth according to Raymond is inverted. Contorted. Skewed to give him a starring role as the hero in the film of our life. Well, enough's enough. I'll be doing everyone a favour putting the twisted cunt back inside. He just can't see that yet. Neither can Nancy, but she will.

∩

Raymond's like a drug.

I hadn't thought of my brother in those terms, but I know what she means. His reappearance a few days ago was surprising but entirely predictable. He was quiet, and complicit initially, but I noticed his leg constantly shaking under the table. He showed up looking for money, naturally. Some barely believable rubbish about an unlicensed boxing match Rocco Quinn is putting on, giving him the opportunity to repay his debts and to get out of the life for good; to let him go back to Nancy and Damo. Have a normal future. There's a fundraising cash tin in my office. It hasn't yet been transferred to the club's account. That's another of my jobs. Something else someone trusts me with.

But in the hope that it buys me time, I gave him the money. If we win the final, I'll replace it with my bonus. I couldn't tell Nancy any of this obviously. I haven't seen my brother, as far as she and Higgy are aware. I return to something I can fix. Something that might help get Nancy and me back to where I want us to be.

'Mrs Reid?' She hasn't answered the door, although I'm sure she's in. The telly is flickering in the front room. I'm shouting through the front door's letter box. Not too loudly though. I don't want to give her a fright.

I see a shadow coming from the kitchen and tap the door again.

'Oh, hullo, son. How are ye? Come in, son, come in.'

I follow her through to her living room. She puts the television set off, even though the sound from it was barely audible.

'Do ye want a cuppa tea?' She asks.

I decline. Tea – so often the soother of stresses and anxieties – isn't going to help me here. I'm here to unburden myself. While I still can.

'Ah've been lookin' up some ae Jock's matches. Some ae the records an' that.'

'Have ye?' she asks.

I pass her the second manila folder. The one with Jock Reid's achievements recorded in it. 'Aye. The club are hopin' tae honour him at the cup final. It's a massive match for us.' I'm yet to clear this with Billy the Kidd. 'Hopin' you'll come too ... as our guest.' I really mean *my* guest.

But she shakes her head. 'Och, son. I haven't been at a football match for years ... since Jock an' me were courtin'.' She smiles, presumably at the memory of doing something that she most definitely wouldn't have done out of personal choice. *The things we do for love.*

'Well, will ye come to this one? Please?'

'Ye've done so much for me, son. So much that Jock would've been pleased about.'

'Ah feel ah owe it tae him,' I say. And I can see her puzzled at this. It isn't the first time. But it's the first time we've being sitting here, in his living room, his framed pictures surrounding me. My need to lay down this momentous weight that has crippled me for thirteen years.

'You're a kind lad,' she says. 'My Jock an' you would've got on like a house on fire.' My face reddens, and it feels like my head might explode under the pressure of the memories that start invading it.

Aul' Jock Reid's aff his heid. His wife's a hoor an' his daughter's deid.

And it's me singing this at the top of my voice. At the dump. In the street. Throwing things. That fucking piano playing along to the words. I feel like I'll vomit right there in her living room. On their worn, shaggy rug. But I can't back out now. There's no future for me and Nancy unless I get this off my back; this horrendous burden I've carried for so long.

'Mrs Reid, ah was there when yer husband died.'

It's out before I know it. It's true that nothing hurts the way you think it's going to. This is only part of it; the first part, but thankfully some of that pressure has eased. There's a silence that lasts for minutes as it sinks in. Her face changes in slow motion. Finally, she speaks and it's as if I'd spoken in a foreign language that she almost recognises but isn't entirely sure of.

'What d'ye mean?' As if she hasn't properly heard. The confused look on her face doesn't change.

'Ah'm really sorry.' And then it does. Her eyes narrow. Delayed reaction. I see her slump a bit. She grips the arm of the chair. *His* chair.

She now looks horrified. I'd imagined the passing of time might've made this moment easier, but perhaps only for me. She stands. A first indication that I'm no longer welcome in his house.

'I don't really know you, do I? Why is that? Why have ah never seen you before?' The question momentarily throws me. And then I realise she doesn't mean recently.

'Why are you doing this tae me?' Her tone is stern. It reminds me of the time me and Scud Meikle got caught stealing seven-inch singles from Woolworths in Ayr by an irate and out-of-breath shop assistant.

'No,' I say, head lowered. 'Ye don't understand, Mrs Reid. I don't want tae ... ah just wanted ye tae know! I needed to tell you.'

'Tell me what?'

'That, em...' I stutter. The hours of rehearsing this speech in front of the mirror hasn't properly prepared me for the real thing; just like practising penalties in training can't simulate taking one in front of a terracing full of opposing fans.

I start reassessing the wisdom of what I'm about to say. Images flash through my mind. Me with Nancy. Me with Damo. Me visiting my brother behind bars again. It'll be worth it. Keep going. I refocus on the script.

'We didn't mean it, but ah had to tell you. I had tae admit it. I was there. There when he went over the bridge.'

'We?' she asks, catching me off-guard. 'Who else was involved?' The anger is rising. Tears are forming. I recognise the look. I've seen it in others many times before.

'Em ... my big brother. Raymond.' And before I can stop myself, 'He didnae mean it. It was an accident, ye know that, don't you?'

Her face changes. She finally knows who I am; the family I'm part of.

'Ah was only sixteen. Ah was in the car, the night after the semi-final. I was still hungover. Raymond, my brother, he was over-revvin' it in low gear for much ae the journey back. Shakin' with rage, he was. No other vehicles on the road. We approached the Barshaw Bridge bend an' ah sighed with relief, knowin' that in only five minutes, ah'd be back in my own bed.'

Her wrinkled face crumples even more as I recount this. She reaches out with her free hand and grabs the back of the chair.

'"Raymond, fucken slow down!" ah said. I turned tae look at him. When ah turned back, a man had appeared fae nowhere. An old man, one that ah recognised. He was walkin' along the narrowest part ae the bridge; on the hump. He turned round an' I could see it was him.'

Her hand goes to her mouth. Covering a silent scream.

Aul' Jock Reid ... he's no' right in the heid. His wife's a hoor, an' his daughter's deid.

'Raymond was unsure ae the pedals. He panicked. Rather than brakin', he accelerated. Rather than turnin' away, he veered the car towards him. Ah still don't know why.'

I'm suddenly composed, telling her this. There's no point now in false emotion. It was years ago after all and we've all suffered. My contrition has been evident.

'But Raymond pulled the handbrake. The car didnae hit him. To get out of the way yer husband leaned backwards. But he overbalanced an' fell over the low wall. My head hit the top ae the dashboard. When ah looked up an' over to the right, the door was open. My brother had gone. Ah got out. Ah half expected the old man to be under the wheel, but he wasn't. Ah looked over the wall. Mr Reid was lying sprawled. His head sat at an awkward angle to his shoulders. His head had hit a boulder. A terrible accident. My brother was next tae him.'

Mrs Reid is struggling for breath.

'A terrible accident,' I repeat.

'Are you aw'right?' I ask her. She doesn't reply. It's like she's staring right through me; like she's not fully grasping what I'm telling her. I motion towards her, but she recoils sharply, the speed of it belying her age. She's crying now. And hyperventilating. I'm worried she might have a heart attack before I can get this out.

She's still making the noises, but I need to get it out of me. To release it into the wild. To set it free so I still have a chance with Nancy.

'Ah saw Raymond pull gloves on an' then reach intae the old man's jacket. He opened a wallet an' it looked like he took some money from it.'

Mrs Reid makes this weird yelping noise. It shocks me. It sounds like a wee dog getting repeatedly kicked by someone with steel-capped boots. She's started screaming. I keep going, unsure of what she's hearing but this is for me now.

'My brother examined the motor. We got back in, an' he drove it back to this woman's house. He told me tae go back tae where I'd been sleepin' earlier. Ah just did what he told me to.'

I must sound like a child to her. I certainly feel like one again. I'd spoken like this a lot when we were young. Recounting an incident; blaming Raymond for the outcome. And then suddenly, and unexpectedly, her screeching stops. She isn't making a sound. Her face is contorted, and I briefly think this must be what having a stroke is like. If she dies, I'll still have atoned, right? It'll still count. I'll be able to look Nancy in the eye and know I've done the right thing. There will be no more secrets. No more running. No more hiding in fucking freezing Arbroath. I'll be able to be normal. Not special, just normal. I'll be fixed.

Minutes pass with no sound other than the metronomic pendulum of the tall mahogany clock in the hall. My heart beats in syncopated rhythm. I'm calmer than I expected I'd be. It's because I now know I'm doing the right thing. That I'm the one fixing this. I notice her hands are trembling, and I wonder how long we'll remain here, contemplating what comes next. I'm not telling her about the building site. About where wee Louise-Anne is, or might be. That's someone else's confession, not mine.

'Get out!' she screams suddenly. She's not having a stroke. 'Get out of my house now before ah phone the police.'

I stand and head to her living-room door. As I pass her, she hits me. It's a weak, badly aimed slap and it neither connects with its intended target nor hurts. But I still wish she hadn't done it. I move past the gallery of heartaches. I've caused her this pain she's feeling. It's only the start. When she hears – as she will any day now – that her granddaughter's remains may lie under the foundations of a farm outbuilding less than half a mile from this house, my admission might hurt less. It might be seen in a different light. But I had to tell her first. For my conscience to be completely clear. Who knows, I'll maybe be able to come back once she regains a bit of perspective. It would be nice to make sure she was okay before Nancy, Damo and I leave Barshaw.

I hear something landing at my feet. I turn from the front door. She has thrown the folder at me. All that work assembling a tribute to her husband. It's now blowing gently in the breeze at my feet.

'You should've gone tae prison along with your brother.'

I look around to see if anyone might've heard. Or if the woman from across the street is watching. Would she act more decisively this time? Or would she still consider this to be someone else's business?

Mrs Reid is still crying. I didn't think old people wept as much. The door slams shut in my face. I look around at the garden, up at the guttering. At the shadow moving away from the frosted glass. My handiwork. There's nothing I can do about this situation now. I have apologised. Done what I came here to do. And I have tried to atone. I'm sure she'll appreciate that in the weeks ahead.

⌂

I'm spending more and more time these days with Anne Macdonald. She's the only person that understands me. We shouldn't really get on – the class polarity between us. But there's something magnetic about her. We're the same age but her life experience is so much more expansive than mine. I've found it easy to open myself up to her fully, and the advice she's been giving me lately has been invaluable.

She picks me up and we drive through the Ayrshire country-side. I made a second copy of Nancy's mix tape and it sounds magnificent bursting through these fantastic speakers that she's had installed.

We don't converse, we just listen. Comet Gain, The Auteurs, Moose, The Go-Betweens. From her reaction, it's clear she's coming around to my way of thinking about music. I knew she would.

Don't worry too much about Mrs Reid, says Anne, eventually. *You did the right thing. She just needs time to come to terms with it. It'll be a shock after all these years.*

I know she's right. She's always been right.

We've driven to The Esplanade at Ayr. The car's parked facing out and we can see the water over the top of the low wall separating the promenade from the sand.

Did you speak to Nancy? she asks.

'No' yet,' I reply.

You need to, Danny. Soon.

'Ah know. Ah've just got tae find the right time. It's a big step, movin' her away fae her ma' an' uprootin' the wee yin fae the school.'

But, it's not the school he should be in, she knows that now. You told her.

'Ah know.'

And you need to do anything you can to get her away from your brother.

'Aye.' We get interrupted by the mobile phone. I put my finger to my lips to ensure her silence.

'Hi.

...

Aye, it's me.

...

236 DAVID F. ROSS

Oh, how ye doin', Alan?

...

Ah'm good, thanks.

...

Aw, man ... that's great. Just the right time, Alan.

...

Aye. We've got the final comin' up but after that, I'm totally free. The chairman's cool wi' it tae.

...

What's that?

...

Aye. Nae problem. Ah'll phone him before ah'm headin' up.

...

Thanks. Ah mean that, Alan. Ah'm really grateful.

...

Aw'right. Aw the best.

...

Aye.

...

See ye.'

Well? asks Anne.

'Formal offer ae a job coachin' the youth team at Ross County. Up in the Highlands.'

They were my local team, she says, excitedly. *How great is that?*

'Well ... haven't got it officially yet, but y'know?'

Yes. I do. It's great, Danny. Really. I'm so pleased it's all working out for you. She kisses my cheek, like the sister I never had. Or the mother I wished I'd had.

She drives me back to The Barn. I have a meeting with the committee, and it'll be an opportunity for me to give them the good news.

'Come in, son,' says Billy the Kidd. There's a concerned look on his face, which is surprising given our achievements this year. He's become a hard man to please, that's for sure.

The full committee is assembled. Not sitting as formally as when I first met them. They all shake my hand. All mumble a word of encouragement about the two matches ahead; the last league game of the season and then the cup final itself.

'Sit down, Danny,' says Phil Dick, quietly.

'Ye've done a brilliant job wi' the team, this year, son ... ye have,' says Billy the Kidd. 'But we're no' goin' tae renew yer post for next season.'

He stands and approaches me. Puts a hand on my shoulder. He's a good man, is Billy the Kidd. He cares for the club, and I'm sure he cares for me too.

'We've ironed out that problem you had at the hotel, so ye dinnae need tae stress about that anymore, okay? An apology was enough.'

'Well, if Anne's okay wi' it, Mr Kidd, then ah'm prepared tae forget all about it tae.'

The American was out of order, and someone like Anne shouldn't have to put up with lecherous bastards like him when she's doing her job. But if the chairman feels that it's best swept under the carpet, for the greater good, then I'm not someone to bear a grudge.

He gives me a strange look. Perhaps I shouldn't have mentioned her by name.

'Yer uncle asked about the remaining games ... the final.'

'Aye,' I reply. 'He cannae wait. It's given him somethin' tae live for after, y'know, my mam dyin'.'

'Well, we've given this some thought. I've spoken to Harry Doyle tae. The squad ... they're keen for ye tae see it...'

'Listen, Mr Kidd. There's nae way ah'm walkin' out on this club before its biggest game in thirteen years. Ah might've done it once but ah was young an' daft back then.'

'Aye,' says Phil Dick. He rolls his eyes and I'm not sure what that means. Then again, he's never liked me much.

'So, after the final ... win or lose, ah want ye tae promise us somethin'.'

'Anythin', Mr Kidd.'

'Ye'll go an' see somebody, son. Get some help. Take a break. Get yerself in order.'

'Aw in hand, Mr Chairman. Ah've got a place lined up. Up north again. Middle ae nowhere. Fresh, cold air ... peace an' quiet, y'know?' I laugh nervously.

No-one from the committee responds. This is a serious business.

'Okay son. Thanks for comin' in. For makin' this so easy on us.'

'Listen, Mr Kidd, ah should be thankin' you. Ah never wanted this job tae start wi', tae come back tae Barshaw ... tail between my legs, an' that. But you've given me a bit ae self-respect back. A bit ae redemption.'

He escorts me to the door, as his colleagues exchange glances.

'Ah need tae ask ye,' I say.

'What is it, son?'

'How's yer stepdaughter takin' aw this, em, crap ... wi' the Yanks?'

He looks at me and sighs deeply. He puts his hand to his mouth. He's disappointed. I can tell. Like I've just broken a code of honour.

'Danny, son, ah don't *have* a stepdaughter.'

∩

As I ran this morning, I considered my unlikely season here; the personal achievements that it represented. Barshaw Bridge will finish fourth in the league, regardless of today's result. We're in a major cup final for the first time since 1983. Jock Reid's name is back, chiselled in gold again on the wooden board in the committee room. I've acknowledged his death to his wife, and I've made reparations. Scud Meikle has benefitted from my return. It's given him somewhere to be and a purpose that has stabilised his decline. I've outlined a much more positive future for my nephew, Damo, than his mother thought possible. And I've buried my mother, along with my memories of her. Deek Henderson is already dead. I can do no more with that one.

I'm at The Barn earlier than normal. Earlier than everyone else, other than the groundsman. I may well miss it next season; not something I had ever expected to feel. There are good people surrounding this club. People who deserve to have some of their passion and determination rewarded. When we won the semifinal, Billy the Kidd couldn't speak to me for the tears. Higgy too ... this club is in his blood. He remembers the days when the club kept the village spirit going. When the bypass came, when the pits started closing and the jobs disappeared, when all that the disenfranchised men had left to give direction and purpose to their lives was this club. A team filled with local men who'd grown up watching men exactly like them. Hoping – mostly in vain – for a win against local rivals like Auchinleck Talbot, or Cumnock, or a wee run to the edges of the Scottish Cup. All of this is now wrapped up in one vital game. The Ayrshire Cup Final. Our last of the season. *My* last of the season. The ghosts excised, I can finally leave here.

But before that, it's our final home league game. Saltcoats Vics, who have somehow limped on through the worst of the season's ravages, are the visitors. They are level at the bottom with Lugar Boswell Thistle. They'll be desperate to win, despite the odds being against it. I've used this – and the competition for places for the cup final – as the motivation for our performance. No complacency.

The team are out warming up. All present and correct, except Tony McIntosh, who hasn't even called to offer an excuse. It's disappointing, but I've been expecting it. His mind's not on it. His appearances at training are becoming scarcer and his weight is fluctuating wildly. Harry Doyle recently made everyone laugh by suggesting we send him to Edinburgh and have him cloned, like the sheep the scientists have named Dolly.

'What? Then we'd have two fat, lazy cunts tae pick from,' Gilhooly joked.

And then I'm on the pitch. That sixty- by one hundred-yard rectangle where no-one can touch me. I can't remember crossing the touchline to get here. But I'm walking around, inspecting the turf. Watching Harry conduct the drills along with Andy Meikle, who has adapted well to a role as Harry's assistant. I'm almost redundant, so polished is the routine now. I look over at the dugouts. I see Nancy in the van, serving food to Anne Macdonald, who is standing beside her. Both wave and I wave back. As does Higgy, standing to the side of it. And Damo. He waves too. And suddenly I'm in the centre circle. There's a ball at my feet. And everyone is waving towards me. Billy the Kidd, his fellow committee members. They are there with the big Texan. He has brought a horse. Damo is feeding it hay. And there's Mrs Reid. She came! But ... how is that possible? She's standing with Jock, her husband. And he's waving at me too. Libby appears from behind him. Waving. Wishing me well. The only one not here is Raymond.

—*I barely fucking touched him. Yet he went down like a sniper had shot him. He's always been a bloody drama queen. But he more than deserves this, the devious wee cunt.*

The pain in the back of my head. It's hard to focus. But eventually he drifts into view.

'Get up, ya wee prick,' he tells me.

'What the fuck happened there?'

'Ah belted ye,' he says.

'Why?'

'Cos ah fucken felt like it!' My brother stands over me. Shouting at me. We're in the home dressing-room showers. I'm disorientated.

'Fuck sake. What time is it?'

'Fucken *Hammer*-time. What difference does it make?'

'We've got a game … Jesus, Raymond. The team'll be in here in a minute.'

'It's fucken by, son,' he says. 'An' so'll you be in a minute.' His fist is clenched. He put me down. He's waiting for me to get up so he can do it again. How sporting of him.

'Wh-what are ye doin' here?' I stutter.

'You an' me, boy. We've got some real fucken shite tae sort out here.' He's prowling. Like a wild animal with its cornered prey.

'Ah know,' I say. It's been a long time coming.

—Right back to when he was a wee boy, he could always compart-mentalise the football; it was everything else that was the problem. Those years of me taking the rap for things he'd done. Everyone feeling sorry for him … 'the wean wi' nae da'. Well, I was the same. Nobody gave a fuck about me though. I was expected to be his da, his ma, his brother, his fucking guardian … all rolled into one.

'Ye told that auld Reid woman an' that fucken bastard journalist cunt that ah was drivin' the car the killed auld Jock Reid,' he yells. 'An' now he's runnin' a fucken story about it, sayin' ah lifted money out his wallet while he's lyin' dead in the river.'

'That's what ah saw.'

'Is it fuck, Danny! An' you fucken know that. Why are ye doin' this tae me? Ah got his address. Took you back tae that auld bag's place tae fucken keep ye out the road. An' ah went tae the polis. Ah've already done the time for it … for *you!* Or have ye fucken forgot that? Nine months for causin' death by dangerous drivin'. Ah took that time for you! So you could get a clean break. Fucken make somethin' ae yersel wi' the fitba up in Aberdeen.' His anger is ramping. 'An' ye couldnae even dae that! Fuck sake, the library books, the obsession with missing weans … Jesus Christ, Danny, you need fucken help, son. You're fucken mental, you!'

And I summon up the strength to punch him. My knuckles

connect with his mouth and my hand immediately stings. He takes the jab well. His boxer's training coming to the fore. But he doesn't retaliate as I'd hoped he would. He smiles at me, before pulling out a tooth that I've dislodged. He stares at it before a look crosses his face. It's almost as if he's finally proud of me. Proud of me for being like him. And then it dawns on me. He thinks he's won. The cunt thinks he's beaten me.

'Finally, a wee bit ae backbone,' he slurs.

'Ah'm wi' Nancy now,' I say, hoping it hurts as much as I suspect he's about to hurt me.

It shuts him up. Stuns him.

'Wi' slept wi' each other. Her an' Damo are comin' away wi' me. Away fae you!'

He laughs at this. As if I've just told him the funniest line he's ever heard. Or maybe just the most unbelievable.

—She admitted she'd been spending time with him. Told me it was because she was worried about him. That he was unravelling. She only went with him the one night to get back at me. Because of what I'd reduced her to. Maybe I deserved it. I've not been a model of loyalty over the years. But that's going to change. And this little prick isn't getting away with it. Fuck it, I'm done with him.

'Connivin' wee cunt,' he snarls at me. He spits blood from the missing tooth into my face. 'Ah'm in the fucken jail, countin' down the bastardin' days, an' aw the while, you're out here shaggin' ma missus...'

He kicks me hard in the stomach. The wind goes straight out of me. It makes me cough repeatedly and eventually some blood appears. Can't remember if I told him about Damo hating him. Hating men with beards. Can't remember anything.

'After everythin' ah've done for ye ... aw the shit ah took tae protect ye when ye were a wee bastard? Ah looked after ye. Did what a brother should. Stopped aw they wee pricks bullyin' ye, an' got the fucken jail for that tae. It's you that owes me, ya cunt!' Ah, our obligations. Our deep desire to have them settled. 'An' now ye think ye can just fucken swan in … take ma place?'

He's yelling at me. Punching my ribs repeatedly. Laughing like a maniac. The apologetic desperation of our last meeting has gone. Rage and aggression are back in the driving seat. 'Yer ain wee family, eh? Aw sorted? Fuck off! Yer a fucken freak, son. A lucky fucken escape fae the abortion clinic. Everythin' ye've ever had is down tae me. Every opportunity … every break … aw because ah created them for ye. An' this is how ye fucken repay me? Ya snidey wee cunt, ye!'

His fist connects with my jaw. He may have broken it, and perhaps his own knuckles. The crack reverberates around the cold, empty shower room. We both moan in pain.

'How the fuck d'ye think ye got intae the first team here in the first place?'

I don't answer. Don't want to know it. This thing he's desperate to tell me.

'What d'ye mean?' I mumble, barely audible, tears forming. Eyes watering.

I'm ashamed of the things I've been put through, I'm ashamed of the person I am.

But he tells me.

—*I did the two of them a favour. Danny got his shot in the first team. Wouldn't have happened otherwise. He was only fifteen, for fuck's sake. Deek Henderson got a warning. I gave him the chance to sort out his fucking weirdo behaviour. I could easily have gone to the cops and reported him. But that's not what we do here. We deal with our own. Nobody runs to the police. And everybody liked Deek Henderson, especially Higgy. I didn't blackmail him. If any of that 'touching up the young boys' shite had continued with my brother, I wouldn't have needed to go to anyone else for help. That's something I'd have dealt with. I'd have battered seven shades of fuck out of the cunt myself. It wasn't my fault that he couldn't live with himself. I didn't lock the bastard in a garage and switch his motor's engine on. Henderson fucking did those things himself.*

'Ye want more money?' I splutter. I can't think of anything else to hurt him with. '"Ah better fucken have some for ye" ... That it, Raymond?'

—He thinks this is about money. He always thinks I'm after money. I'm not. He's spiralling out of control again. And when that happens, I always take the fall for it. Not this time. I can't go back there.

His damaged honour over Nancy is a sideshow; an avenue to justify the violence. The mobility is returning to my jaw. It can't be broken. Isn't diminishing the pain though.

'Ah don't have any more ... so why no' just fuck right off, Raymond?'

—Any more of what?

He lifts me up by the collar. Both hands holding me in place. Getting ready to smash his forehead into my face.

'Danny?' It's Higgy. He comes into the room and the look on his face is one of horror. I see it before Raymond. My brother turns. Drops me.

'An' as for you ... ya auld cunt!' he says. The focus of anger temporarily shifts.

'Raymond! What the bloody hell are ye doin' here, son?'

I watch my brother push the old man backwards. He staggers over an upstand in the tiling and tilts over. He goes down in instalments. His head cracks off a sink. Higgy's down, his body folded in half like a discarded ventriloquist's dummy. Harry Doyle, who's followed him in, barrels into Raymond. His squat, army-honed physique is a match for my brother's taller, leaner frame.

Raymond is too open. Too wired. Harry Doyle thumps him into the dressing-room door, which comes off its hinges.

As Harry tends to Higgy, Raymond slopes out. He's a lost cause, corrupt and futile. This won't be the last I see of him. It won't end until he's back inside, or dead. Even if Nancy and Damo and I disappear, as Doreen and her once did, he won't stop looking for us.

We take Higgy to hospital in a taxi. His head wound will need stitches, and lots of them. Fragments are returning to me, prompted by Harry Doyle. We won easily. Five–nil. The team playing some excellent stuff. Sharp movement and high percentages of possession. The only black spot came in the first half. Billy Gilmour was carried off injured. Knowing that I wouldn't answer the phone, Higgy and Harry Doyle were returning to The Barn to let me know the good news that Gilmour hadn't suffered ankle ligament damage, as first feared.

⌂

I finally get home around 11.00 pm. The taxis to and from Crosshouse Hospital were charged to Kidd's Carpets' accounts, since I didn't have the thirty pounds on me. Higgy has been kept in for observation. He'll eat better there and that might explain his contentment at being told of his inpatient status.

I need to clear my head. Thoughts of ways to get back at my brother have been building for days. Tonight's drama tipped the scales. I bought some cigarettes. I light one and the fog clears a bit. I'm tempted by whisky but resist, for now. Even though I've stopped taking the pills, it'll still unsettle my stomach.

I change my shoes and head back out for a run. My skull feels like it's being slowly crushed in a vice. Tightening and squeezing until there's no more give. The blackness envelopes the village. I see no-one. *How many times before could you tell I didn't care? When you turned your back on me, I knew we'd get nowhere.*

I'm clinging to this. I just need to find the right way to get her and the wee man away from him for good. I get back to Higgy's place with no immediate memory of the previous hour. Like someone robotically driving a car across the country on characterless roads and having no ability to recall any defining moment of their journey. I do feel calmer though when I turn the key in the lock.

I'm in bed barely an hour when the irritating mobile phone rings. Rather than ignoring it, I get up and look for it. It could be a worrying update from the hospital, or more threatening abuse from my brother. It is neither. It's a distraught Anne Macdonald. She's phoning me to tell me that The Barn is on fire.

∩

We're in Anne's car, staring across at the smoking Barn. I don't know how we got here. In fact, I have little recollection of the last few days. There are too many things happening. Too many sequences of activity that I can't control. And they are all colliding into each other. I know it's the morning of the cup final, but I can't seem to focus on the match ahead.

Danny, there was somebody in the building, says Anne. *The firemen don't know if he started it or not. But he's in a bad way. This is really terrible.*

'Fuck sake, Anne. Ah think Raymond did this.'

There isn't as much damage as I expected. The structure and the fabric of the building is intact. A fire engine is still attending, and an ambulance has just left the scene. Siren on, alerting the remainder of the villagers who didn't already know. Scud Meikle could still be saved, the poor bastard.

Collateral damage, unfortunately. A small crowd is assembling on the pitch. Villagers, supporters of the club mostly. Even from this distance, I recognise most of them from the terracing or from The King's Arms.

My parents don't know yet. They were at a business dinner over-night at the Turnberry Hotel.

'Maybe ye should head down there. Tell yer da face tae face, like. Maybe that's better than hearin' it over the phone, or fae somebody else,' I suggest.

Perhaps. I need to find out a bit more about the extent of the damage first, I think, she says. *I'm going over to speak to the police now. Are you coming?*

'No,' I say, too firmly.

You're the club's manager, though, she says. She seems angry with me. I don't like it. *Take some responsibility, Danny.* My head hurts when she says this.

'That's no' fair,' I protest. I didn't sign up for this. My responsibility is for the results. For the team's performance. It's a fucking part-time job. I'm running a second-division junior outfit from Ayrshire, not drilling the Galacticos at the fucking Bernabeu.

She's out the car. Impatiently waiting for me.

'Anne, get back in,' I say. 'Please!'

She does. *What is it?* She grabs my shoulder. *Danny tell me! What do you know about this?*

'Ah'm sure my brother started this fire. Ah don't know what tae do about it.' I have my head in my hands. She may think I'm about to cry, but the sheer weight of it is suddenly sapping my neck muscles. I'm losing control. I thump the steering wheel repeatedly with my forehead, only stopping when I accidently hit the horn. It draws attention. Anne puts her hand on the back of my neck. She calms me.

Anne starts the VW's engine. It reverses, and we drive off.

I don't know how we got here. But we're back, at Ayr's Low Green, looking out over the calming water at Arran away in the distance.

'We had a fight,' I tell her. 'Ah thought he was gonnae kill me. He cannae stand it that Nancy's wi' me now.'

Are you sure you can trust her, Danny? She says this as if she has information that I'm not privy to. I give her an odd look before nodding. *You have to tell someone. It doesn't matter that he's your brother. If it was him who started the fire, he might've killed somebody.*

'I can't go tae the police, Anne. Ah just cannae. It'd destroy Higgy. Ah've got tae get through this final. For him.' I'm pleading with her. 'Only another day, an' then it's over.'

I'm annoyed at her. I needed her support. I've supported her all these years. I've given her the future everyone else denied her. Louise-Anne Macdonald ... missing presumed dead. But I knew she wasn't. I was the only one who still believed she was safe. Living a different life – a happier life somewhere else with people that cared about her. What kind of friend takes someone else's side? I need some air. I also need a drink. I tell her to wait in the car for me. She was driving, but it's me with the keys in my hand.

The newsagent is well stocked with the Saturday papers. Most of the nationals are still running with the extraordinary aftermath of a momentous general election landslide victory for the Labour Party under Tony Blair. His smile beams out from most of the front covers. He comes across as a cooler Bill Clinton. A politician who says he likes Oasis and The Smiths and The Jam and actually means it. I didn't vote. Didn't really see the point, given my own future plans, but if I had, I'd have voted for New Labour. And not just because I now know they won; that had been anticipated. No, because Blair seems to be offering hope of a new beginning, and sometimes that's all any of us crave after a depression, isn't it?

I pick up some sweets. A few wee things for Damo. A can of Irn-Bru, and the *Kilmarnock Standard*. Just to check if there's anything further from Sandy Buchanan.

There is.

'Ye buyin' that, son ... or just checkin' if yer bingo numbers are up?'

'Aye ... aye, sorry.' I hand over the money and head outside to read Sandy's report.

Missing Ayrshire child, Louise-Anne Macdonald 'most likely' died in a tragic accident near to where she disappeared in 1972.

Little Louise, from Barshaw Village, was five years old when she went missing. Fears that she had been abducted sparked one of the largest police operations in Scottish history.

Fragments of a distinctive toy believed to have been in Louise's possession at the time were found during recent fresh searches in the grounds of a farmhouse on the edge of Barshaw Woods. A spokesman for Strathclyde Police said that the force was pursuing a new line of inquiry, which suggested that the little girl was most likely killed accidentally.

The spokesman confirmed that the force remained committed to the investigation to provide closure for Louise's remaining family. He stressed that the case remained open.

Detective Constable Bob Palmer, who is leading this new stage of the inquiry, said: 'During the course of the inquiries we have made over the last year, we have closed off several theories about what happened to Louise. Some of these have been circulating speculatively for over twenty years.

'My team and I know that a number of items of heavy machinery were used to clear building land in the renovation of a series of farmhouse outbuildings on 4th May 1972.

'We are investigating the possibility that young Louise died as a result of an accident at the farm, which is near to her grandparents' house, where she was last seen playing.'

It is believed that a workman, operating a large digger at the time, may have been responsible for the young girl's death. It is also believed that the unidentified man had been assisting police with their inquiries until he passed away in hospital in March this year.

A team of forensic specialists, archaeologists and rescue professionals have spent the last month excavating the site. The remnants of the doll found at the site has been shown to little Lou's grandmother, Alice Reid, and she has confirmed it had been in her granddaughter's possession around the time she went missing.

This Sunday marks the twenty-fifth anniversary of Louise-Anne Macdonald's disappearance.

By the time I reach the car, she is gone. Missing. She won't be coming back. And I'm alone again.

⌢

The Ayrshire Cup Final, 1997. Barshaw is deserted. Buses organised by The King's Arms left for Townhead Park at 10.00 am. People are looking for me. In no particular order: Higgy, Raymond, Billy the Kidd, Harry Doyle, Sandy Buchanan, Tony McIntosh, the police.

All have left urgent messages for me on this annoying piece of plastic. All stressing that I should turn myself in for starting the fire at The Barn. Fuck it. Time to move on. Tony McIntosh is the only one I reply to. He doesn't give a fuck about my problems; he has enough of his own:

'Boss, ah'm sorry. Ah cannae make the final. It's Ellen,' his message says. His voice is breaking. 'She's in the hospital. Tried tae dae away wi' herself. She cannae cope wi' the weans.' I hear him sighing on the recording. As if trying to compose himself. 'Dunno if ah'm gonnae be back. Tell the boys good luck fae me, will ye?'

Poor fucker. His name has been shite around the village. After his wife's public pitch intervention, it's been widely assumed he's been playing away. He looks the type. But then appearances are often deceiving.

I watched some top-class deception myself only an hour earlier. From behind a hedge, at the bottom of her street, I saw Nancy. I watched her stand on her front step, looking left and right, before opening the door behind her to let my brother slip past her. He came out. She said something I couldn't hear. He went back towards her and kissed her. And she kissed him back. He's shaved that fucking beard off. As if that's all it would take. This doesn't completely surprise me. Anne Macdonald always said she was one for the watching. I should've listened to her.

A heart that's left at home becomes a heart of stone.

I'd refused to see it; what was right in front of my face. I've been used by both of them. He's a cunt, she's a duplicitous bitch. They deserve each other. Damo is the only one left; the only one who's honest and true and innocent. The only one I can still save. I jump back into my car, where I've spent the last forty-eight hours, hiding out in the shadows like I was a bloody fugitive. It still smells of petrol from the can in the boot, but I'll get it cleaned on the way to Cumnock, where the final is being held. I'll buy one of those perfumed hanging-card air-fresheners for the long journey north. My possessions – a bag of clothes and the records, mainly – are on the back seat. So is the box of memories that Libby maintained in my honour. With that retrieved, I have nothing connecting me to Barshaw.

Higgy will be fine, especially if we win today. He'll die happy. The club too will survive. Attendances are up, the sponsorship deal with the Texan's hotel chain will see the fire damage repaired and, most likely, a new interior fit-out that upgrades the frozen changing rooms, sorts the dilapidated plumbing, replaces the horrendously gauche carpets.

Harry Doyle will become the new team manager. He deserves it. If I'm honest, the drilling of this squad into one capable of lifting a regional cup is down to him. I understand tactics and formations, but so much of the junior game is about having the strength and stamina to out-muscle your opponents. He has imbued that army attitude into them. Even the skilful ones like young Gilmour – who'll surely be playing at a higher level next season – now compete with a fair degree of dig.

Raymond and Nancy will grow older; chained to this joyless village environment, chaperoned by vengeful old Doreen, hating each other more with every passing year. Him, yo-yo-ing backwards and forwards from spells in Barlinnie, getting caught running 'errands' for his boss, Rocco Quinn. Her, forever a doormat.

Fuck them. I've washed my hands of the lot of them. Apart from one last act of salvation, I'm done.

⌒

The capacity of the ground – home to the beaten semi-finalists, Cumnock Juniors – is three thousand. There must be more than that here today. The small stand is packed, and the grass banks around the other three sides are teeming with the black and gold of Auchinleck Talbot. There are smatterings of red and white in two corners but the Barshaw fans are outnumbered by about ten to one. It's the type of beautiful sunny day that, even in Ayrshire, makes you believe that anything is possible. Especially new beginnings.

The tannoy sounds, and, to add to my sense of dislocation, it seems to be a playing a song directed at me. A rough, bouncy song, and then a gentle female voice wafts above the crowd:

'Oh Danny boy, Danny boy, Danny boy.

I get knocked down, but I get up again, you are never gonna keep me down.'

And those surrounding me sing my name. Egging me on.

'Oh Danny boy, Danny boy, Danny boy.'

From my place, hidden amongst the Talbot supporters, I can see Damo's space helmet. He's in his normal position just right of the dugouts. Higgy is beside him, and so too is my brother.

—*He's here. I fucking know it. He's unhinged. I need to find him before the police do. I can't save him this time but if he hands himself in, he might have a better chance. Despite everything he's done, he's still blood.*

Harry Doyle has set the team up well, I see. He's using a formation we talked about many times. It's essentially 5-3-1-1. Defensive, admittedly, but designed to frustrate them, to keep us in it as far as the third quarter, and to give us a slugger's chance. Absorbing everything they can throw at us and then landing a late counterattack when it's too late for them to come back. All good on paper, but then, as the great ones know, the game isn't played on paper. Nevertheless, with Billy Gilmour out injured, he's done what I'd have done. Good luck to them. I desperately want them to win. I say 'them', because it already feels like I've left. Not my choice of course, but that's the way it is. No regrets. No looking back. Too late for that now.

The ref gets it under way, right on 3.00 pm. My interest is less on the game, more on the actions of the crowd. Unlikely I'll be recognised, but you never know. Fifteen minutes in and Barshaw are on the ropes. Last-gasp challenges, goal-line clearances and, miraculously, Josey Monsanto has saved a penalty. It was poorly struck, down the middle, and it ricocheted off his foot as he dived, but he did his job. He kept it out.

Twenty minutes in and the game gets stopped. A drunken woman staggers onto the pitch from the Barshaw end and takes off her top. Large breasts bounce freely, and no-one is quite sure what to do. The predominantly male crowd roars its approval until two stewards give chase. A rugby tackle ends the pursuit and the crowd boo loudly.

When play resumes, the break seems to have benefitted Barshaw. A run of consecutive corners ends with a Gilhooly header cracking off the bar. Despite the early Talbot pressure and a missed spot kick, the first half ends with that being the closest anyone has come to a goal.

During the break, I keep watch on Higgy, Raymond and Damo. Raymond is not interested in the match, I can tell. He's only here for me. When he deduces that I'm not here, he'll leave his son with Higgy, an old man unrelated to the boy.

Raymond Garvey, Dad of the Year. My protector. My guardian. My fucking role model.

A needless free kick conceded out on the left. Billy Young, Talbot's captain and best player, drops off a few yards. His marker doesn't go with him. A clever short ball played square and he doesn't even need to break stride. He rattles it low into the right-hand corner with Josey rooted to the spot.

Auchinleck Talbot 1-0 Barshaw Bridge

The section of the crowd I'm in salute the goal but their impatience can still be detected. A walkover would've been anticipated, and Talbot have struggled to make a breakthrough against a side from the lower division.

'C'mon Talbot, get intae this fucken shower ae shite,' yells the deep-voiced man immediately to my right. 'Ah've a bloody tenner on five nil,' he tells me by way of explanation.

'Aye, this lot are fucken pish!' I find myself replying. I push the black-and-gold scarf I bought on the way in further up around my neck. It partially conceals my mouth.

For fifteen minutes, it's astonishing how Talbot don't add to their tally. The woodwork comes to Barshaw's rescue twice. And another penalty – *a fucken cast iron-stonewaller* according to those around me – is denied the current cup-holders.

Sixty-seven minutes, or thereby, arrives. No goal, but a moment that could change the game. Harry Doyle takes Stevie Smith off, and replaces him with Billy Gilmour. Gilmour dallies on the touchline, returning to kiss Damo's helmet before going on.

'Whit the fuck is that wee prick dain', Boaby?'

'Christ knows, Kirky. Team full ae fucken village idiots, ye ask me!'

'Fucken beam me up, Scotty!'

Those around me jeer at the time being taken to make the substitution; an act I don't quite comprehend since it's only Barshaw time being wasted.

Five minutes pass, and Gilmour hasn't touched the ball. He's being starved of it. He doesn't look fit. Talbot are growing in possession, power and – although they barely need it – confidence. There's ten minutes to go and the only astonishing fact about this game is that it's only one-nil. If it'd been a boxing match, it'd have been stopped, the towel having been thrown in. All the Barshaw subs have been used. A late challenge by Davie Russell, who's suffering from cramp, is rewarded with a straight red card. He limps off the pitch and I see Higgy's bandaged head slump.

The one thing I wanted for him – the *only* thing – was this victory. As unlikely as it seemed, football is full of moments that surprise. Teams that overachieve and pass into legend. It's why those who love the game love it so much. The relentless drudgery of following a team on the slide, living in the slim hope of clambering to the top of that sheer, impenetrable wall of reason ... just once. In order to experience the view from the top. The reality of that is crushing, but easily forgotten. There's always next week. There's always next season. There's always the hope. But it's the hope that kills them.

And then, just as the Talbot supporters around me start to count down the minutes, agitated that their normally all-conquering team have made such a meal of this final. Just as they are preparing for a drunken night back at their social club; the very heart of the Talbot community. Just as everyone assumes Barshaw are out on their feet. It happens. A sharp, passing movement between O'Halloran and Peters. I can see the pass before they do. Swept out left to Ramage.

Pass it to Garvey.

Dib beats his man; faints left and slides it to Gilmour.

Take them on, son!

Billy Gilmour swivels his hips and glides past one. Nutmegs another...

Shoot, Danny, shoot!

...and unleashes an unstoppable shot into the top left-hand corner.

Garvey will burst your net.
Auchinleck Talbot 1-1 Barshaw Bridge
(Gilmour)

Time seems to stand still. I'm looking at those around me. Disbelieving. Open-mouthed. I manage to control myself. The fireworks are internalised. The Talbot players argue amongst themselves. The Barshaw fans are on the pitch. Stewards struggling to hold them back. In the melee, I've lost sight of Raymond, Higgy and Damo.

Eventually the game restarts with fans on both sides stood on the touchline. The Cumnock stewarding is woefully insufficient. The predominant Talbot mood is now one of anger.

We must be well into six minutes of injury time and a resurgent Barshaw force a corner. It could be the last kick of the game. I see Josey bouncing around like an incontinent man outside a locked toilet. A subtle nod from Harry Doyle and he's off like a sprinter. Up to the Talbot goalmouth for the set piece. All twenty-one players left on the pitch are in the penalty box, apart from Gilmour who's about to take the kick.

I glance around the ground. Every pair of eyes bar mine is trained on the action. Angry, reddened faces on one side; tearful expectant ones on the other. I didn't know what to do when I got here, but I do now.

The ball curls over, almost in slow motion. Five players leap for it. The Talbot keeper comes for it. A gust of wind seems to catch it and lift it gently over them all. It drops down, head height, at the back post. Josey Monsanto, in the bright-yellow jersey, throws a head forward. But misses the flight. The ball connects with his shoulder. It glances awkwardly. It rises. Over the head of their right back. Off the underside of the bar. And down into the net.

It's a fucking goal! No-one can believe what has just happened. It's Spinks beating Ali. It's Norway winning the Eurovision Song Contest. It's Benny from fucking *Crossroads* winning *Mastermind*.

And seconds later the pitch is swamped. Both colours, both

sides. Fights breaking out. Stewards trying to stop them. Turf being dug up. The nets being stolen. Barshaw's players are being carried shoulder high. The match won't restart, even for the seconds that can only remain. I see the referee being cajoled and then dragged.

FT.
Auchinleck Talbot 1-2 Barshaw Bridge
(Gilmour, Monsanto)

And I see Higgy. On the grass, on his knees kissing it. All reason and responsibility deserting him in this euphoric moment. Damo is behind him, his expressionless face through the visor. The boy sees me, and what I'm holding and comes towards me through the throng. Higgy's lost in this moment. His moment. He'll get over my betrayal, I reason. He'll always have this, and I gave it to him. Raymond fades into view in the distance. But he's too late. He's too far away. He won't reach us. The crowd is too boisterous. And we're closer to the gates than him. We both know what's happening. From fifty yards away, I see his face. I smile at him. One last time. And I think he smiles back. He finally knows he's beaten.

'It's good to be on the road back home again.'
We drive fast along the road. We pass three police cars driving faster in the other direction. In the rear-view mirror, I see the last of them turn sharply and switch on the siren and flashing lights. Damo is implacable, studying the new team of football men I gave him to entice him to come with me. The tape is playing. Nancy's tape. I turn up the volume to protect him.

'Wanna go faster, Damo?'

'Faster Damo,' he says.

He's such a great kid. They don't appreciate him, or how gifted he is. They just take him for granted or moan about him when he holds them back; prevents them from going out or doing the selfish things that they want to do.

They don't fucking deserve him. They don't deserve happiness.

We pull into the Barshaw main street, a police car still on our tail. The speed of the purple VW is impressive. I'd forgotten just how nippy it was. Its handling is good too, I ponder, as we swerve tightly around a woman pushing a pram laden with bags full of messages.

We pass The King's, bedecked in red and white. As is the church, its pews no doubt temporarily swelled in the days leading up to the game by agnostics reaching out for the fine margins that Higgy and Harry and I used to talk about. Anything that might help.

The car behind is close. Twenty yards or so as we head downwards; down the hill. That gradual decline. The straight road that bends sharply and suddenly at the famous Barshaw Bridge. Everything we do is an echo of a previous time. We're just damned to repeat the same patterns.

'Let's see how high this rocket can fly, Damo?'

'I know it's over, and it never really began

But in my heart, it was so real.'

I put my right foot down, take my hands off the wheel and close my eyes.

A – Songs For Nancy

01: Magellan, by Felt – *(Duffy)*
Available on Creation Records, 1990

02: Couldn't Bear To Be Special, by Prefab Sprout – *(McAloon)*
Available on Kitchenware Records, 1984

03: My Sister, by Tindersticks – *(Mark, Staples, Boulter, MacAuley, Fraser, Hinchliffe, Colwill)* Available on This Way Up Records, 1995

04: Heart of Darkness, by Sparklehorse – *(Linkous)*
Available on Capitol Records, 1995

05: It's a Shame about Ray, by The Lemonheads – *(Dando, Morgan)*
Available on Atlantic Records, 1992

06: Low Expectations, by Edwyn Collins – *(Collins)*
Available on Setanta Records, 1994

07: It Just Came To Pieces in My Hands, by The Style Council – *(Weller)* Available on Polydor Records, 1985

08: Unsolved Child Murder, by The Auteurs – *(Haines)*
Available on Hut Records, 1996

09: Tongue, by REM – *(Berry, Buck, Mills, Stipe)*
Available on Warner Bros. Records, 1994

10: Bill Is Dead, by The Fall – *(Scanlon, Smith)*
Available on Fontana Records, 1990

11: The First Big Weekend, by Arab Strap – *(Moffat, Middleton)*
Available on Chemikal Underground Records, 1996

12: Teenage Riot, by Sonic Youth – *(Gordon, Moore, Ranaldo, Shelley)*
Available on Blast First Records, 1988

Songs For Nancy – B

01: A Pair of Brown Eyes, by The Pogues – *(MacGowan)*
Available on Stiff Records, 1985

02: Good To Be on the Road Back Home Again, by Cornershop –
(Singh) Available on Wiiija Records, 1997

03: Little Bird (Are You Happy in Your Cage), by Moose –
(Fletcher, Davis) Available on Hut Recordings, 1992

04: I Want You, by Spiritualized – *(Pierce)*
Available on Dedicated Records, 1992

05: These Are the Dreams of the Working Girl, by Comet Gain –
(Feck) Available on Wiiija Records, 1997

06: Isolation, by Joy Division – *(Sumner, Hook, Morris, Curtis)*
Available on Factory Records, 1980

07: Bizarre Love Triangle, by Frente – *(Gilbert, Hook, Morris, Sumner)*
Available on Mushroom Records, 1994

08: Bachelor Kisses, by The Go-Betweens – *(McLennan, Forster)*
Available on Sire Records, 1984

09: Live Forever, by Oasis – *(Gallagher)*
Available on Creation Records, 1994

10: Lonesome Tonight, by New Order *(Gilbert, Hook, Morris, Sumner)*
Available on Factory Records, 1984

11: I Know It's Over, by The Smiths – *(Morrissey, Marr)*
Available on Rough Trade Records, 1986

12: White Love – Piano Reprise, by One Dove –
(Allison, Carmichael, McInven) Available on FFRR Records, 1993

Acknowledgements

Sincere thanks to the following people who kindly gave me their time – and recollections – of the brilliantly bonkers world of mid-90s junior football in Ayrshire:

Billy Young, Charles Adam, Kevin Toner, Peter Dallas and of course, the one and only Alan Rough.

Thanks to my family, as always, but particularly Nathan, whose love of the game – and dedication to it – I find truly inspiring. Thanks also to Stuart Cosgrove, Dani Garavelli, John Carnochan, David Logue, Alistair Braidwood and Markus Naegele. And to the brilliant community of writers in Scotland for their selfless encouragement and support.

I'm indebted to Anne Macdonald who bid to become a character in the book to benefit the fantastic work being done by Marie Curie UK. If you wish to follow Anne's inspirational lead, or if you would simply like some information and support about care through terminal illness, you can do so at the following address: https://www.mariecurie.org.uk/

And last but certainly not least, massive thanks and love to Karen Sullivan, West Camel, Anne Cater, Cole Sullivan and everyone at Orenda Books, without whom these words would have represented yet another collection of rough ideas and sketches rattling around my skull, looking for a way out.